Praise for *The S*

'Wonderful...If *Out of the Line of Fire*
mind and senses, *The Snow Kimono* is a fine champagne...a novel of detection, a thriller of the intellect.' *Sydney Morning Herald*

'Gripping...Like a Japanese puzzle, prized for their infinite solutions and depth of revelation, each chapter builds on the one before, unfolding through levels of story to unpack deeper and deeper truths...Henshaw's ability to combine such cultural and aesthetic diversity in his fiction is not only an example of what a period of dedicated study can do, but a marker of his ability as a writer.' *Guardian*

'The writing is beautiful: pellucid and wonderfully visual, painting memorable landscape cameos. The reader is compliant, willingly engaged with a story that starts in medias res and branches in unexpected and seemingly unconnected yet complementary directions.' *Advertiser*

'The novel questions authorship and the slipperiness of memory... [Its] narrative twists are challengingly clever.' *Australian Book Review*

'Henshaw's prose [is] luminous and crisp, like the snowy countryside of Japan or the barren lanes of Algiers...When I finished *The Snow Kimono*, I raised my head, vaguely surprised that I was at home, in familiar surrounds, and it was still daylight outside. I turned straight back to page one and began again.' *Saturday Paper*

'*The Snow Kimono* stands out as an extraordinary, clever and exquisitely executed fiction.' *Hoopla*

'Engrossing...With agile intelligence, with boldness in what he has imagined and tight control over how it is developed, Henshaw has announced triumphantly that he is no longer a ghost on the Australian literary scene, but one of its most substantial talents.' *Weekend Australian*

Mark Henshaw has lived in France, Germany, Yugoslavia and the United States. He currently lives in Canberra. His first novel, *Out of the Line of Fire* (1988), won the FAW Barbara Ramsden Award and the NBC New Writers Award. It was also shortlisted for the Miles Franklin Literary Award and the *Age* Book of the Year Award. *Out of the Line of Fire* was one of the biggest selling Australian literary novels of the decade, and is being republished in the Text Classics series.

In 1989 Mark was awarded a Commonwealth Literary Fellowship, and in 1994 he won the ACT Literary Award. Under the pseudonym J. M. Calder, in collaboration with John Clanchy, he has written two crime novels, *If God Sleeps* (1996) and *And Hope to Die* (2007). His work has been widely translated. For many years he was a Curator of International Art at the National Gallery of Australia. He recently returned to writing fiction full-time.

THE SNOW KIMONO

MARK HENSHAW

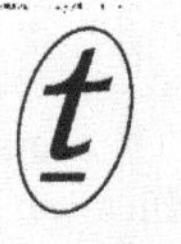

TEXT PUBLISHING
MELBOURNE AUSTRALIA

textpublishing.com.au

The Text Publishing Company
Swann House
22 William Street
Melbourne Victoria 3000 Australia

First published in 2014 by The Text Publishing Company
Reprinted 2014

Cover and page design by W. H. Chong
Typeset in Guardi by J&M Typesetting

Printed in Australia by Griffin Press, an Accredited ISO AS/NZS 14001:2004 Environmental Management System printer.

National Library of Australia Cataloguing-in-Publication entry:
Author: Henshaw, Mark, 1951–
Title: The snow kimono / by Mark Henshaw
ISBN: 9781922182340 (paperback)
ISBN: 9781925095326 (ebook)
Dewey Number: A823.3

This book is printed on paper certified against the Forest Stewardship Council® Standards. Griffin Press holds FSC chain-of-custody certification SGS-COC-005088. FSC promotes environmentally responsible, socially beneficial and economically viable management of the world's forests.

To my wife, Lee.
I could not have a better companion
with whom to share this great adventure.

I can be sure that even in this tiny, insignificant episode
there is implicit everything I have experienced,
all the past, the multiple pasts I have tried in vain
to leave behind me...

ITALO CALVINO
If on a Winter's Night a Traveller

❀

On his return, after many years' absence,
Kenji-san went to see his blind friend.
He told him of Abyssinia, that mysterious land,
of his many adventures there.
'So, Keiichi,' he said, when he had finished.
'What do you think of Abyssinia?'
'It sounds like a magical place,' his friend said,
as if returning from a dream.
'But I lied to you,' Kenji-san said. 'I was never there.'
'I know,' his friend replied. 'But I was.'

OTOMO NO TSURAYUKI
The Night of a Thousand Brocades

Part I

FUMIKO

❀

Chapter 1

THERE are times in your life when something happens after which you're never the same. It may be something direct or indirect, or something someone says to you. But whatever it is, there is no going back. And inevitably, when it happens, it happens suddenly, without warning.

❀

Paris: July 1989

When Auguste Jovert stepped out of his apartment building on rue St Antoine to get his evening paper, it was dusk. The streetlamps were lit. Rain still fell in a thin mist. The roads shone. To anybody else it would have been obvious—accidents hovered like hawks in the air.

As he made his way along the wet pavement, in his coat, his umbrella unfurled above his head, he was thinking about a letter he had received that day. It was from a young woman, someone he had never met before, who had made an extraordinary claim. She claimed she was his daughter.

He had stood that morning in the cool, empty foyer of his apartment building reading and re-reading the letter. He did not at first see the small photograph caught in the corner of the envelope. When he did, he raised it to his face. One look into the young woman's eyes and he knew that it was true.

For thirty years, Jovert had worked as an Inspector of Police. Before that, he worked for the French Territorial Police in Algiers. Recently he had retired, and ever since then he had had the strangest feeling, the feeling that he was lost. While he worked, he barely had time to think. Things kept at bay. Now, however, fragments from his past had begun to replay themselves in his head. It was as if, now that he was approaching the end of his life, the overall pattern of his existence was about to be revealed to him. But the moment of revelation never came. Instead, he began to have doubts, to wake up at night. What's more, he constantly had the impression that something was about to happen. Then something did happen. The letter arrived.

❀

It seemed to him later, recalling the accident, that at one moment he had been thinking about the letter, and the next he was lying flat on his back in the gutter looking up at the intricate expanse of the underside of a car. He could feel the heat from the engine on his face and hear the tiny tinking sounds of its cooling pipes. Odd drops of water fell about him and onto his forehead. One wheel of the car rested on the pavement above his head.

In the distance, he could hear the urgent rise and fall of a siren. He turned his head tentatively to his right. There, suspended beneath the rim of the car, was a man's face. He was wearing glasses. His upturned hat lay on the roadway beside him.

The man was kneeling down, staring at him. Jovert saw now that he was bald, that his perfectly burnished head was studded with thousands of tiny, incandescent hemispheres of light. He looked from one tiny dazzling world to the next. He saw the man's mouth moving. The tip of his tie rested on the wet roadway. A dark circle had begun to form about his knee. Jovert had wanted to tell him. Then a peculiar thing happened. All the lights went out.

❀

Two days later, Jovert left his apartment once again to get his evening paper. This time on crutches. Six weeks, the doctor had said. He had held the X-rays of Jovert's knee up to the hospital window. Maybe more, he said.

On his way home, Jovert sat down on the bench opposite St Paul's to rest. He took the envelope he had received earlier that week out of his coat pocket, read the address.

Inspector A. Jovert
Le Commissariat de Police
36 Quai des Orfèvres
75001 PARIS, FRANCE

He looked at the stamp, brought it up close to his face. Only now did he see that it had been franked some months before.

He took the letter out and read it through once again. She did not know whether he was still alive, she said. She had only recently discovered that he was her father. She wanted him to know that she existed. She did not say why. I make no demands on you, she wrote. But then, at the end: *Perhaps, if you wanted, you could write to me*. And she gave him a name, an address—Mathilde Soukhane, 10 rue Duhamel, Algiers.

He took the photograph out of the envelope. He recalled the day almost thirty years before when he had seen her mother for the first time. It had been in Sétif, in a narrow side street. He had been walking up the chipped stone stairs. She had emerged suddenly, like an apparition, from an unseen door in the wall, her dress so white, so dazzling in the light that it was like some momentary disturbance in the air itself.

Even after all these years, the image of her face, her skin, dark against her blazing dress, still lingered. He remembered she had been carrying a bundle of papers in her arms. When he turned to look after her, she was gone.

The girl in the photograph had the same face, the same eyes. She had the same dark skin.

He sat for a long time thinking.

Then, all at once, as though he had only just made up his mind, he took the photograph, and the letter, and crushed them into a tight ball in his hand. He rose, threw the wad of paper into the bin beside the bench, and walked off.

It's too late, he said to himself. It's too late.

That evening, however, things began to change. Afterwards, months later, the letter, the accident, came to seem to him precursors of an even greater shift in his life, one that had been lying in wait for him for years.

❀

When he arrived back at his apartment building, he punched his code into the panel by the door, listened for the click. His building was old. The door was heavy, its thick black paint cracked. He had to push with his shoulder to get it open. The hospital staff had been right. His crutches *were* too short.

Inside, in the foyer, the lift was out of order once again. He stood looking at the note taped to its wire cage. It was the third time this month. He pushed in the light switch beside the stairwell. He would have three minutes to climb the five flights of stairs to his apartment before the light went out. Reluctantly he began to climb.

By the time he heaved himself up over the last step to his landing, his right leg had begun to ache. Then, as he took his keys from his pocket, they slipped from his fingers and fell to the floor.

Jesus, Mother of God, he said under his breath.

A door closed beneath him. He heard footsteps receding down the hallway. He thought of calling out, but it was already too late. Whoever it was had begun descending the stairs. He leaned against the wall, looked up at the globe glowing dimly above his head. Its shade—dusty, discoloured, suspended on a length of twisted cord—was oscillating minutely. He pictured the tiny convected eddies whirling at its rim. He could see the movement of its shadow on the wall opposite. Any moment now, he knew, the light would go out. He waited, counting the seconds, until it did.

He closed his eyes.

Standing like this in the darkened hallway, he could hear the thinning evening traffic, the muffled subterranean rumble of the Metro, the sound of a distant siren. He thought of his own accident, took a deep breath. The air smelt musty now.

Beneath his door a thin fissure of light hovered in the darkness. In it he could just see his fallen keys. He prodded them with the end of one of his crutches. Then he heard a rustle at the far end of the corridor and, suddenly, a voice.

May I help you, Inspector?

The sound startled him. It seemed to come out of nowhere.

The light switch, he said. I've dropped my keys.

Instantly the light came on. It flared up around him for a moment before dying down. He stood there blinking. He could just make out the shape of someone standing in the shadows at the top of the stairs.

Permit me, Inspector, the stranger said, coming forward. He stooped to pick up the keys. As he raised his head, light fell across his face and Jovert registered for the first time that his saviour was Oriental—from China, or Japan.

He could see him clearly now—an impeccably dressed, sharp-featured little man in his fifties. A pair of wire-rimmed spectacles poked out from the top of his coat pocket. In his hands, he held a hat. There was something about him that reminded Jovert of the Emperor Hirohito.

Thank you, Jovert said.

You're welcome, Inspector. I have been waiting for you.

Waiting? he said.

Yes. Permit me to introduce myself. I am Omura. Tadashi Omura, former Professor of Law at the Imperial University of Japan. And you are Inspector Jovaire, are you not?

With this he bowed slightly. It had been like an announcement.

Now I am here, he said.

Jovert half-expected Omura to go on, but instead, he stood there silently, with Jovert's keys still in his hand.

Jovert, he said. Auguste Jovert.

He felt compelled to bow himself, but instantly he realised how impossible that would have been. Instead, he turned awkwardly on his crutches to face Omura, inclined his head.

Your keys, Omura said.

Yes, thank you.

Omura, however, made no attempt to leave. As they stood there in the empty hallway, Jovert began to feel increasingly under some obligation to this odd little man who had helped him, and who was still standing, expectantly it now seemed, in front of him.

He unlocked his door and pushed it open with his elbow. As he did so, Omura leaned forward. He stood, half-stooped for a moment, surveying the room. Then he straightened. Looked up at Jovert. Smiled.

Yes, he said.

The two men stood there on the threshold for a moment.

Would you like to come in, Jovert said.

Yes, yes, Omura replied. I have been waiting. Please.

And with this, he stretched out his arm, inviting Jovert to precede him, as if, in fact, the apartment belonged to him.

❀

Later, when Jovert tried to recall what had taken place between this moment and the next, he could not. One instant, it seemed to him, he was standing in the open doorway to his apartment, leaning on his crutches, and the next he was sitting opposite his lounge-room window listening to Tadashi Omura's strangely mesmerising voice.

One afternoon, Omura was saying, I decided to take Fumiko to see her mother's grave. Fumiko must have been about three at the time. It was the middle of winter and there was still snow in the streets. I remember the sky being a uniform, dull white, which meant it would snow again later in the afternoon.

We must have spent some time getting ready. Going to

the cemetery was no easy matter. Katsuo had wanted Sachiko buried in the old cemetery outside of Osaka. We had to take the bus, then the train. Not that this was a problem. We lived on the outskirts of Osaka, in any case. But afterwards we would have to walk the one or two kilometres through the woods. I myself loved this walk, even in winter. Often I would be the only person on the path. I loved the absolute stillness, the sound of my own footfall on the fresh snow, the feeling of my fogged breath on my face. Sometimes one would see a fox, or an owl perched on a tree limb. There was a stone bridge across the stream which led up to the temple gates, and I used to look forward to the odd hollow echo of my boots on it as I crossed. A short distance away, downstream, was a pond which froze over in winter. From the bridge you could see the children who came there sometimes to skate.

I had never taken Fumiko to the cemetery before. My housekeeper, Mrs Muramoto, had called at the last minute to say that she was ill, that she could not come to take care of Fumiko after all. I remember I suspected her of lying, and later I found out she had gone to visit relatives in Nara. I remember being angry. She knew I was depending on her, that I could not leave Fumiko alone in the apartment. I already had my coat and gloves on, and I could tell immediately by the tone of her voice that she was lying.

Then I remember standing on the steps outside our apartment building, with Fumiko beside me, all dressed up in her coat and fur hat.

It's like yesterday, he said. I can still feel her child's gloved hands in mine. Fumiko wanted to know where we were going. She was turning from side to side, waiting. I knew she was excited because she was humming to herself.

Omura stopped for a moment. Took out a packet of cigarettes, shook one loose.

But I am not explaining myself well, he said. And there is something I have forgotten to tell you. You see, Fumiko was not my daughter. In fact, I have never been married. First there were my studies, then establishing my legal practice. I never seemed to find the time. How I came to have Fumiko is rather complicated. I will get to that. At the time I am talking about, Fumiko had been with me for about a year. In general, Mrs Muramoto looked after her. Already, however, I had begun looking towards the future, when things, explanations, would be difficult. As a consequence, I had decided, at least for the time being, to bring Fumiko up believing that she was my own daughter. In other words, that I was her father.

As you can imagine, Fumiko had been talking for some time, and yet, despite all of my and Mrs Muramoto's encouragement, she had never once called me Father. I cannot tell you how important this had become for me. At the time, it seemed as if the whole future of our lives together depended on Fumiko uttering this one word. Without this, the world I had decided to build for her would never, could never, exist.

Omura fell silent again. He leaned forward, flicked the end of his cigarette into the small bowl on the table in front of him. He raised the cigarette to his lips, inhaled.

Where was I, he said.

Standing on the doorstep outside your apartment, Jovert replied.

Yes, yes, he said. You see, I was still not used to going out with Fumiko on my own. A three-year-old child. What if something happened? I wasn't even sure if she was properly dressed. I remember looking down at my watch. It was already almost two. It was so still. I knew it was going to snow again. Not heavily. There was no danger. Nothing like that. It's just that I didn't know whether to take Fumiko or not. Usually there was Mrs Muramoto with us when we went out, or someone else.

I knelt down to look at Fumiko.

So, Fumiko, I said, shall we go?

Why not? she said, shrugging her shoulders and smiling.

I stayed there, half-kneeling, looking at her. I remember how sweet she looked in her coat and hat.

Are you warm enough?

She nodded.

Sure?

Sure, she said.

She had never been on a train before. It was all new to her. We sat in the warmth of the station waiting room. Fumiko sat next to me, her stockinged legs dangling over the edge of the seat. I had never realised how curious children are. It's odd, I think it was only then that I began to realise how being the head of a law firm had cut me off from…well, from everything, from the world around me. From life. Here I was, I must have been forty or forty-one at the time and, all at once, it seemed to me that I knew nothing about the world, nothing.

Suddenly, I was glad Mrs Muramoto had phoned to say she could not come. For the first time since Fumiko had come to stay with me, I began to feel what it might have been like to really have a child of my own.

Is she your daughter? an old woman on the train asked. She was carrying a wicker basket full of frozen fish.

Yes, I said.

She didn't appear at all surprised. I had always assumed it was obvious that Fumiko was not my child. I was old enough to be her grandfather.

Yes, I repeated, she's my daughter.

Such a beautiful child, the old woman said.

But all of this is not what I set out to tell you. It is so difficult not to get sidetracked. And I am sure there are many other things I have forgotten. What I remember happening, happened later.

At Togetsu, we got out. At the time, Togetsu was the end of the line. A series of small, lightly cultivated fields separated it from the surrounding woods. It is mainly tenant farmers who live there. Anyone who gets off at Togetsu is either a farm worker or on their way to the cemetery.

Only half a dozen people stepped down from the train when we pulled into the station. Almost instantly, they were gone.

I don't know how to explain this, he said. How to explain what I felt as we walked through the snow-covered fields and into the woods. It was so still, you see. So absolutely still. There was no one else about. It was as if the whole world consisted of just Fumiko and me.

Because of the snow, Fumiko's shoes were soon wet. As we entered the path through the woods to the cemetery, I hoisted her up onto my shoulders. I was holding her ankles with my gloved hands. I could feel her fingertips on my head. Far off, we could hear the dull thud of a woodsman's axe. All about us stood the wet-dark trunks of trees, stark against the surrounding whiteness.

As we walked, I was thinking of Fumiko's weight on my shoulders, what a new experience this was for me, how alive her legs felt. I had already begun to plan what I would do, that I would take the opportunity I had been offered to move to Tokyo after all. I know that for some minutes I must have become completely absorbed in my thoughts.

Then, all at once, Fumiko said: It's snowing! And I felt her change position. I looked up to see her outstretched hand trying to catch the large scattered snowflakes that had begun floating down towards us. I thought briefly of turning back. I knew, however, that it would be some time before it began to snow in earnest.

Are you all right, Fumiko? I asked.

Yes, she said.

Shall we turn back?

No, she said emphatically.

It was only when a loud crack rang out close by that I

realised that the sound of the chopping we had heard as we entered the path had ceased. Now it had resumed. We stood and listened for a moment. I could tell that it must be coming from near the stone bridge ahead of us, the one that crossed the stream at the foot of the stairs that led up to the cemetery.

We walked on. The sound came louder now. Every two or three seconds, a loud crack followed by an echo up the mountainside. And now that we were close, I could tell it was not the clean, sharp sound of an axe on wood. There was something different, something muffled about it. A different after-tone. With each step, this sound—regular, thick, solid—filled the air around us. I thought I could feel it through the earth. After one particularly loud crack, I felt Fumiko's body stiffen.

What is it, Father? she asked.

Father. You know, it caught me almost completely unawares. I had been concentrating so much on the sound echoing around us that I nearly missed it. But she had said it at last. The word I had been waiting for.

What is it, Father? I repeated to myself. You cannot imagine how I felt.

I don't know, I said. But I'm sure it's nothing we have to worry about. Shall we go and have a look?

Maybe I'm wrong, he said. Maybe I didn't say that. I was so surprised by Fumiko saying Father that I'm not sure that I said anything at all.

Omura got up out of his chair and went to stand by the

window. The room had fallen into semi-darkness. Jovert sat looking across at him. He could no longer see Omura's features, just his silhouette against the cool blue evening light. A lamp came on in the window of one of the apartments opposite. Jovert saw the figure of a woman appear briefly, raise her arms, then pull the curtains closed.

The evening light was beginning to fade. Jovert felt them both drawing into themselves as the light ebbed from the sky.

When Omura began speaking again, Jovert looked up to find that he had shifted away from the window, so that he could no longer see him. Now, Omura's voice came to him from out of the darkness. Disconnected, invisible, incorporeal. He was speaking slowly now, as if he were back there, back in a place Jovert had never been. And yet, at the same time, he felt Omura's voice drawing him closer to a place within himself that he had never left.

Jovert tried to place him in the shadows, but could not. Maybe it was a trick of light, the square of fading sky beside which Omura must have been standing, and his oddly melancholy voice, hanging suspended in the darkness, slow, still, concentrated.

I do not know if you can imagine what it was like, Omura was saying. It must be difficult for you. You have never been there. So how could I expect you to understand?

He sounded disappointed.

It's strange, he continued. When I recall this moment, I do not remember it as if it was actually me. Of course, I can still feel Fumiko's weight on my shoulders. I can feel the collar of my coat against my neck. I must have taken my gloves off because, even now, I can feel the texture of Fumiko's stockinged legs, and her shoes. They were new, and black, with silver clasps.

I must have put Fumiko down because I can see myself kneeling beside her, adjusting her jacket, looking into her face. She has the darkest, darkest eyes. There is some snow caught on my cap. Fumiko wants to dislodge it. She tells me to bend my head down. I feel her brushing it away. I look up to see her assessing how good a job she has done. For some reason she laughs, her head to one side. As I stand, I can see, as my hand reaches down, her hand reaches up. I watch as the two of us, me, a tiny—I can't believe how small I am—concentrated little man, already in middle age, and this little girl...as the two of us set off again up the snow-covered path.

You see, Inspector, this is what is so extraordinary. I remember this moment as though I was a spectator, looking on. I see these two figures, a man and his tiny daughter. I see the snow drifting down through the bare, wooded canopy. I can see it settling on my back. I can see our breaths. And even now, inexplicably, I can feel the tension building. Then, without warning, a mighty crash fractures the stillness around us. It is a frightening, terrifying sound.

And yet we press on.

We can hear their voices long before we see them. The sound reverberating off the mountains has led us astray. Gradually, however, muffled voices betray them. Dwarfed by the trees, a group of huddle-dark figures is gathered at the edge of the frozen pond. One figure, larger than the rest, someone whom I can tell is powerfully built, stands on the frozen surface. He is a little apart from the others, almost facing them.

He has an axe in his hands. Its blade rests on the ice. He seems to be catching his breath. He leans the handle of the axe against his thigh. He says something to the others, shakes his head. He raises his hands to his face, blows on them. I can see his fogged breath. He rubs his palms against his trouser legs and picks up the axe again. He is wearing heavy, studded boots.

I remember watching as he scored the surface of the ice. He steadied himself. For a moment the axe is high above his head, its giant, polished curve hovering. And then the cracking blade is in the ice. Then again. Four or five crashing blows in quick succession. The sound echoes away from us up through the hills.

With each powerful blow, the axeman grunted as he brought the blade down. And each time, a small spray of ice leapt up from the surface of the pond.

It was difficult to tell what he was doing. He appeared to be making a line in the ice. I remember him stopping again for a moment.

We were quite close to them by this stage. But no one seemed to have noticed us, or to care that we were there.

We halted a few metres short of this semicircle of dark figures. For some irrational reason, I felt a surge of panic pass through me, as though I should just turn around and go, that what was happening here did not concern me.

One of the figures, a man of about my own age, at the edge of the semicircle and half-facing me, glanced up and caught my eye. One or two of the others turned to look at me. There was a moment of absolute silence.

I cannot describe the look on their faces, not hostile, barely curious, immobile. You see, it was as if, all along, they had been waiting there for me.

Omura broke off again, and as he did so, Jovert felt a similar wave of panic pass through his own body, as though what Omura was saying presaged a moment of catastrophic revelation not only for Omura, but for him as well.

It was as if, now that I had arrived, they could finish what they had begun. I was aware of Fumiko tugging at my hand, trying to pull me away. And yet I could not leave. My eyes kept passing from one face to another.

In that strange, hallucinatory state, I bent down to pick Fumiko up. When I looked around again, I saw that they had all turned away from me. I was about to turn away myself—the axeman had picked up his axe once again and was repositioning himself on the ice—when I heard a single cry, a cry so desperate, so lost, that it reached into me and closed around my heart.

I saw the axe blade rise once more, watched it come crashing down. Now, however, between each blow, inescapably, I could hear the low, primitive sound of a woman crying. The group of figures too had come to life. I stood transfixed by the falling of the axe blade.

As the last blow fell, a sudden movement convulsed the group. From their midst one of them, the woman I assumed had been crying, broke free and fell upon the ice. With wild, almost demented sweeps of her arms, she began frantically trying to clear the shards of broken ice from the frozen surface of the pond. I could not see her face, and it took me a moment to realise that for some reason her hands were bound. As a consequence, each new sweep seemed to obscure what she had just uncovered. This in turn increased her desperation. After two or three sweeps she would pause and lower her head to the ice, as if she was trying to see into its molecular depths. All of a sudden, defeated by what she was doing, she collapsed onto the icy surface.

Inevitably, her actions had drawn me closer, so that now I too stood on the periphery of this semicircle of dark figures looking down on her. No one seemed able to move. I have no idea how long she lay there, half a minute, a minute. I don't know. Then, one of the group, the man who had earlier met my eye, stepped forward. He leaned down and grasped her under the arm. As he raised her to her feet I caught a glimpse of her face. She wasn't a woman at all. She was just a girl.

I was so taken aback that I hardly had time to register her features. Moreover, immediately my gaze fell upon her face, one of the onlookers, an old woman, uttered a loud cry and began clutching at her mouth. It was a moment before I realised that she was staring at something at her feet. Almost simultaneously, each of us turned to look at the spot where the young girl had lain. I did not, at first, see what the old woman had seen. It was the surface of the ice that struck me first. Where the girl had fallen the thin frosted layer of snow that covered the pond had melted, revealing the hard molten transparency beneath.

I no longer remember, the effect was so overwhelming, the exact instant when the bleached and twisted tree root that I could see trapped just centimetres below this solid surface resolved itself into what it actually was: the foot and leg of a tiny, newborn child.

In a moment of powerful revulsion, I felt myself turning away, and it is now only as an after-image that I can see beyond the perfection of this tiny foot, with its odd node-like arrangement of toes, perfectly ordered, so close to the surface, to see that the rest of the child's body is also more or less visible. It was as though the child had been frozen at the instant it had hit the water. One arm was oddly turned back, as if to break its fall. I can still see part of the crown of a tiny head, with its constellations of fine, dark hair.

What is more extraordinary, however, is that I can see its eyes. They are open. It's as if the child had fallen in such a manner that it appeared to be looking back over its shoulder at the mother who had just flung it from her arms.

By the time I realised this, I had already begun to move away from the group. I could hear the agonised wailing of the girl who by now must have seen what we all had seen.

Fumiko was saying, What is it, Father? What is it?

But I was too shaken to reply, and we set off back down the track in the direction from which we had come.

Omura's voice trailed off. The room was completely dark now. Outside, in the distance, Jovert could see the faint silhouette of the towers of Notre-Dame lit up momentarily by the floodlights of a passing *bateau-mouche*. Then they were gone.

Chapter 2

AT exactly 2.56 the next morning, as though some hinged reflex had been triggered in his sleep, Jovert found himself abruptly sitting up in his bed, staring into the darkness, the pale-green bloom from the clock on his bedside table the only thing that lit the room. He had been dreaming, although what it was he had been dreaming about now eluded him.

Then he was up out of his bed, pulling on his coat, reaching for his crutches. Five minutes later, he was standing in the vitreous stillness of the street outside. A solitary figure moving through the sleeping sepia city.

Even as he approached, he knew the bin would be empty. He peered in, trying to pry the inner gloom apart. Nothing. He looked around, at the deserted streets, at the silent stone façade of St Paul's, the abandoned newsstand. The green neon sign of the pharmacy opposite was blinking fitfully on and off. He watched it come instantly to life. Then, like someone exhaling in their sleep, it began to flicker. Went off. Came on. Somewhere, a car alarm began to sound.

He leaned down, touched the top of the bin with his hand. His shadow made to go. Then he saw it, hidden in the darkness at the base of the bin: a piece of crumpled paper, lying like a half-unfolded flower. He reached in, retrieved it. It was her photograph. The letter was gone. But he had her photograph. It was something.

❀

When Jovert awoke later that morning, his bedside light was on. He reached for his cigarettes, saw the crumpled photograph waiting for him beneath the lamp. He picked it up. Smoothed it out. Her face looked back at him now through a web of pale, thin creases.

He lay there thinking. About the photograph. About the night before—Omura. He tried to recall, exactly, what Omura had said, what he had been wearing, every floating gesture of his hand, every intonation of his voice. Most of it he could retrieve. But when he tried to recall what Omura had said to him after he had turned to walk back down the snow-covered path, he could not.

He leaned over, flicked the ash from his cigarette into the cup on his bedside table. Once again, he circled back. And once again he found himself teetering on the brink of the same abyss, staring into the same void. All he could see before him was the image of Omura and his little daughter walking down the path, away from him. He watched them recede into the falling snow, until they disappeared.

He lay in his bed, the smoke from his cigarette curling lazily towards the ceiling the only thing in the room that moved.

❀

It had been winter when Jovert first saw the apartment. Early evening. The agent had been late. Jovert was forced to wait in the cold.

When he finally arrived, the agent, an astonishingly fat man, grasped his hand. He was wearing a voluminous olive-green suit. His cheeks were flushed. He had begun to sweat.

The Metro, the Metro, he said, pointing to the stairs.

The man would not look Jovert in the eye. Instead, his mad gaze seemed to bounce off him. Jovert watched it skid across the road and up the wall of the building opposite.

The apartment? Jovert said.

Yes, yes, the apartment, the man said. He spoke to Jovert's shirt front, ran a finger around his damp collar.

Then they were inside, waiting for the lift.

The apartment opened directly onto a sitting room. It was larger than Jovert had expected. On the far side of the room, beyond two glassed doors, a small balcony. Two old, once elegant leather sofas sat facing each other. A frayed Oriental carpet, its reds and blues muted in the lamplight. Against one wall, an enormous, squat-legged cabinet, the dimpled grey surface of which looked as though it had been carved from elephant hide.

The advertisement had said: *Apartment for sale. As is.*

There were two bedrooms. A small, dated kitchen.

Then they were out on the balcony.

The view, the view, the agent was saying. Jovert nodded. He had heard it all before.

He had turned distractedly to look in the other direction. It was then that he saw it, the thing that would make all the apartment's charmlessness seem irrelevant, temporary, surmountable. Two hundred metres away, suspended against the dimming, sickle-mooned sky, hovered the floodlit image of a golden-winged youth, fleeing, Nijinsky-like, across a dark and chimney-potted plain.

Of course, he thought, the Bastille Column. The Spirit of Liberty, Dumont's gilded youth standing naked on top of it. He remembered a school assignment he had written about it. How the statue had almost toppled to the ground when it was being hoisted into place, the boy's golden wings useless against its fall.

He stood looking at this magical form, at its newly polished wings, the boy's triumphantly upraised torch, the broken chains that had once shackled him, the six-pointed star above his head. Here was a different kind of Icarus. Permanently frozen, improbable, ludicrous perhaps, but magical nonetheless.

Victor Hugo lived nearby, the agent was saying.

I'll take it, Jovert said.

The agent stopped talking.

You will? he said.

Bewildered, he turned to look in the same direction as Jovert.

I see, he said.

But he didn't, hadn't, and probably never would.

❀

Now Jovert was standing in the bathroom, leaning down, looking at his face in the mirror. He ran his hand across his stubbled chin. He pulled each eyelid down, examined the whites of each eye. He touched the wound where his head had hit the gutter. He pictured the impact, his head rebounding silently off the curb's concrete edge, the broken-fleshed furrow slowly filling with blood, saw its first small overflowing, saw the first crimson drop drop to the roadway. The wound had crusted over now. He ran the tips of his fingers cautiously across its jagged surface.

He sat on the edge of the bath, undid the brace on his knee. The swelling had begun to subside but the bruising looked worse than ever. It reminded him of something by Monet.

Fifteen minutes later he was back in his living room, drawing the curtains aside. It was early, the sky churlish. Banks of cloud the colour of egg white hung low and flat on the horizon. In the guttered lee of the dome of St Paul's sat a row of dismal pigeons.

He made himself a pot of coffee. He carried first it, then a cup, out onto the balcony. Below him, where the street curved around to Place de la Bastille, a solitary green-and-white street-cleaning machine was crawling along the curb. The monotonous drone of its engine floated up to him. A man, tall, thin, North African, wearing overalls and a cap, carrying a long green-bristled broom, was jiving along beside it.

❀

It occurred to him that to see his inability to recall what Omura had said the night before—after he had turned to walk back down the path—as a gap, a void, was the wrong way to see things. What he should do was not to search for what had dropped out of his memory, but to look more closely at what had come so insistently to inhabit it—the image of Omura and his little daughter standing on the snow-covered path.

He spent much of the rest of the day moving from his balcony to the kitchen, to the sofa, to his bedroom, smoking cigarette after cigarette, thinking about this. About the letter, the accident. Omura. He picked up the photograph from his bedside table, put it down, picked it up—stared into her eyes.

As the day wore on, he became more and more convinced that later that evening Omura would appear outside his door once again, unannounced and uninvited. In his present frame of mind, Omura was the last person he wanted to see. He decided he would go to watch the Bastille Day fireworks after all. Besides, he had just remembered—it was his birthday. He was sixty-three.

Chapter 3

THAT evening, at nine, Jovert picked up his keys from the kitchen table. He put on his coat, gathered up his crutches, and stepped out into the corridor. He could hear the clack-clack-clack of a typewriter coming from the floor beneath him. As the lift descended, the sound rose for a moment, then drifted away above his head.

On the darkening street, the same mist-like rain. It had been like this for almost a week now. Clumps of people were moving beneath the saffron-haloed streetlamps. He joined the slow tide drifting Bastille-wards in the cataracted light.

Ten minutes later he was standing under the awning of Le Bar l'Anise. Chairs knelt like penitents against the polished rims of the tabletops outside. Through the window, he saw that the café was still only half-full.

When he opened the door, the sudden sound of people

talking, laughter, a glass breaking, flooded past him. A group of men at the far end of the bar looked over at him, nodded. He recognised some of their faces. They were former colleagues, from Special Operations Branch—riot police, anti-terrorists, bomb disposal. Normally they'd be padded up like armadillos. Now, in civilian clothes, they appeared almost weightless. He saw them take in his crutches, saw them filing this piece of information away, for later, for tomorrow, for when he wasn't there. Did you see Jovert? On crutches? Not sorry. Some people *never* forgave you. Besides, you retire. Things change. You're no longer one of them. It was almost a treacherous act to leave. More treacherous. He was surprised how quickly the phone had stopped ringing. If it ever had.

He chose an empty table by the window and ordered a bottle of Gigondas. Daudet, the owner, tall, thin, thin-faced, in his fifties, with bulging, hurt eyes, came over.

Daudet was an old acquaintance. Two years earlier his only son had been killed in a freak car accident. There had been a police investigation. A gun found hidden in the glove compartment. There was some issue about what his son had been up to. Jovert had helped it go away. There was nothing to find, in any case. A gun—hidden? Not hidden? Who knew whose it was? It could have been anyone's. Unregistered, untraceable. No criminal record. Nowhere to go.

A year ago, he'd heard that Daudet's wife had died. Of grief, cancer, resignation? He didn't know. He remembered her—vivacious, dark-skinned, part Dutch, part Indonesian.

A mole above her right eye. She had always been friendly to him: Hello, Mister Inspector Jo-Jo. You like a table? How is business? If only she knew.

Now he looked around the bar. Gone were the shadow puppets from the walls, the gamelan music, the advertisements for Bintang beer. Only the name had remained unchanged. Le Bar l'Anise. Some people never knew.

So, Daudet said, picking up one of his crutches. Citroën?

Jovert laughed.

No, he said. It was a Fiat.

Ah, *les Italiens*. And let me guess. He didn't stop.

No, he stopped, Jovert said. He stretched out his leg. It's nothing really. A scratch. It could have been worse.

Yes, Daudet said. He could have been Swiss.

He gave a short laugh, flicked his tea towel over his shoulder. He leaned down and picked up Jovert's bottle, topped up his glass.

We don't see much of you these days, he said. I heard you had retired.

Jovert nodded.

You know, I never thought I'd see the day. Jovert, Inspector of Police, retired. It's hard to believe.

He shrugged. What could he say. He had never thought he'd see the day himself.

Life, Daudet said, and walked off.

❀

At midnight, the fireworks start without warning. Five or six booming explosions, like mortar fire, echo around the square. For one frightening, chaotic moment—it is as though a trapdoor has suddenly opened beneath him—he is back on the streets of Algiers, in a police car, hurtling through the labyrinthine darkness, his arm outstretched against the dashboard. He can see figures running. Cars overturned. Buildings on fire. A man reaches out to them as they pass; his face is imprinted on Jovert's brain. Beseeching them to stop. His splayed hands burst up in front of the car like two white pigeons. Thibaud swerves to avoid him. All around them, there is artillery fire.

Thibaud is saying: What if she's not there? What if she's already left?

He strikes the steering wheel with the palm of his hand.

This is crazy, crazy. *Merde*.

Then he is back in the café, listening to the last thunderous report dying away. This, he knows, is just the prelude. Four or five eerily quiet seconds pass. He can see the crowd gathered on the pavement. The rain has cleared. Suddenly, the curved darkness above them explodes. Dozens of splintering spheres of light burst silently overhead. A moment later, like an afterthought, a muted, antiphonal boom, boom-boom echoes across the square. He can feel the reverberations through the floor, see the minute tremblings of the window pane.

With each burst of light, a vast sea of upturned faces is lit up. It is like something primitive, he thinks. This primeval noise, these sky-shattering eruptions of light, the transfixed human mass beneath. The building façades on the opposite side of the square flicker on and off, as insubstantial as opera sets.

As he turns away from the window, someone bumps his table. A small red archipelago of wine spills from his glass. He looks up. A young woman is leaning across his table, her hand pressed flat against the window. She is wearing a close-fitting black dress and dark glasses.

I'm sorry, she says.

She barely glances at him. But then she turns back, takes her glasses off.

Don't I know you? she says.

I don't think so, he replies.

She frowns down at him, as if she is searching her memory, trying to place where she might know him from. He begins to feel uncomfortable. Perhaps she does know him. It *is* possible. He had been an Inspector of Police for thirty years. He had met thousands of people. He's sixty-three. She looks back over her shoulder.

Merde, she says. *Ne-poussez-pas*. Don't push. There's a table here.

She turns back to him.

Maybe you're right, she says.

Then she leans across his table again. Perhaps it is the effect of the wine, or the combination of her black dress and the darkness of the café, but with her suspended above him like this, it is difficult to tell where her body ends and the night sky begins. It is as though he is looking through her into the star-clustered heavens above. It is only intermittently, when the sky lights up outside, that he can see this odd inverted horizon for what it is—an outstretched arm and a body clad in black.

He found himself wondering about this young woman, what her life was like. Was she a student? Did she work? Where did she live? Did she have a lover? What was *he* like? Or she. And why was she here alone? He thought about the photograph. Mathilde. Not that they were the same: they weren't. This girl was younger. Still, he thought, change a few details, a time, a location, and this young woman could easily have been her—the daughter he had never known.

He watched her raise her hand to shade her eyes. She seemed to be searching the fugitive shapes of the buildings opposite, moving intently from one to another. He followed her gaze. Through the plane trees he could see the packed balconies. On one, a group of young people were singing, boys and girls with their arms around each other. He could see their mouths moving, the cans of beer in their hands. A good-looking boy—someone he could imagine a girl like her with—was keeping time with a bottle of champagne.

But there were so many balconies it was impossible to tell where exactly she was looking. His gaze fell distractedly to the crowded street, and to the moment which, in retrospect, seemed inevitably to be there, waiting for him. Standing on the pavement, standing so close that he could almost have reached through the glass to touch him, was Omura. He was wearing the same suit, the same spectacles, as the evening before.

His umbrella hung from his arm. He was staring into the momentary darkness above him, his head tilted so far back that his hat was balancing precariously on the edge of his collar. At any moment Jovert half-expected it to fall end over end to the ground.

He leaned back into the shadows, watched as Omura took off his glasses and wiped them clean. He saw him retrieve a small notebook from his coat pocket and begin to write something into it. Another constellation of light lit up the square. Two old women as thin as circus dogs stepped unsteadily back, their handbags raised above their heads. One of them half-stumbled into Omura. He barely seemed to notice, merely stepped aside, continued writing. Then he glanced down at the pavement, looked around, folded his notebook and put it back inside his coat pocket.

As Jovert reached out to pick up his glass, the young woman who had been leaning over his table pushed herself away from the window. Their eyes met once again. She smiled.

Au revoir, Monsieur, she said.

Au revoir, Mademoiselle. He raised his glass.

When he looked back into the street, Omura was no longer there.

❀

Half an hour after the fireworks had finished, Jovert reached for his crutches, stood. Daudet was busy polishing glasses behind the bar. He nodded to him over the remaining crowd, and left.

The air outside was thick with the smell of exploded fireworks. Jovert stood on the curb for a second or two, adjusting his grip on his crutches, then levered himself cautiously across the intersection. Ahead of him, thickets of people lingered on the pavement. Talking, laughing, negotiating the remains of the night. Here and there they spilled out onto the roadway. Jovert was forced to step off the curbside from time to time to get around them.

Outside Le Soleil Noir another group. All young. Some drunk. A young man in jeans and studded jacket was looking at him with a kind of cool detachment as he approached, as though he were some kind of exotic insect. The young man turned back to his friends. Jovert was close enough to hear him say: No, no, you're wrong. It was at Serge's.

A young woman at his side grasped his sleeve.

Frédéric? she said. She leaned into him, tugged at his arm. Frédéric, there's someone here, someone who wants to get by.

But instead of moving aside, the young man brushed her hand away.

Wait, he said sharply. Can't you see, Solange, I'm talking here.

He glanced at Jovert.

You're wrong, he said again. I am absolutely sure it was at Serge's.

The young woman looked at her companion, her mouth open, her dismissed hand still raised.

Merde, she said. She cuffed his shoulder. Why are you *such* a jerk, Frédéric? She looked at Jovert, shrugged her shoulders.

It's okay, he mouthed.

He looked across the road to the dark archway of rue de Lesdiguières. He would be better off taking the long way home, he thought, walking through the deserted back streets, where he did not have to contend with arseholes like this.

Twenty minutes later, when he turned the corner of rue St Paul and stepped out into rue St Antoine, Omura was standing in front of their building. He had his notebook out. He was flipping through its pages. Jovert saw him peer at the notebook, then at the keypad; watched him plug in his security code. The door opened and Omura disappeared inside.

Then Jovert was standing outside the same door, punching in his own security code. He listened for the familiar click. Pushed the door open. The light over the lift was on. The door was ajar. He stepped in and pushed the button. As the lift began to ascend, it half-crossed his mind that Omura might be waiting for him outside his apartment. But when he arrived at his floor and stepped out into the corridor, the hallway was empty.

Chapter 4

THREE days later, there *was* a knock at his door.

Ah, Inspector, Omura said when he opened it.

Professor Omura.

Omura. Just Omura, please, Omura said.

Omura.

Would you care to join me for dinner, Inspector?

Professor Omura, Jovert said, that is very kind. Thank you. But I am exhausted. He looked down at his leg, held out one of his crutches. Perhaps anoth—

I have booked a table for us, Omura said. You would be my guest. I would be honoured by your presence.

Jovert looked at Omura's smiling face. In a way he could not quite explain, he was aware that the decision whether to go or not had already been made for him, that the present moment contained the next, the moment in which he would reach for his coat and step out into the corridor to follow Omura down the hallway to the waiting lift. He was surprised, however, by how simply he had been caught.

My coat, he said.

He reached behind the door, handed his crutches to Omura, and stood on one leg pulling his coat on. He gestured with his hand for Omura to lead the way.

Please, he said.

Outside, it was raining again. A cool wind had sprung up. Jovert stood in the lee of the building adjusting his collar. Omura opened his umbrella, held it above Jovert's head. The remnants of the evening rush hour, heads bowed, brushed past them.

It's supposed to be summer, Jovert said. Look at this weather.

Omura nodded, looked about.

There were tiny specks of rain on Omura's glasses. He was holding his hat against his head with his left hand. Jovert could see two nicotine-stained fingers and the speckled skin on the back of Omura's hand. His skin was so translucent he could see through it to the white bones and the fine network of veins beneath.

This way, Inspector, Omura said.

❀

Twenty-five minutes later they stepped up out of the Metro onto the twilit streets of Belleville. This was an area Jovert knew well. It was the Algerian part of town. The rain had ceased, but the roadways were still glassy. They had barely crossed the intersection when Omura retrieved a small blue guidebook from his coat pocket. They were standing at the entrance to a narrow elbow-kinked street. At its far end, where it disappeared, a series of neon lights were blinking on and off. Their reflection spilled down the roadway to where the two of them stood. Above their heads, a familiar sinuous melody wound its way into the night.

One moment, Professor Omura, he said. Where, exactly, are we going?

Not far, Inspector. Just a few steps. Omura pointed to the row of neon lights.

Yes, yes, Jovert said. He could hear the irritation in his voice. But which restaurant are we going to?

Le Sétif, Omura said.

Le Sétif! Jovert almost shouted. A man and a young woman walking in the opposite direction on the other side of the street looked across at them. He saw the man's arm come up to the woman's shoulder, registered the soft collision of their bodies as he pulled her closer.

Why Le Sétif? he said. Why there?

It was the one recommended, Omura said.

Recommended? Recommended by whom?

Not by whom, Inspector.

He reached into his inside pocket again and pulled out the guidebook. He flipped through its pages until he came to an entry which had been asterisked in red.

See, he said, tapping the page. Le Sétif—best Algerian food. Best service. Best value. Four stars.

Jovert took the book from him. He read the entry.

But why there, of all places?

I do not understand, Inspector.

Why Le Sétif? Why Algerian?

The other night. You said you had spent some time in Algeria. I myself have not eaten food from this part of the world.

And that's the only reason?

The only reason, Inspector.

He stood thinking about what Omura had said.

I'm sorry, Omura, he said eventually. I can't go there. An unhappy coincidence. Is there somewhere else?

❀

In the end, they went to Le Chapeau Tombé, a restaurant on the other side of town, somewhere far from the tainted streets of Belleville, somewhere Jovert took his associates. Used to take.

Jovert recalled later that, immediately the waiter had left, Omura began asking him questions: about his life, his past, what he had done, where he had been. There was a peculiar urgency about it, a directness he had found unnerving.

Were you ever married, Inspector? Omura asked.

Once.

May I ask what happened?

We...we grew apart, he said.

And children?

Yes, one.

A daughter?

No, a son.

Jovert shifted in his seat. He glanced across at a young woman who was sitting alone by the window. She was wearing a red scarf. Her hair was freshly cut. Her skin lightly tanned. She was twisting a ring distractedly on one of her fingers. He saw her look at her watch. She leaned forward on her elbows, looked out the window, first one way, then the other. The street outside was deserted. It had begun to rain again.

And you see your son often? Omura asked. He lives in Paris?

No.

No?

No, Jovert said evenly. He's dead. He died as a child.

Omura paused.

I'm so sorry, Inspector. I did not know, he said.

Now it was Omura's turn to look away.

You know, Inspector, he said after some minutes, when I was a child, my father loved jigsaw puzzles. This may strike you as odd in a grown man. But jigsaws mean something different for us. Ours is an ancient tradition, quite distinct from what you have here in Europe. Each piece of a puzzle is considered individually. No shape is repeated, unless for some special purpose. Some pieces are small, others large, but all are calculated to deceive, to lead one astray, in order to make the solution of the puzzle as difficult, as challenging, as possible. In our tradition, how a puzzle is made, and how it is solved, reveals some greater truth about the world. Puzzles are not toys to us, but objects of contemplation. Do you understand what I mean?

I think so, Jovert said.

In any case, my father was fascinated by them. He was a connoisseur, an expert. He had a huge collection. All of them from China or Japan. He had a number of extremely rare, one-of-a-kind puzzles that were centuries old. They were beautiful things, made from combinations of exotic woods, with inlays of ivory, or mother of pearl, or gold and enamel. They were works of art in their own right, exquisite things.

But the puzzles my father prized above all others were the ones he loved for the ingenuity of their construction. Perhaps you have heard of them. They are the so-called *himitsu-e* puzzles, puzzles so cunningly made that they have either an infinite number of solutions or solutions which are mutually contradictory.

Then, one day—I must have been eleven or twelve at the time—my father came home waving a magazine about above his head. He called for my mother and me to come and look at what he had bought. I can still see us gathered around him, looking at an advertisement in the magazine for European jigsaw puzzles.

Five thousand pieces, he was saying. Five thousand! Can you imagine that?

He sent away for one. While he was waiting, he even had a wooden box specially made for it.

In the intervening weeks our whole household became caught up in my father's excitement. I think we all began to pace to and fro with him as he waited. Finally he received a message from the post office that a package had arrived, and he set off to fetch it.

An hour later, my father came home carrying a large carefully wrapped carton in his outstretched arms, as though it was an offering.

We all crowded round while my father placed it on the table. I can see him sitting there contemplating it.

Aren't you going to open it? my mother asked.

Shh, my father said, holding up his hand.

You know, it makes me laugh now. I remember when my father eventually unwrapped the box how impressed he had been with the beautiful picture of water-lilies on its lid.

You would have to know my father, Omura said. You see, after he had emptied the contents out onto the table, in a state of ecstasy, seeing the enormous pile of pieces in front of him, he handed me the box they had come in.

Here, Tadashi, he said. You can have this.

My poor, dear father.

He was so agitated, and so unfamiliar with how one put such puzzles together that his first, tentative efforts to assemble it were agonisingly laborious. He spent ages contemplating individual pieces, turning them this way and that, saying: Look at this, look at this. Then later, much later, when the picture began to emerge, he could barely contain himself. Until, of course, it dawned on him.

Tadashi, Tadashi, I remember him calling.

Yes, Father, I said, when I arrived.

What did you do with the box?

At first I wasn't sure what he meant.

The box that contained the puzzle, he said.

I brought it to him. He sat for a long time looking at the picture on the cover and the partially completed puzzle that lay before him. He seemed unable to believe that they were the same.

You cannot comprehend how disillusioned he was. The fact that these images were identical went against everything he had ever understood about jigsaw puzzles.

The experience changed my father. He went back to the jigsaws he had known all his life. Then, one day, these too he put away. He had become obsessed with the idea that lay behind these mass-produced European puzzles.

No matter where you start, he said. You always end up in the same place. And you always know beforehand.

I think he felt trapped.

Perhaps, Father, I said, there's another way of looking at it. Perhaps it means something like this—it doesn't matter where you start, if you keep going, you will always find completion. What is important is that you start.

I thought that this would appeal to his way of thinking. Instead, a strange sort of pessimism seemed to take hold of him.

What if what you discover, Tadashi, is not what you want to know? he said.

And I had no answer for this.

❀

When Omura finished telling him about his father, Jovert found that, as if by magic, their meals were already there in front of them. He glanced over to where the young woman had been sitting. But she was no longer there. Her empty chair was pushed back from the table as if she had only just got up. A half-drunk glass of wine stood beside her untouched plate. He could just make out a faint smudge of lipstick at its rim.

❀

When they left the restaurant, the wind had died down. The rain had eased. Light still trickled in the gutters.

I thought you might have asked about the girl, Omura said.

They were standing at the corner of rue du Jardinet. On the truncated end of the building facing them was an enormous billboard. It showed a woman's face. Beneath her lips, a telephone number. *Call* ME, it said.

What girl? Jovert said.

The girl on the ice.

Jovert stood looking at Omura. The street was empty. The sounds of the city had retreated.

What would you have done? Omura said.

What do you mean, Professor Omura?

Would you have gone on? When I first heard the axe falling, I had a choice. I could have turned around and gone back. I already knew, instinctively, that this was no place for me. If it had been you, what would you have done?

I don't know, he said.

Jovert had never liked conversations like these, conversations he did not control, which reversed the natural order of things.

But you must know, Omura said abruptly.

Why must I know? Jovert replied. It's got nothing to do with me.

Jovert watched as a gust of wind scooped up a plastic bag lying in the gutter opposite. Its ghostly form swept up through the lamp light. For a moment, it skimmed back and forth across the façade of the building opposite, as though it was pursuing something. Then, without warning, it shot up into the sky above their heads and disappeared.

Rain had begun to mist down again.

Listen, Omura, Jovert said. I don't mean to be rude, but why are you asking me this?

How else am I to know, Inspector? he said. In Japan, we have a saying: If you want to see your life, you have to see it through the eyes of another. Perhaps you can help me. And I can help you.

What do you mean—help me? he said. Help in what way?

That is for you to decide, Inspector.

And if I don't want your help, Professor Omura?

Omura stood looking into the funnelling darkness.

You? You have no choice, Inspector. Not now. Why do you resist?

Resist, he said. What, exactly, am I resisting?

I do not know, Inspector, Omura said calmly. Perhaps one day you will tell me.

Jovert could see that hundreds of tiny droplets of water had begun to gather on Omura's shoulders, and the crown of his hat. He watched the nimbussed headlights of a taxi approach from further down the street. The taxi slowed for a moment. He caught a glimpse of the driver's face turned briefly towards them before it sped on.

And, Professor Omura, if I ask you to leave me alone? What then?

Then, of course, Inspector. I will leave you alone. If that is what you want.

Now, standing on this dimly lit corner, with rain misting down, Jovert felt the events of the last few days descend upon him like a weight. The night had been long. His shoulders were aching. He looked at his watch. It was almost midnight.

I am sorry, Professor Omura. I do not know what you want from me. But please, please, leave me alone.

As you wish, Inspector.

With this, Jovert stepped out from beneath Omura's umbrella. He poled himself across the intersection and up onto the pavement on the other side. Kept going. He could see his projected shadow on the wall of the building opposite folding and unfolding like a giant calliper. When he got to the end of the street, he glanced back. Omura was still standing in the middle of the empty intersection. He had his notebook out. Half a dozen leaves were swirling eerily above his head. He could almost hear Omura saying: Four days, Inspector. I give you four days.

Chapter 5

FOUR days, Inspector. I give you four days. If Omura *had* said that, he was wrong. It was three weeks before Jovert saw him again.

Later, Jovert asked himself why. Why had he waited so long? Not that he couldn't guess. In his experience, strangers turning up on your doorstep, unannounced and uninvited, never augured well. How many times had he had to do this himself, knock on someone's door? The bearer of bad tidings. Your son. Your daughter, husband, child. He no island of solace in a sea of weeping. Unable to take back the forever time-locked moment. How long *did* you wait before you went? Was there ever long enough?

He went to see his doctor again. His afflicted knee an endless dull discomfort. He sat once more on the hard-edged examination table. He flexed and unflexed his leg.

You need more exercise, Inspector. Swimming, treading water, hydrotherapy. His doctor's hand cold on his hot knee.

He surrendered his crutches. Got a walking stick. Gargoyletopped, antique, something with history. From the same place he had abandoned his squat-footed cabinet. His *hippopotamane*. Who would have imagined that there was a word for things like this?

He went to the pool on rue de Pontoise to exercise, the famous one, the one with the glass roof and the tiers of pale-blue cubicles coliseumed above the water.

He called an old friend at Police Headquarters. Asked for a favour, two. He wanted him to locate someone.

Yes, that's right. Algiers, he said.

He was sure his friend would still have the necessary contacts.

Who?

Haifa Soukhane.

I thought that was ancient history, his friend said.

It is. He did not elaborate.

And?

And any information you can find out about a Mathilde Soukhane, he said.

Mathilde, his friend repeated, writing it down. Jovert could picture him in his office, already configuring, calculating, reconfiguring.

And who is she?

Her daughter, he said.

Her daughter, his friend repeated. The three syllables written.

Anything else I should know?

No, he said.

❀

Three days later, a return phone call.

Haifa Soukhane...He could hear papers rustling. Haifa Soukhane was killed in a car accident. Last year. No suspicious circumstances.

No suspicious circumstances?

That's what it says.

Okay, he said.

She'd become a judge, you know. In Algiers. Much admired. He paused. For what it's worth, his friend said, I'm sorry.

Jovert was at a loss to know what to say. Haifa. Killed. The year before. So recent.

On the other hand, it *was* a long time ago. Anything could have happened in between. Still, he should have prepared himself.

The past is the past, he said. And Mathilde?

Mathilde. Once again he could hear papers being shuffled. Mathilde. What, in particular, did you want to know?

I'm not sure, he said. An address, date of birth. Anything.

Let me see. Last known address: 30 rue Amar el-Kama—same as the mother's. Date of birth: 22 June 1960. Studied jurisprudence in Marseille. Current whereabouts, occupation...unknown.

Married?

No. Not that I can see.

Siblings?

None listed.

Thanks, he said, and rang off.

So, rue Amar el-Kama. Not rue Duhamel.

He did a quick calculation. 22 June 1960. Yes, it was possible. Just. He had left Algiers on 3 October 1959. June 1960 to July 1989. That would make her twenty-nine.

He needed time to think. He went back to rue de Pontoise.

❀

Jovert wondered if the sound bothered his neighbours. Omura's typing. It was him he could hear whenever he went up, or down, in the lift. The dull, brain-stuck clack-clack, clack-clack-clack. At eleven in the evening. Midnight. Sometimes later. Lying in bed. The sound filtering up through the floorboards. Clack, clack-clack. Awake. Listening for the next key to strike. The noise reminding him that Omura was there, that he was waiting. Until it stopped.

So he went.

❀

Inspector? Omura said, when he opened the door.

Omura. Besuited. Bespectacled. But the bow tie new.

He had expected Omura's apartment to be different. What he found was spare, ordered, interim. The floor plan a mirror image of his. The same ageing light-stained curtains. A wooden desk by the window. On it, an old manual typewriter—a

Bresson—its body as polished, as flawless as a museum exhibit, its silver-rimmed keys now silent. A single lamp. Beneath it, a ream of paper, radiant in the white light.

Omura made coffee.

Jovert had gone there hoping to resolve something. Exactly what, he did not know. He remembered standing. Sitting. Then… the same hypnotic thing. Without knowing how it happened, or when, he found himself once again floating in a conversation that appeared to have no beginning, no antecedent. As if it had always been there.

You must think me foolish, Omura was saying. An obsessed old man.

He paused to re-light his cigarette. In any case, after much reflection, he went on, Fumiko and I finally moved to Tokyo. I had been offered a partnership in one of Japan's most respected legal firms. We rented an apartment on the top floor of one of the new high-rise buildings overlooking the city. I had a space in the basement where I set up a workshop—a small private world of my own where I could make things. I had an intercom installed connecting it to my apartment. Three or four nights a week, after I had put Fumiko to bed, I would go down there. To make things—toys, wooden boxes, that sort of thing. It was a release for me, an escape from my workaday life.

Occasionally, seeing my workbench, with my tools all gleamingly arrayed above me, I used to think I had missed my vocation—that I would have been better off doing something with my hands than trying to deal with something as elusive, as intangible, as the law. If it hadn't been for Fumiko, perhaps I would have. Not that Fumiko was the reason I kept practising. On the contrary, with Fumiko in my life, there was no need to look for anything else. Besides, most of what I made in my workshop, I made for her.

The year Fumiko turned five, I decided to take her to Kamakura. To see the famous kite festival. I knew what to expect. I had been there many times before. But I wanted this to be a special occasion for her, one she would never forget. So I set about making a present for her, something I had once seen in a Kyoto toy store.

Each night, after work, I went down to my workshop. Of course, Fumiko guessed that I was down there making something new for her. She began questioning me. In the morning, before school. In the evening when I arrived home from work. I remember on the third or fourth evening I heard the intercom buzz.

I raised my protective goggles, pushed the button. It was Fumiko.

Father? I heard her say.

Yes, Fumiko.

Can I come down? Please?

I looked at my watch. It was already 10.30.

You should be in bed, I said.

I was, but I can't sleep.

I took my glasses off, rubbed my eyes. I was tired myself.

All right, I said. But just for a few minutes.

I went over to my bench and pulled a clean cloth out from one of the drawers and used it to cover what I had been working on. I had just finished tidying my tools when I heard a tap, tap-tap-tap on my door.

Fumiko was in her pyjamas, her hands behind her back. She was smiling, looking up at me. As I reached up to pull the cord to extinguish the last remaining light over my workbench, she tried to peek past me.

Oh, no you don't, I said.

But you said you'd finish it tonight.

No, I didn't. I said I'd finish putting it together tonight. I still have quite a bit to do. And besides, what did I tell you—not until Kamakura.

Ooh, she said.

Whenever I was down there, I used to tie a piece of white cloth around my head to keep the sawdust off. I remember stepping out into the basement and hoisting Fumiko up onto my hip. She had her arm around my neck. When we reached the lift, she took a deep breath and blew. A cloud of dust billowed up from my head.

There, she said, and her clear, bell-like laughter filled the emptiness around me.

❀

You know, Inspector, Omura said. I still have it. What I made her. I brought it with me. Would you like to see it?

Before Jovert could answer, Omura had risen from his chair and disappeared into one of the bedrooms. A few minutes later, he returned carrying a small rectangular wooden case the size of a shoebox. Its burnished surface had been embellished with a series of thin, shallow brushstroke inlays. It could have been a thousand years old.

Omura handed him the box. It was heavier than Jovert had anticipated. He turned it over, looked for a clasp. There wasn't one. It appeared to have been cut from a solid block of wood. He glanced at Omura.

Press here with your thumb, Omura said. Now, slide the top.

The wood seemed magically to separate.

That is beautiful, he said. Ingenious.

The case was lined with silk. Fitted snugly into this was a long, thin, trapezoid-shaped object. At its centre, there was a folded handle. Jovert lifted it up and pulled the object out. There were eyepieces at one end.

It's a viewer, a mirror scope, Omura said.

Jovert held the instrument up to his eyes. Instantly, the room began to spin.

Oh, he said, shaking his head.

I know, Omura said. In here is not the right place. But outside...you should see it outside.

Jovert took a closer look at the viewer. The end opposite the eyepieces was open. Inside, it was lined with mirrors. Externally, the sides had been lacquered a rich, multilayered red.

Beneath the lacquer, in the wood itself, he could see what looked like flecks of gold. Long, sweeping brushstrokes ran the length of each side. Down the centre, there was a single column of beautifully formed Japanese characters.

Here, Omura said, rising from his chair and taking the viewer from him. He walked over to the lamp, held the viewer under it. Its lacquered surface suddenly came to life, almost as if the wood was translucent, lit from within.

I remember the moment I finished it, Omura said, when, finally, it existed free of me. He ran his fingertips across its embered surface. Its beauty exceeded even my own expectations.

❀

The following weekend, we went to Kamakura, to view the kites. We took the train. Then the bus. We disembarked high above the beach. It was spring. The sun was shining. Fumiko was walking or half-skipping along beside me. She carried our straw mat under her arm. I carried our picnic basket.

We sat on a grassy embankment somewhat away from the rest of the crowd. Fumiko was chattering away to me like a bird. I remember laughing at something she said.

Most of the crowd had already gathered at the foot of the slope which ran the length of the beach. The mood was festive. Laughter floated on the air. Banners high on poles swam eel-like in the breeze. There were vendors pushing their brightly canopied carts back and forth. We could hear their strange cries coming up to us intermittently on the breeze. A bird seller, his cages hoisted like a giant corn cob over his shoulder, was wandering from group to group.

Below us, on the beach itself, the kite flyers and their assistants were busy making the final adjustments to their crafts. A few kites, not many, had already taken to the air. Beyond them was the ocean. The repeated rise and fall of a small surf. To the west I could see the velvet-blue mountains, where they rose abruptly out of the narrow coastal plain.

Couldn't we go a little closer, Fumiko said.

Let's see what it looks like from here first, shall we. Then, if we don't like it, we can move. But, I said, I think you'll find that this is the perfect spot.

I laid the straw mat on the ground, pulled its corners straight. Fumiko slipped her shoes off, then sat in the middle of it.

We were protected from the wind, and the sun quickly began to warm us. As we sat looking down at the beach, each new instant saw yet another kite—a swallow, a dragon, a butterfly, a frowning face—take to the sky. It was only when you looked down to see the tiny tent-peg figures of the kite flyers struggling beneath them on the beach, their crab-like arms working away in front of them, that you realised just how enormous these kites were. As one of them took to the sky, it lifted the man holding its ropes three or four metres off the ground. I could see his legs running in the air.

Look, I said to Fumiko, pointing to him. She watched the man bounding along the sand, his assistants running after him, trying to catch the guy ropes dragging along the ground.

Half an hour later, as I had anticipated, the wind began to change. Within minutes, five gigantic samurai faces were ducking and weaving through the air above us. They would swoop down, one after another, descending so rapidly, their sails roaring in the wind, that it seemed impossible that they would not come crashing down on us. But at the last moment, barely metres above our heads, they veered away across the slope, then climbed serenely up into the sky again. Fumiko was lying on the blanket in front of me, following the zigzagging trajectories of the duelling kites. I remember her eyes, how closely they followed the changing fortunes of the battle, and her mouth—now smiling, now with breath held.

This *is* the perfect spot, Father, she said.

Aren't you forgetting something? I reached into the basket and held up the case.

She sat up.

Of course, she said.

I handed the case to her, showed her how to open it. She put it in her lap, pushed the lid aside. The viewer lay snug and lustrous in its silk lining. She began to prise it out with her child's fingers. She held it up, examined first one end, then the other.

But what is it, Father? she said.

It's a viewer, I said. Here, if you hold it like this. I folded her fingers around the opened handle. Now, if you look through these two holes.

I brought the viewer up to her eyes.

Now look through here, I said.

She drew in her breath.

Oh, Father, she said. It's wonderful. Just wonderful.

She stayed like this for some time, looking at the soaring kites. Then she took the viewer away from her face and closed her eyes.

It's as though the whole world is just sky, and you're floating in the middle of it, she said. Just floating. And all these kites are spinning around and around and around you.

She opened her eyes again. She held the viewer up in front of her. She turned it around, and looked at its open end.

It's beautiful, Fumiko said. Beautiful.

Perhaps I *am* a foolish old man, Omura said. But seeing Fumiko lying there, seeing her smiling, I cannot tell you, Inspector, how much I had come to love this child.

That evening, on the way home, in the train, Fumiko sat by the window. At some point I caught a glimpse of her reflection. Her face seemed to be floating in the darkness outside. Seeing her like this, I was reminded of the first time I saw Sachiko, her mother. And I was reminded yet again of all the terrible events that followed.

Chapter 6

AFTER that day at the beach, time seemed to evaporate. Years slipped by like days. My legal practice at Fujimoto, Fujimoto and Co. expanded. I became a senior partner. I began publishing articles in a number of legal journals. My reputation grew. As a consequence, I was offered a professorship at the Imperial University. It was a difficult decision. I enjoyed my work. There was also the question of loyalty. Fujimoto and Co. had been good to me. And Fumiko. So I put a proposition to the university. I would accept their offer on the condition that I was able to continue my private practice. They agreed.

So, two days a week, I continued walking the kilometre and a half to my office, just as I had been doing for years. And for a long time my life with Fumiko was settled. Of course, there *were* times when she was curious about her mother. This was only to be expected. I answered her questions by telling her that her mother had died in childbirth, which was true. I showed her a black-and-white photograph of Katsuo and Mariko, his fiancée, and myself that had been taken on the terrace of Katsuo's house overlooking Osaka Bay. This was at a time when Katsuo and Mariko were still happy.

In the photo, the bay was at our backs. I remember Katsuo showing Ume, his housekeeper, how to operate the camera. It was late afternoon. Katsuo and I were wearing our dark suits. He was holding his hat in his left hand by his side. Mariko was wearing a long, white, pleated dress, like something from the twenties. A row of dark pearls at her neck. On the stone balustrade beside us were two glasses of saké, each still half-full.

In the photograph, Mariko's dress glows in the late afternoon sun. I am standing next to her. My right hand is resting on her shoulder. She has a small scar there, like a tiny map of Japan, which she does nothing to conceal. Katsuo is standing off to one side.

I used to look at this photograph from time to time. And every time I did so, I could see why Katsuo had fallen in love with Mariko. With her half-smile, her self-possessed gaze, Mariko was extraordinarily beautiful.

I told Fumiko that this was Sachiko, her mother. Who had died in childbirth. It was a lie, but a small lie, one which she seemed happy to accept.

On the other hand, she never once questioned the monstrous lie that lay dormant just below the surface of our lives, the lie that I was her father, a lie that I knew would come back to haunt us. But by then, her childhood memories, if they had ever existed, had been erased.

Occasionally, little things would even conspire to reinforce this deception. Once, I remember, we were eating our evening meal when Fumiko—she must have been twelve at the time—turned to me and said: Do you remember, Father, how some months ago I said I had noticed that in the afternoon the shadow of our apartment building climbed your office tower, and that on the day of my birthday the corner seemed to pass right through your window? And you said, well, in that case it would have to pass through your window *twice* in one year. Do you remember?

Yes, I said.

I glanced up. Fumiko's eyes were wide with excitement.

Well, she said. You were right. I've been watching and I've worked out that tomorrow it's going to pass through your window once again.

You mean to say you've been watching my window all this time?

Well, no, she said. Not really. But a month ago I noticed that the shadow had begun to move back across your building.

I went to go on with my meal but when she didn't continue I realised that we were playing a familiar game, only now the roles had been reversed.

Go on, I said smiling.

Well, remember I said how strange it was that the shadow should pass through your window on the very day of my birthday. I said it must mean something. You said it wasn't strange at all, it was just a coincidence.

Yes, I said.

Well, it's tomorrow, she said. Tomorrow it's going to happen again.

I must have looked puzzled.

Tomorrow! she said.

She looked at me with her eyes bright, as if she were stating something obvious.

Tomorrow it's *your* birthday. Don't you see, Father? So it must mean something, after all.

❀

Father. As the day of Katsuo's release drew near, each time Fumiko said the word I had so longed to hear it was like a blade being plunged into my heart. It astonished me how often she said it. Father, could we go to the markets? Father, shall I pour your tea? Father, there's a letter here for you. And each time she said it, I was reminded again of the lie my life had become, and of the inevitability of what lay ahead, the moment when I would have to tell Fumiko the truth. About our life together. And who her father really was.

Exactly three years to the day that Fumiko had reminded me of the shadow passing down my building, the day of my birthday—it made me wonder whether Katsuo had planned this, it would have been so characteristic of him—the letter which would undo my life finally arrived. Fumiko was fifteen, just two years younger than Sachiko was when she died.

After years of vigilance, its arrival caught me completely by surprise. As I knew it would. Every morning I used to go through my mail expecting it to be there. You cannot imagine what that did to me. How much my walk to work was coloured by the expectation that today would be the day it arrived. How it—this waiting—tortured me. Perhaps, I hoped, there would be another solution: Katsuo might die in jail, he might disappear as he had done in the past, he might relinquish her. In my heart, however, I knew that there was no escaping what was about to unfold—it had been written into both our lives years before.

And now, on the morning of my fifty-fifth birthday, here it was.

I had taken the bus to my office instead of walking. It had been raining and I was eager to finish the article I was writing.

I began working as soon as I arrived. At ten, Mrs Akimoto, my secretary, brought me my mail. It lay bundled up in the tray on my desk. I looked up some minutes later to see the thin sharp edge of a pale-blue envelope projecting slightly from the pile. I sat looking at it, this edge, refusing to believe what I knew I was seeing. And seeing it, I felt as though a vice was closing about my chest. I reached out, picked up the bundle. My hand was shaking. I could barely breathe. I undid the piece of string that bound the bundle together. I retrieved the envelope, held it up to my face.

I recognised his handwriting immediately, the characters still beautiful, still perfectly formed. And yet, the more closely I looked, I could see, here and there, an unmistakable tremor, a momentary loss of control, as if death were already stalking him. This observation shocked me. I had never thought of Katsuo growing old. I had been aware of my own decline. But Katsuo. I had always thought of him as young, immutable.

I could not open it. Not at first. I left it all day. I spoke to Mrs Akimoto. Cancelled all my appointments. She had seemed perplexed. At one point, she knocked on my door. I was by the window, looking out over the city, thinking that Fumiko would be home from school by now. Then she knocked again. When she opened the door she was holding a number of files in her arms.

Is everything all right, Mr Omura?

I saw her glance at the unopened letter lying on my desk.

Yes, thank you, Mrs Akimoto, I said.

Is there anything I can get you? she said.

No, I'm fine, I said. Thank you. Have Ryuichi call me tomorrow, will you.

Eventually, I sat down at my desk. I reached into my drawer, drew out my letter opener. I inserted the blade under the flap of the envelope. A thin blue curl, like a tiny breaking wave, began to unfold along its edge.

The writing paper took my breath away. A gift from me years before. I had no idea he had kept it—the texture so beautiful, the grain so fine, the irony so perfect. So characteristic. I *could* see him planning all of this. His foresight was, as always, so cruelly precise.

The letter was exactly as I had expected.

My dear Tadashi,

I have known for some time that it was you who took Fumiko in. I had always hoped it would be. I want you to know—I bear you no malice.

And then, the words I feared.

I would like to see my daughter. I think only of her. Indulge an old man, your one-time friend, this one wish.

How many times had I imagined seeing those words? Imagined Katsuo writing them? *I think only of her, I think only of her…*

This would be how my world ended, I thought. I would be alone, with everything over, all questions answered. And Fumiko, my beloved daughter, would be gone.

As I put the letter down, I felt a death-like chill pass through me. Without Fumiko, my beautiful, beautiful child, life meant nothing to me.

❀

That night, walking home through the crowded streets alone, I wondered what I would do. We were supposed to go to Kamakura the following weekend to watch the kites. It had become a yearly pilgrimage. We always enjoyed ourselves. I could not tell her about Katsuo before then. It would have to wait, even though it had already begun to crush my heart.

So, Fumiko, I said during our evening meal. Are we still going to Kamakura?

We don't have to, Father, she said. Not if you don't want to. We have been so many times before.

And we lapsed into silence, falling back into our own separate worlds, hers with its unknown future, and mine with its inescapable past.

Chapter 7

WE went to Kamakura in any case. I carried the viewer—we had taken it every year since I had made it for her—and my collapsible chair. Fumiko carried the mat, as she always did, and our basket of provisions. We went to our favourite spot overlooking the beach.

But I was not myself. I was preoccupied with how to break the truth to Fumiko. I could not think of anything else. I decided I would tell her later that evening, when we returned home. She, for her part, seemed to have picked up on my mood. I caught her glancing at me from time to time. I could not bring myself to meet her eye.

We sat without speaking for most of the afternoon, me in my chair, with Fumiko on the mat a little way in front of me, her hands around her knees. She had worn her hair up. Her neck was exposed, her earlobe faintly translucent against the sun. A wisp of dark hair kept fluttering beside it in the wind.

The sight of it was more than I could bear.

I do not know whether I dozed off or whether I was daydreaming, nor do I know what brought me back to myself. Perhaps it was a shout from the beach, or the sound of thunder in the distance. Whatever it was, when I next looked up, hours had passed. The beach below was in turmoil. Fumiko lay curled up asleep. Behind us, a tremendous storm had begun to build. Already a dark underbelly of cloud had spilled over the mountains and was beginning to loom over us. The light had begun to change. It was growing darker by the minute.

All around us, people were packing up, folding rugs, reorganising picnic baskets, running this way and that. Some were already leaving, carrying their hastily collected belongings under their arms. The vendors and their carts had already gone. On the beach, the kite flyers were urgently hauling in the few remaining kites. I could see their arms working. Near them, anxious parents were trying to shepherd half a dozen children together who had strayed onto the beach. Somewhere a man was calling, *A-ki-o, A-ki-o,* his voice all but lost in the thunder that now rumbled towards us across the narrow plain.

I watched a lightning bolt dance crazily along the mountain tops. It was alarmingly close. Then another. I looked down and saw the light flicker across Fumiko's face. Almost instantly the thunder detonated above us with a tremendous buffeting thump. I felt the ground shake, as though the earth itself were recoiling. A sharp metallic smell permeated the air. People were beginning to run. The storm was upon us.

Fumiko, Fumiko, I said. I leaned down, shook her shoulder. She sat up, dazed. Hurry. There's a storm coming, I said. We have to go.

❀

The storm broke just as the train pulled out of the station. It was already dark. The rain came slashing down. Fumiko and I sat huddled opposite each other in the crowded compartment. I remember the train gathering speed. I remember a level crossing flashing by, rain-swept windows lighting up, the warning bells rising and falling. A dimly lit station appeared, was gone.

Fumiko was staring into the darkness outside, her head rocking back and forth as the train sped on towards home, and the moment that awaited us there.

We took a taxi from the station to our apartment. It was still raining when we pulled up. We held the straw mat above our heads as we ran along the rain-soaked path towards the entrance.

I no longer remember what happened next, the exact order. But I can still feel the twisted knot in my chest. I can see us in our living room. The curtains are open. The rain has stopped. The glistening city lies spread out below us in the clean sharp air.

Fumiko has changed. She is wearing a simple dark-blue cotton kimono. She is seated opposite me, drying her hair. In her lap, there is a book.

A teapot rests on the stand in front of us. My cup sits

beside it, still full, untouched. Fumiko puts down her brush, reaches for hers.

Fumiko, I say.

I hear my voice. It sounds strangled. I hesitate. The blood is hammering in my head.

I have to talk to you, I say. There is something I have to tell you, something I've been meaning to tell you for a long time...

I look at her. She sits watching me.

But the opportunity never seemed to present itself. Now... now there is no choice, now it's too late.

I thought that, once I had begun, the words would tumble out. But I was wrong. Barely had I begun to speak when my nerve failed me. Where *did* I begin? With Katsuo—her real father? Sachiko—her mother? What had happened to her? Did I tell her first that I was not her father?

I fell silent. I stared at my hands, my grotesquely intertwined fingers, while all the complicated events of my life swirled around and around in my head.

You must understand, I said.

Now, more than ever, I felt ashamed of what I had done. How could I have lied to Fumiko, to my child who was not my child, for so long?

I stopped.

It must have become obvious to her that I could not go on.

It's all right, Father, she said. She opened the book in her lap and pulled out an envelope.

You see, she said. He wrote to me as well.

❀

Why won't you tell me? she says.

It's not up to me, I say.

I had no idea how much time had elapsed. Fumiko was still sitting opposite me. Katsuo's letter was open beside her. She had been crying.

Not even why he was in jail? Not who my mother was? Is it so terrible?

I can't.

Why can't you? You should have told me years ago who my father was. It would have changed everything.

How could I tell her that that is what I had feared most.

I tried, I said.

I told her that it had crossed my mind that Katsuo might die in jail. What would have been the point in telling her then? No one knew except me. No one had ever found out. No one had ever asked any questions. Why risk destroying the happiness we had built together?

Because it was a lie, she said. A lie.

❀

Katsuo's letter to Fumiko was different from the one he sent me. I no longer care what people think of me, he said. Whether what I did was right or wrong. I have paid a terrible price. But you are still my daughter. I would like to see you. I ask nothing more.

What happened after this, over the next few days, I don't remember. Katsuo was due to be released the following week. In his letter to me, he had made one request: the first person he wanted to see as he walked out of the prison gates was Fumiko.

I offered to accompany her to Osaka. She refused.

She booked the ticket herself. Her train departed from one of the small outer-suburban stations. She agreed to let me take her there. It was late in the afternoon when we arrived. Knots of people had gathered on the platform, waiting to board. The weather had turned cold; the warmth of the day had gone. Now a pitiless wind had sprung up. It buffeted us, first this way then that. It would die down for a while, then come back to howl and snap at my coattails. It was so strong that I had difficulty maintaining my balance. Fumiko's small suitcase lay at my feet. I remember turning away from the wind, my eyes watering. Squinting behind my glasses. Reaching up for my hat. I recall looking off into the distance. I walked a few paces to relieve the stiffness in my legs. I tried in vain to light a cigarette, but each time I put the cupped match up to my face the flame was instantly extinguished.

The station master stuck his head out of his watch post, looked up and down the tracks. I felt like a man awaiting his own execution.

Fumiko came to stand beside me, sheltering her face with the collar of her coat. An image of her as a three-year-old came back to me. It was the afternoon we had gone to see Sachiko's grave. She was dressed in her coat and fur hat, and we were standing on the old Togetsu platform.

The whistle blew.

I have to go, Fumiko said.

I stood awkwardly before her. I could not believe that this moment had finally arrived. I am ashamed to admit it, Inspector, but I stood there silent, not knowing what to say.

Goodbye…Father, she said.

She stooped to pick up her suitcase. I went to help.

It's all right, she said. It's not heavy. I can manage.

I struggled to find the simplest words.

Goodbye, Fumiko. I—

But what I was going to say then, if indeed I was going to say anything, was lost, cut off by another shrill blast from the train whistle.

I went to reach out to touch her shoulder, but couldn't. I was frozen to the spot.

Then she was in the carriage. The train was already full. She was having difficulty making her way down the narrow aisle. I saw her looking at the seat numbers. When she found hers, she lifted her bag into the overhead rack.

I must have turned to look down the platform then. I hadn't expected the train to leave. Not yet. But when I looked back up it was already moving. There was a great confusion now beside me—the wheels squealing against the polished tracks, an incomprehensible announcement over the loudspeaker, the whistle blowing. I looked up to where I thought Fumiko was, but suddenly all of the carriages looked alike. I couldn't tell which was which. I started to move along the platform, my hand outstretched. I don't know what people must have thought. It must have appeared as though I was reaching out to try and stop the train. I scanned the windows of the carriage in front of me. Then the next. The one behind. The whistle sounded one last time.

Fumiko! I called.

A gust of wind snatched my hat off and sent it bounding along the platform, as though it was racing crazily along ahead of me. All at once, it changed direction and veered into the path of the train. Disappeared. One instant, it was there, the next it was not. The train was gathering speed. There was nothing I could do, and I came to a stop.

As the sound of the train died away, a stillness, vast and desolate, descended upon the platform. And I was lost, and utterly, utterly alone.

Part II

KATSUO

❀

Chapter 8

YOU asked me, Inspector, about Katsuo. What he was like.

Where do I begin? We were childhood friends. Katsuo was a little older than me. Like me, he was an only child. But when his father was killed in the war—in a bomb explosion—and his mother died not long afterwards, he was taken in by an uncle who lived in a different part of the city. An uncle on his mother's side. A poor uncle. For a couple of years after that I hardly saw him.

Katsuo proved to be a gifted student. As a consequence, as was not unusual at that time, particularly for children who had been orphaned by the war, an anonymous benefactor arranged to pay the fees for him to go to a good Middle School. My school.

He arrived midyear, in the ninth grade. I can still picture him standing at the classroom doorway with the principal, Mr Nakajima. I was overjoyed to see him again. I could hardly wait to tell my parents. For his part, Katsuo barely glanced at me.

It was as if he no longer knew me.

This is Master Katsuo Ikeda, the headmaster said to our teacher.

She too seemed a little surprised to see him. They exchanged a few words. And then the headmaster introduced him to the rest of us. After which, with a gentle prod, Katsuo went to sit at the back of the class.

After the bell, Katsuo stayed behind, I assumed to talk to the teacher about where he was up to, and to sort out his books.

Guess who's come back, I said to my parents when I returned home from school that afternoon. Of course, they had no idea.

Katsuo, I said. He's back. And he's in my class.

And so we resumed our friendship. He started to visit us again. In fact, he was always at our house. It almost seemed as if he lived there. His father and my father had been old friends. We were like brothers again. Both my parents loved Katsuo, loved him as if he was a second son. If only we had adopted him, my mother would say. As if they could have taken legal precedence over Katsuo's own flesh and blood.

For a long time, I thought it was my father who had provided the money for Katsuo's education. Years later, when I asked him about this, he became very angry. One does not ask such questions, Tadashi, he said. I should know better.

I never knew—until much later—whether he was angry because he had provided the money, but it was a matter of family honour that this not be revealed; or whether he was angry because he had never thought to do so, and wished he had.

But that was later. At the time, when Katsuo came to my school, and we resumed our friendship, he reignited a joy in my parent's life which had long been absent. Not that my parents were unhappy. They weren't. But he seemed to bring them closer together again, to remind them that good things in life still existed after all.

Of course, Katsuo did brilliantly at school—we both did, except that Katsuo did so effortlessly. Moreover, unlike me—I have always been somewhat reserved—Katsuo always seemed to know what to say. How to win favour with people. Teachers, his fellow students, other adults. Even when it was clear that what he was saying was exaggerated, or could not possibly have been the case, people did not take offence. Instead, they laughed at his audacity, became affectionately complicit, as though they enjoyed being taken in. He had the happy knack of stealing the limelight, by some witty remark or droll observation. But he did so in a way that almost always won him friends. Perhaps we thought that by being around him some of his brilliance might rub off on us. It was exciting. Nobody got hurt. At least not in the beginning.

The next year, in the tenth grade, Katsuo published a series of daring haiku in one of Osaka's leading literary magazines. After that, our teachers began talking about the great future which lay ahead of him. They treated Katsuo with renewed respect, fear almost.

Later, before we went to university, Katsuo made me swear never to reveal his straitened circumstances, how poor his uncle was, or that his parents were dead. In particular, I was never to reveal to anyone that he was dependent on the generosity of others for his success.

But you're not dependent on anyone, Katsuo, I said. Any success you've had you've earned yourself.

Don't be foolish, Tadashi, he said. Only someone in your position would say that. If you could spend a minute in my shoes you would see how privileged you are to be you.

As you can probably gather, there was, behind the perpetual smile, something harder in Katsuo, which his eyes betrayed. He was a merciless observer of people. He had a sixth sense about a person's weaknesses, their foibles, their fears. I would find myself watching him when we were out together. One of us would be recounting something they had seen or done, and we would all be listening, nodding our heads to show we were following them. But not Katsuo. He would fall back into the shadows and listen in a way that was entirely different from ours. In comparison, we were hardly there. Katsuo, on the other hand, was not merely listening, he was imprinting. Everything. Every gesture, every intonation, every tiny detail. He used to entertain us with his impersonations of people—teachers, politicians, movie stars. We all thought he was a fantastic mimic. But when his stories began to appear, we realised that he had been observing us as well, and not one of us had escaped his cruel scrutiny.

Much later, he would say to me: Look at people, Tadashi. Just watch them. If you want power over people, you have to get inside them, find out what they are afraid of. Be them. It's the only way.

And I remember responding: What if I don't want power over people, Katsuo. What then?

We all want power over people, one way or another, Tadashi, he said. Including you.

Chapter 9

WE were in our third year of university when the scandal broke. Katsuo had humiliated one of our most respected teachers, an old professor named Todo. After which, instead of waiting to find out if he was going to be expelled, he simply left.

Then, one afternoon, over a year later, a telegram was delivered to my door.

My dear Tadashi, it said. *Urgently need to see you. Am at The Three Willows in Shirahama. Please come by earliest train.*

The telegram was signed: *Your faithful friend Katsuo*.

I wondered, after the Todo incident of the year before, what trouble he was in now.

The next morning I took the first available train. Shirahama was a fashionable seaside town about a hundred kilometres south of Osaka. I sent him a message telling him what time I would arrive.

When I got off the train, there was no one waiting for me.

I walked up and down the platform a number of times, in case I had missed him. I waited an additional twenty minutes, then caught a taxi to The Three Willows. I introduced myself at the desk, got his room number, left my bag. When I knocked on his door, there was no answer. I went back downstairs.

I was expecting to meet Mr Ikeda here, I told the innkeeper. But he's not answering his door.

Well, I can tell you he's still a guest here, the innkeeper said. I saw him go out late last night myself. Perhaps he is yet to return.

This was typical of Katsuo. I had lost count of the number of times he had left me waiting.

If he arrives, I said, could you tell him that I am in the garden. And could you have someone bring me some tea?

The Three Willows was old, but its cedar framework, its sliding screen doors, its beautiful garden, with its koi pools, miniature waterfalls and its sculptures, had all been lovingly restored some years earlier. It was just the place I would have expected Katsuo, with his perverse love of ancient things, to stay.

It was 4.15 before I saw him walk through the wooden archway and into the shaded inner courtyard. He stood for a moment at the top of the stairs, casting about for me. I was shocked by his appearance, however. At university Katsuo had, as part of the shedding of his past, taken to portraying himself as someone who came from a wealthy family. He wore white linen suits, hand-stitched shoes, expensive shirts, and he always, always wore a bow tie. I liked to think it was something he had got from me. Now, standing at the top of the steps, he looked exhausted, unkempt, disreputable.

I signalled to him.

What happened to you? I said, when he sat down. His suit was mud-encrusted, stained all along one side. The sleeve of his jacket was torn. A sliver of red lining was visible. It looked as though someone had tried to tear it from him.

I lost my way, he said. On one of the forest paths, up by the temple gates. I tripped, on a tree root or something. I couldn't tell, it was so dark.

I looked at my watch. It was late afternoon. Still light.

And then, don't tell me, the tree tried to steal your coat?

He didn't reply. He was clearly in no mood for banter. Instead he glanced across at a young couple sitting on the opposite side of the courtyard. They were leaning in to each other. The girl, young, pretty, moist-eyed, was smiling. I saw her catch Katsuo's eye and then look quickly away.

I don't have time for this, Tadashi, he said, turning back to me. I need to get myself cleaned up. Have you got yourself a room?

No, I said. I thought perhaps you might have booked one for me. Didn't you get my message?

What message? he said, looking distractedly about. Oh, yes, yes, that message. I'm sorry, Tadashi. I have had so much to think about lately. And then, last night something urgent came up.

He inspected his trousers.

I should know by now not to wear white, he said. He brushed

at a patch of dirt on his trouser leg.

What a week, he said. What a week.

As we walked back to the foyer he put a hand on my shoulder in his familiar way. I had often wondered where he had picked this gesture up from. Some foreign movie, perhaps. But feeling the weight of his hand on my shoulder made me instantly feel better. Like we *were* old friends, happy to see each other again.

I'm going up to my room, he said. I need to change. Why don't you book yourself in. You're lucky, if you'd come next week, you wouldn't have stood a chance. Not in a place like this. But at the moment, it's almost empty. The rooms either side of mine are vacant. Ask if you can have one of those.

He told me his room number.

I know, I said. The innkeeper gave it to me. I went up earlier and knocked on your door.

Yamada?

Yamada?

Yes, Yamada, the innkeeper. He gave you my room number?

Yes, I said.

A look of anger flickered across his face. He half-turned towards the reception desk, where the innkeeper was chatting to a man, and a woman in a wheelchair.

Is something wrong, Katsuo?

He patted me on my shoulder again.

No, he said. No, it's nothing. I'll see you in half an hour.

And he headed for the stairs, leaving me in the almost empty foyer.

An hour and a half later we were walking amongst Shirahama's market stalls, the ones that sold worthless trinkets, summer clothing, hats, wax-paper umbrellas, song birds in cages, collapsible lanterns.

And Professor Todo? I said.

Haven't you been listening, Tadashi?

We had come to a stall selling cheap jewellery. Katsuo took down a pair of earrings that was hanging from a wire stand. He laid them out in the palm of his hand. He made a small adjustment to the way they lay.

Is this real mother of pearl? he said to the stallholder.

It is, Master Ikeda.

He turned his hand this way, then that, in the light.

So, did you hear me, Tadashi? he said, looking at the earrings. I've finished it. My manuscript.

So you said.

In fact, he had talked about nothing else since he had come down into the foyer looking like the Katsuo of old. Handsomely dressed in a new white suit—despite what he had said earlier. His dark hair slicked back. His cheeks freshly shaved. A gorgeous deep-blue butterfly at his throat.

What do you think? he had said, tugging at his lapels and giving a knowing, new-garment kind of shrug.

Impressive, Katsuo. As always, I said.

He removed a piece of lint from his sleeve.

Todo? I said.

Todo is a fool, Katsuo replied. I've told you that before.

I think he's…was a kind old man. There's a rumour going around that he committed suicide.

I'll take these, Katsuo said to the stallholder. He held up the earrings.

Are they for Miss Yumiko, Master Ikeda? the stallholder asked. He was smiling, but almost instantly his smile faded. I glanced at Katsuo. I saw the same murderous look pass across his face as had passed across it when I mentioned his room number. It lingered for a moment in his eyes. And then he too was smiling.

Todo is no great loss, Tadashi.

How can you be so callous? I said.

He shrugged.

I don't know. I've never really thought about it. Weren't we going somewhere for a drink?

❀

You mean to tell me you're *not* in trouble?

No.

Of any kind?

No, not at all. Why would I be in trouble?

Why, then, the appeal for me to come to Shirahama? Why so urgent?

Because, as I said to you before, Tadashi, I've finished it. My manuscript.

I'm not sure I follow, I said.

I need you to read it. I wrote to you as soon as I had finished.

You mean to say that you summoned me here, to Shirahama, on the train, for the sole purpose of getting me to read your manuscript?

You make it sound as though it's nothing, Tadashi. It's not. You, of all people, should know that.

I took this to be a barbed reference to my own long-dead ambition to become a writer, an ambition my parents had not encouraged, and one that, eventually, I had relinquished myself.

So, that evening, I read Katsuo's manuscript while he paced up and down in my room, smoking cigarette after cigarette. In the end, the air became so thick with smoke that I had difficulty breathing, and I had to ask Katsuo to go out onto the balcony.

Occasionally I'd look up and see the glow of his cigarette. Or I'd catch the embered arc of a burning butt cartwheeling into the darkness, flicked by a preoccupied Katsuo into the lily pond below.

It was two in the morning when I stopped reading. I sat there thinking about what I had just read. Five minutes passed before Katsuo turned and saw that I had finished.

So, what do you think? he said. Do you like the title?

Spring Promise?

Yes.

Spring Promise, I said. It's perfect. The irony heartbreaking. So exquisite, so complete.

It is, isn't it, Tadashi? he said. It *is* the perfect title. I know it sounds conceited, but I needed to hear it. From you. You know how much I trust your judgement. I knew you would see how perfect it was.

He poured himself another drink, lit another cigarette.

Oh, I'm sorry, he said.

He headed for the balcony.

It's okay, Katsuo, I said. I've finished. The air has almost cleared in here, in any case.

He inhaled on his cigarette, looked at its burning end, then threw it over the balcony anyway.

So, he said. Now that you've had some time to think about it, what do you think, overall?

You mean in the five minutes since I put it down?

He shrugged.

I told him again how impressed I was.

And you found it credible?

Very, I said.

He threw his head back. He was exultant.

So, Katsuo, congratulations, I said. Now you've heard it from me.

I knew it, he said. I knew it. I kept saying to myself, if Tadashi approves, I will have achieved what I set out to do.

He sat down, smiling. I think this was the only time I ever saw uncalculated pleasure on his face. Of course, I did not know then what I know now—that the future changes everything.

Chapter 10

TODO, I said.

It was our third evening in Shirahama. We had gone to a small restaurant away from the town centre. When we arrived most of its tables were taken. Not by tourists, but by locals.

You know, Inspector, Omura said, interrupting himself. Isn't that strange. I've forgotten to tell you something, just as I had forgotten it that evening.

You see, when Katsuo came down into the foyer that evening, I was already there waiting for him. I remember him stepping off the stairs and coming over to me. He was adjusting his tie, his cuffs.

What's the matter? he said.

I brought some papers with me, I told him. From Osaka. One of them is missing. I think someone has been through my things.

One of your papers? Why would anyone want to take one of your papers? Are you sure you didn't leave it behind?

It's possible, I suppose, I said. But I could have sworn I brought it with me. It was part of a sequence of documents I've been working on.

Did you tell Yamada?

I did. He asked me what they looked like. They were papers.

What kind of papers?

They were deeds to a property.

Katsuo shrugged.

Are we going? he said. Or would you prefer to stay?

Half an hour later we were pushing on the door of the small restaurant in Shirahama's back streets.

The owner came over to Katsuo when we entered.

Ah, Mr Ikeda. Back so soon?

Katsuo grasped his hand, smiled.

Once we had ordered and the waiter had departed, I returned to the subject I had raised the day I arrived, determined to have an answer once and for all.

Professor Todo? I said.

Like I said, Tadashi, Todo was a fool.

And if it's true, this rumour going around that he committed suicide?

Wouldn't you?

Wouldn't I what?

Commit suicide. If you were T-T-To-d-do, he said, imitating Professor Todo's tortured stutter.

Don't you care?

About what?

T-T-To-d-do, I said pointedly.

No, Tadashi. I don't. And don't look at me like that.

Like what?

Like you're judging me.

He waited.

I see nothing's changed, has it, Tadashi, he said. You think you are such a man of principle. Good, honourable Tadashi, who can do no wrong.

He uttered the words with such bitterness, such venom, that I felt as though I had been slapped.

What happened to us being brothers? he said.

I don't know, Katsuo, I said. Perhaps you could tell me.

❀

How memory waylays us. His comment about being brothers, and what I had been thinking about in that rundown back-street restaurant, resurrected for me, from the undifferentiated mass of otherwise similar memories, the precise moment the scandal had begun to unfold.

Katsuo and I were sitting on one of the stone benches in the old courtyard of the university. Katsuo had returned from Osaka only that morning.

You know, Tadashi, he was saying, Etsuko is probably the most intelligent person I have ever met.

Etsuko was his girlfriend at the time, although I was yet to meet her.

What, more intelligent than you? I said.

Well, at least as intelligent.

And I'm sure she's beautiful too.

Katsuo seemed to consider what I said for a moment. It was unlike him to have missed my irony.

I've never really thought about it, he said. But yes, I suppose you could say she is beautiful. In her own way.

And what way is that? I said.

In *her* way, Tadashi. Not that you would know anything about that.

Again, his comment, and the coldness with which he delivered it, stung me. I had thought that my reserve with women was something known only to me.

Will you look at old T-T-T-Todo, the st-star-star-stuttering old fool, he said. I don't think I've met anyone so blind to everything that goes on in the world.

Professor Todo was one of Katsuo's teachers. He had just emerged from the archway at the far end of the courtyard. I knew him. He occasionally came over to talk to us. Or, more accurately, to talk to Katsuo. He *was* old. He should have been pensioned off years before. But he was harmless. Whenever he came over, he always seemed nervous. He would refer to Katsuo as Master Katsuo. How are you today, Master Katsuo? And you, Mr Omura? he would say with a nervous smile.

He likes you, Katsuo. He treats you like a son, you said so yourself.

Todo is a fool.

I thought you said it was Todo who encouraged you.

Oh yes, I remember. You ma-ma-must r-read, K-K-Katsuo. You m-must analyse, always analyse. Above all, you ma-ma-must work. You have t-t-t-talent, Katsuo. But t-talent is nothing. For every writer who creates s-s-something lasting, there are a thou-thousand young m-men of t-talent who do nothing, whose only accomplishment is d-d-daydreaming.

You know, he came to me a week ago, Katsuo said. But how can you respect a man who can't even pronounce his own n-n-name? To discuss Shiga's poetry.

Katsuo laughed. We were still watching Todo crossing the courtyard. He seemed as preoccupied as ever, gesturing to himself as he walked.

Shiga! Another fraud, he said.

Shiga was a previously unknown nineteenth-century poet whose works had been unearthed by a Tokyo academic the year before. The literary journals were full of him. Already the canon of seventeenth-century poetry was being reassessed in the light of his work. Katsuo had been scathing.

You know what I think of Shiga, he said. Anyway, Todo came to me. To me, can you believe it? To discuss his own 'observations' about Shiga's work. The old fool wants to write an article himself. He thinks he can see some connections between Shiga's poetry and the great Utamaro.

It's possible, I said. I have noticed echoes there myself.

You've read Shiga?

Yes. Like everybody else, I read the poems when they came out.

And, don't tell me, *you* think there are connections between Shiga and Utamaro.

Yes. I do, in fact.

Don't be ridiculous, Tadashi. It's not possible.

Why? I said.

Katsuo just looked at me.

I shrugged. Sometimes, most times, there was no point in arguing with Katsuo.

So, what did you do? I said.

What do you think I did? I encouraged him.

What for, Katsuo? Todo is an old man.

He's a fool, Tadashi. He kept on saying he wanted to write one last significant piece before he died. As if he's written anything significant before in his life. He's an ignorant buffoon. He needs to be taught a lesson.

And you're going to teach him?

Yes, I am. T-Todo is in for a big fall, he said bitterly.

Todo had disappeared by now. I, too, went to get up and leave, but Katsuo held me back.

I offered to help him, you know, to write his article, Katsuo said. I quoted Shiga's poetry at length. I made the occasional mistake, of course. Deliberately. Which, amazingly, the old fool corrected. I pointed out some flaws in his argument. Suggested some alternatives. I was able to convince Todo that what I said was superior, and that it was he who had led me to these insights. Insights that even Shiga, fine poet that he was, had failed to grasp. And yes, indeed, there *were* parallels after all between Shiga's poetry and the works of Utamaro. So many, in fact, that I felt ashamed that I had not seen them myself.

Ah, Tadashi, you have no idea how conceited old Todo is. When he left, he could scarcely get the words of fawning gratitude out, so indebted to me was he for my help.

I protested. I told him that what I had said was merely in response to what he had already been thinking, that really I had said nothing at all. His Shiga article, he told me, would be the one thing that guaranteed his rightful place amongst his intellectual peers. Katsuo snorted. His rightful place amongst his intellectual peers! At least he was right about that.

A month or two went by. I didn't hear any more from Katsuo after this conversation. But then he came to see me in my room.

Read this, he said.

He handed me a magazine. A literary magazine. It was open at Professor Todo's article.

The article was long, and quite dense. There were many footnotes. It took me some time to read as Katsuo paced up and down. Todo's arguments seemed, I have to confess, very lucid. And his style was surprisingly elegant, not what I had expected at all.

This is quite good, I said. I'm impressed.

Katsuo raised his eyebrows, laughed. He took the journal from me and flipped through a couple of pages.

Now read this.

It was the last article in the magazine. It was a lengthy and devastating analysis which proved that the whole Shiga discovery was a hoax. The poems were made up of a range of misquotations and distortions of sixteenth- and seventeenth-century so-called rustic school poets.

The crux of the article, however, was what followed. Further investigations by its author, over a period of some months, involving a forensic process of backtracking and hole-plugging, had revealed that Etsuko Kaida, the leading Tokyo academic who had made the initial discovery, did not, in fact, exist.

What—and this was the article's closing argument, delivered with a chilling nonchalance—had convinced the author that the Shiga poems were fake was the certain knowledge that they had been written by the author of the present article himself. He had constructed the poems. And he was, in addition, the mystery Tokyo academic who claimed to have discovered the poems in the first place. Etsuko Kaida was, in fact, Katsuo Ikeda.

I just rearranged the letters of my name, Katsuo said.

I was staring at him.

Oh, come on, Tadashi. Etsuko! Who is, let me remind you, just as smart as I am.

I can see that, Katsuo, I said. The name. I'm not stupid, you know. What I can't see is why you could possibly want to do that to Professor Todo. What has he ever done to you?

Who really cares? he said. It wasn't about him. I did it to amuse myself.

But he's an old man, I said. He's harmless.

Katsuo didn't answer. I handed the magazine back to him.

He rolled it up and began tapping it on the top of my desk.

I'm going for a walk, I said. When you've finished, please have the courtesy to pull my door closed when you leave.

❀

Within hours, news of the scandal was circulating in every corridor of the university. How a student had duped one of the university's most senior professors. Todo was publicly humiliated. He had been made a complete laughing stock. The university felt it had been disgraced. While the governors decided what to do about him, Katsuo took matters into his own hands. He disappeared.

This would not have meant much to me if it had not been for Todo. He came to see me the night before the disciplinary tribunal was to meet to decide Katsuo's fate.

When I went to answer my door, Professor Todo was standing outside.

Mr Omura, he said.

Professor Todo.

May I come in?

He sat for a long time holding his hat, looking at the floor.

You know, Mr Omura, he said at last, I was not surprised. Katsuo is the most talented student I ever had, he said. But it is a talent that is poisoned. He does not yet know how to harness it. I tried to help him. Do you understand what I am saying?

I nodded.

But I might as well not have been there. Todo was still looking at the floor. It was as though I was invisible, and he was talking to himself.

He thinks I am stupid, blind.

Todo seemed to have shrunk even further into himself. I could see his left hand shaking.

Katsuo's like a spider, he said. He paralyses people. Then he sucks them dry. It's almost as if he can't help himself. I think I recognised this the moment I first saw him.

He nodded to himself, as though confirming something he had just thought.

I treated him like a son, he said.

He got up, took out his handkerchief and wiped his forehead, replaced his hat.

I have spoken to the tribunal, he said. I've told them I take full responsibility for what happened. I've recommended that they take no action against Katsuo.

He went to the door.

Would you do something for me, Mr Omura? When you next see him, tell Katsuo that I understand.

He bowed and left.

It was only later that I recalled something—the entire time he was in my room, he had not stuttered once!

A few days after this, I heard that Todo had resigned. Then he too disappeared. Rumours started to circulate that he had gone back to his village, that he had committed suicide there.

❀

A week later, there was another knock on my door. This time it was Katsuo.

Where have you been? I said.

Away, he said. He waved his hand in some indeterminate direction. Tell me, he said, is it true? I've just heard they want to expel me. Their best student! Can you believe that? Can't they see it was just a joke?

A joke, I said. What about Professor Todo?

Well, yes. Todo, he said. But Todo's life was over. He's old. Old, Tadashi. What more did he have to contribute?

He brushed his hand through his hair.

He came to see me, you know.

Who?

Professor Todo.

What for?

I think he wanted to know why.

And what did you tell him?

I didn't tell him anything. He warned me to stay away from you. He said you sucked people dry, suffocated them. He said that he had treated you like a son. He said, Tell Katsuo I understand.

Katsuo was staring into space.

Todo was a fool. A stupid, ignorant fool, he said.

Katsuo was about to say something else, but instead, he turned and left. It was not until I went to Shirahama that I saw him again.

Part III

NATSUMI

❀

Chapter 11

AT the beginning of summer, Natsumi took her two children to Shirahama once again to escape the oppressiveness of the capital. Her husband, a successful businessman, was happy to indulge his still-young wife, to pack her off with his best businessman's smile to the seaside for a month or two, so that she could escape her boredom, or her disillusionment, or whatever else it was she called the emptiness of their marriage.

❀

When, eventually, I read these lines, and more or less most of what followed, I recognised them instantly from the letters Katsuo began sending me from Shirahama around this time. It was what had happened to him.

❀

Forgive me, Madame Kanzai. We are very busy. Would you permit someone, a gentleman, to share your table?

Natsumi looked up from her book. She was sitting at her favourite inn, one of the few that overlooked the beach. The sun was shining. Soseki, the innkeeper, bowed to her as was his custom. She nodded politely in return. She held a hand up to shield her eyes, trying to ascertain if there was anyone, a gentleman, someone she did not yet know, standing beside him. But, of course, there was not.

As Madame well knows, Soseki said, we have many customers who come only here. He smiled down at her. On the other hand, if you would prefer to remain alone...

He smiled again. His request had seemed so natural, so considerate. So courteous. And he was right. She knew Soseki's restaurant well. She had been here many, many times before. Soseki was always so welcoming. He looked after her. They shared, she thought, a special understanding. He knew her children's names. How old they were. He spoke to them. She regarded him by now almost as an uncle, someone she could trust.

Her table was a setting for four. And yet here she was, sitting by herself.

She thought again of Soseki talking to her children, how he always brought them sweets after their meal.

Please, she said.

It would not be intruding?

No, she said. And...this gentleman?

From Tokyo. A writer, he said.

I will try not to hold that against him, she said. She smiled her loveliest smile up at him.

It is not always a mark of disrepute, coming from Tokyo, he said. He knew, in part, of Natsumi's troubles there. She laughed at the subtlety of his misunderstanding.

She looked around now, trying to intuit where her imminent companion might be. Wondering if, perhaps, he might be standing in the doorway of the restaurant.

So, are we agreed, Madame?

We are indeed, Soseki.

Thank you, Mrs Kanzai, he said. You are most understanding.

It was like a game, this repartee. This back and forth. She enjoyed playing at it. It made her feel young again.

She watched Soseki disappear inside. She leaned forward to pour herself another cup of tea. Folded her book in her lap. It will be nice, she thought, to have some company. After her year of being alone.

A minute or two later, Soseki returned.

Allow me, Mrs Kanzai, he said, to introduce you. This is Mr Ikeda, Mr Katsuo Ikeda. From Tokyo. He stepped aside to reveal the subject of his introduction. Like you, Madame, Soseki said, Mr Ikeda is one of our most valued customers. Mr Ikeda, Mrs Natsumi Kanzai.

Natsumi looked up to see the surprisingly young man standing beside Soseki bowing formally to her. She knew him, of course. Shirahama was a small place. She had seen him. At the markets. Strolling along the beach. Visiting the shrine above the town late one evening. Only yesterday she had observed him talking earnestly to Mr Soseki. She thought, for a moment, that he had glanced her way. He was shorter than she had imagined. Slimmer. Still, he was beautifully dressed—his linen suit white, his dark hair coiffed, his bow tie brilliant, the kerchief tucked into his top pocket. And how exquisite were his hand-stitched shoes.

She looked back up at his freshly shaven, still-innocent face. Oh dear, she thought, how *very* young he is. Perhaps she had made a terrible mistake.

Mrs Kanzai, Soseki said, has been coming to Shirahama for a number of years now. I think of her almost as a niece.

Katsuo reminded her, standing there beside her table, his hat behind his back, of a young actor, someone you might expect to see in an old American movie, something from the forties.

Mrs Kanzai, he said, extending his hand. I am very pleased to meet you. She raised her perfectly curved hand up to him. He held her long, thin fingers briefly in his. He bowed again.

Beneath his nonchalance, Natsumi discerned a certain nervousness. She had felt it in his hand. It was something she had learned to do years before. Take a potential suitor's hand immediately you meet them. Not later, when they have regained control.

I trust I am not disturbing you, her new table companion said. But...He gestured with his palm to the crowded outdoor sitting area. I came down late this morning, he said. I didn't expect so many people to be out and about so early.

On the other hand, his voice was strong. Not like a young person's voice at all. Rich, measured, like someone older, more experienced. Perhaps he wasn't as young as she thought.

You are welcome, Mr Ikeda, she said. I was just reading. Please.

Katsuo turned to Soseki.

Thank you, Soseki-san, he said. I appreciate what you have done for me. He bowed. Soseki inclined his head.

You are more than welcome, Mr Ikeda, he said.

Soseki bowed to Natsumi.

Thank you, Mrs Kanzai, for accommodating Mr Ikeda, he said. It is most gracious of you.

Natsumi smiled.

You're welcome, as always, Soseki. It is the least I could do.

Once again, she watched Soseki's retreating form. When she turned back to the table she glanced up to take a discreet look at her new companion, but he was already looking directly at her.

❀

The following morning, Katsuo rose from his bed early. He bathed, put on the new suit he had bought the previous afternoon. He went to sit in the garden as he usually did. The air was crisp.

Kenji, the proprietor of The Nine-Tailed Fox, the inn he was staying at, came with his tea.

Another beautiful day, Master Ikeda, Kenji said.

Another beautiful day, Kenji, Katsuo replied. And he thought: How wonderful life can be.

While he sipped his tea he went over what he knew of her. Her name was Natsumi. Natsumi Kanzai. How old did he think she was? Twenty-eight? Thirty, perhaps? Her skin still so lovely. And when she had turned, her hand raised, to look half-squinting out over the beach, towards the sea, how beautiful her profile was.

It had been Natsumi who asked the first question.

Soseki-san tells me you are from Tokyo, Mr Ikeda.

No, I am from Osaka, he said. But I have been working in Tokyo for a number of years now.

Oh, Osaka, she said. I am from Osaka. She hesitated. So, were you born there, in Osaka, Mr Ikeda?

Yes, he said.

He thought that it was both thrilling and strange that it was she who was asking him, someone she had just met, such intimate questions.

Where, she said.

Where? he asked.

Where were you born, in Osaka?

So surprised by the question was he that he gave her the district in which his uncle lived, instead of where he had been born. It was too late, and too complicated, however, to take it back.

What a coincidence, she said. I live quite nearby. Do you know Hamada's?

Hamada's was the famous artists' shop where he had bought his drawing materials when he was a child, when he thought it was an artist that he wanted to be. The shop was centuries old, its high, narrow aisles stocked with all manner of things: special fan-shaped brushes, brushes as fine as a cat's whisker, oil sticks, hundreds of different types of coloured pencil, all with their little heads poking out of their burrows like families of weasels, tiers and tiers of them, inks in tins, woodblocks, carving instruments as sharp as any surgeon's, solvents in glass-stoppered jars. In short, it was a magical place, a place in which he had lost himself for hours and hours as a child.

No, he said. I can't say that I do.

He shifted in his chair.

What a pity, she said. It's a beautiful old shop. And so close to you. You must go there sometime.

He had expected the conversation to cease at this point. They had, after all, already established the polite limits of what each needed to know about the other in order for them both to now fall comfortably silent. A silence which he would soon break. It would give him the upper hand. But she continued: And what is it you do in Tokyo, Mr Ikeda?

I work for a publishing house, he said.

Ah, publishing. A noble profession.

And you, Mrs Kanzai? he asked, now emboldened.

Me? I am a governess, she said. To two lovely children.

Their father is a wealthy businessman. Someone who is very, very busy. Who is often away. Although, it was not always so. Now, however, each summer, he sends me here with the children, to Shirahama, for the holidays.

And the children's mother? he asked.

To tell you the truth, I am not sure what has happened to her, she said. I know that some time ago she disappeared. Now she rarely comes up in conversation. My understanding is that the children's father has not seen her in years.

She sat looking across at the shimmering horizon. Although it was early, there were people already on the beach, with picnic baskets, umbrellas, children. Others—couples, their cuffs half-rolled, white-calved—were walking down to the water's edge. Only to run back laughing. Pursued by the small rippled sea.

So, she was from Osaka. A governess. To two young children. Boys, girls? He did not know. And he did not have the opportunity to ask. It seemed Natsumi had confessed enough.

Would you excuse me, Mr Ikeda? she said, looking at her watch. I have to go and collect the children. I hope you enjoy your stay in Shirahama. Then she added, as an afterthought, something he remembered, because he found it so odd: I hope it is everything you wish it to be, she said.

She gathered up her book, and her bag, placed some money on the table, and left. She departed so quickly that he barely had time enough to stand.

After a few minutes, Soseki came out to the table to pick up the money. So, what do you think, Master Ikeda?

I don't know, Soseki. There is no disputing that she is beautiful...

The truth was that he had no idea what to make of Natsumi. He had never met a woman like her before. Someone older than he was, forthright, in control. Someone who knew her own mind. She was uncharted territory. He did not know where to start. But start, he knew, he must. It was what he had set himself to do. He took his notebook out, tore out a sheet of paper.

My dear Tadashi, he wrote. *I am done with little sparrows. I have finally met her, the woman I told you about. Her name is Natsumi. Would you believe she lived just two streets away from me in Osaka?*

❀

The following morning, hoping to see her, he went to the markets again. It had been here that he had first observed her.

He spent a fruitless hour or two walking up and down the market stalls before deciding, on the spur of the moment, to walk up through the narrow back streets to the mountain shrine. He was thinking about Natsumi as he walked, when, as though it were his thoughts that had summoned her, there she was, standing not more than fifty metres away. She had some parcels under one arm. She was trying to open the gate to one of the summer houses with her free hand.

He thanked the gods for how lucky he had been.

Here, he said. Let me help you.

Oh, it's you, she said, a little startled. Mr Ikeda.

So, she remembered his name.

Mrs Kanzai.

Instead of opening the gate, he reached out and took the parcels from her. Open the gate, and she will thank you, and walk in. Take the parcels, and *she* will open the gate. And you can carry the parcels to the door. Who knew what might happen after that.

Thank you, she said, turning back to him. She reached for the parcels.

I'll carry them to the door if you like, he said. It will save you having to put them on the ground. He smiled.

She looked around nervously, a little unsure. A woman of propriety, he thought. Excellent, excellent. And now that he regarded her as a challenge, his nervousness evaporated.

All right then, she said. But just to the door.

Is this where you're staying? he asked.

Yes, she said, avoiding his eyes. When they reached the top of the stairs, she took her key out from her purse.

This will be fine, she said. Thank you, Mr Ikeda.

Katsuo, he said.

Katsuo.

He placed the parcels in her outstretched arms. She seemed more nervous than ever.

Goodbye, she said.

Clearly she was not going to open the door while he was standing there.

Perhaps we could meet sometime, he said.

No, she said. No, I don't mean to be rude, Mr Ikeda, but I don't think that would be possible. Her back was to the door.

The more Katsuo looked at her, the more attractive he found her. She seemed so vulnerable standing there.

Well, thank you, Mrs Kanzai, for allowing me to help, he said.

Thank you, Mr Ikeda, for helping me. I knew when I met you that you were a man of principle.

As he walked down the path this phrase kept ringing in his ears. A man of principle. How dismayed he was by this coincidence. He was Katsuo Ikeda, not Tadashi Omura. A man of principle!

When he got to the gate he opened it, stepped onto the street, pulled the gate to behind him, turned, and without looking back, began walking towards the centre of town.

❀

My old friend Shigeo gave it to me, Kenji was saying. You remember, the caretaker of the temple gardens, the one with the missing fingers. You met him last year.

Kenji was tending the garden at The Nine-Tailed Fox. He was holding up a small tree in a pot.

It comes from the famous gingko by the temple gates, he said. The one that is a thousand years old. This is one of its children. He held the tree up to the light, the leaves, like miniature fans, suddenly translucent. Perhaps this one will be here too, in this garden, a thousand years from now, he said.

Katsuo was only half-listening to the old man. He was thinking about Shigeo, the temple caretaker. About his right hand. How shocked he had been when he first saw it. The middle three fingers missing. Shigeo had been sitting on his haunches, spreading humus under the shrubs. His hideously maimed hand, as if lured out from his shirt sleeve, looked like a pale crab scuttling about in the leaf litter, as though it was trying to catch some elusive prey that was hiding there. Katsuo had been transfixed by how grotesque it had looked.

There, that should do it, Kenji said, tamping the soil down. He picked up his watering can and began applying a fine incantatory spray to the young gingko tree as though it were a blessing.

There, he said again.

Are the markets open today, Kenji?

Yes, yes. Today, and tomorrow, and the next day.

❀

Katsuo did not see Natsumi the next day. Or the next. He went to talk to Soseki. No, he had not seen her either. A week went by. He walked back to the summer house. The shutters were closed. The place looked deserted. He asked a passerby, an old man, if this was the house of Katsuo Ikeda.

No, the old man said. Mr Ikeda lives two streets back.

He started giving Katsuo directions.

Are you sure? he said. Mr Katsuo Ikeda?

Yes, yes. I'm quite sure, the old man said. I have known him all my life.

Then who lives here? Katsuo asked.

I have no idea, young man, no idea. Someone from the city, I suspect. People come and go. I thought you were looking for Mr Ikeda's house, he said.

I am.

Then why do you want to know who lives here?

Without waiting for him to answer, the old man turned and walked off, shaking his head.

Katsuo came back later that night. To see if the lights were on. But the house lay in darkness.

No matter, he said to himself, as he turned to walk back into town. Maybe he shouldn't have given up on sparrows after all. Sparrows came in flocks, not ones or twos. Move on. There will be others.

Chapter 12

SEEN from above, the central marketplace of Shirahama is like a giant spider. A maze of ancient bent-legged streets radiate out from its small body. Some lead up the mountain, some stretch far out along the coast; others, the shorter, gathering legs, extend only as far as the waterfront.

It was the day after Katsuo had waited outside Natsumi's darkened house. He had been in the marketplace barely ten minutes when he heard a female voice calling: Tadashi... Tadashi-san.

He turned to see who was calling the name of his friend so brazenly. There was a young woman standing on the other side of the stall. She was waving to someone. He looked behind him to see who this Tadashi might be.

Tadashi-san, he heard her call again.

But there was no one there.

He turned back to her. She had stopped waving and now was

looking directly at him. She seemed vaguely familiar. Had he met her the week before? Or perhaps it was the week before that? Or was it, now that he thought about it, last year? Whatever the case, he knew he knew her. But what was her name? And here she was, coming around the market stall towards him. Smiling. Her name, her name? But the blank would not fill.

Tadashi Omura, she said.

Tadashi Omura. He was surprised how natural it sounded. He had done this once or twice before, used Tadashi's name, when he didn't want to be troubled by some young woman who might not leave him alone, afterwards. And what harm was there in doing this? Tadashi would never find out. To do so, he would have to speak to a woman first. And there was never any danger of that.

He remembered now, writing his name down for her on a piece of paper.

Tadashi Omura, she had repeated, as if she too liked the way it rolled off her tongue.

He remembered how timid she'd been. On the other hand, he knew immediately that she was the type of girl who would do anything he asked. Anything. Which always disappointed him. He preferred to be surprised.

Yes, now he remembered. Not her name. But the incident. A month ago, six weeks. A not unrewarding experience. Not at all. She *was* very pretty. It had been a frivolous afternoon's interlude.

How are you? she said. I was hoping to see you.

And so much prettier now that she was close.

As I was you, he said. I've been wondering where you've been.

But I told you. I had to go back to Kobe. To see my friend off.

He looked at her.

And now I'm back, she said.

He recalled her small breasts.

You don't like them, she had said.

I love them, he told her. Which was true. He did. He loved small breasts.

They were still standing by the stall. Other customers had to move around them.

I thought we could meet again, she said shyly.

He thought again of her, her breasts. How they had lain flat against her ribcage, her two nipples like two small Mount Fujis rising out of a new and different plain. How he had enjoyed kissing them! How compliant she'd been. With her pretty, slim body.

I was thinking the same thing, he said. Are you free this evening?

Not this evening, she said. My father is here. But he returns to Osaka tomorrow. What about tomorrow evening? Are you still at The Seven Sisters?

He wasn't, but he soon would be.

I am, he said.

Having boldly agreed to the arrangement, she now seemed unsure of herself. She stood in front of him, her body twisting shyly in the breeze.

He looked at his watch.

I'm so sorry, he said. Is that the time? He extended his hand. He knew how young women never expected this. Shaking hands. It always took them by surprise. But he also knew how much they liked it. Afterwards. The lingering touch. Their skin remembering, remembering again. One hand tracing the outline of the other, a kind of foreshadowing of what might follow.

After the briefest hesitation, she too put her hand out.

Oh yes, she said, only now remembering.

So, till tomorrow evening, he said. At ten.

He was still holding her hand.

Yes, she said. Tomorrow, at ten.

He bowed, released her.

She bowed twice in return. And then he was gone.

❀

The following day, he went to see Soseki. On his way, he bought himself a newspaper from one of the street vendors, a boy who had been shouting out the headlines to passersby. But he had been shocked to see—when the young vendor had turned in response to his *Yes, I'll have one*—that the boy was missing an eye. His walnut-skinned empty socket had unsettled him. It had seemed like a bad omen.

At Soseki's, when he could still hear the boy crying his wares a few streets away, he found himself looking up from his paper and saying, Damn that boy. He said it loud enough for several patrons nearby to look up from their plates and stare at him. He threw the newspaper into the centre of the table.

A few moments later, Soseki came out and Katsuo ordered an apéritif. It was only when Soseki reached down to retrieve his cup that Katsuo noticed the small photograph on the upturned page of his paper. He reached out and picked it up. The photograph was blurred, almost unrecognisable. Laughable really. He would have been one of very few able to recognise that it was a photograph of Tadashi. The accompanying article revealed how he had been appointed to one of Osaka's pre-eminent law firms. 'This unassuming but brilliant young man, already with a string of notable achievements to his name…'

Plodding, unimaginative Tadashi. What notable achievements? Tadashi was a fine human being. He was trustworthy, reliable. But notable achievements?

Have you seen Mrs Kanzai? he asked Soseki when he went to pay his bill.

No, Soseki said.

Do you know if she's still here?

Soseki thought for a moment.

I don't know, he said. She may have gone already. But it seems a little early for her.

I think she's gone, Katsuo said dispiritedly. I think she's gone.

❀

He went back to the summer house each morning and each evening, just to check. But nothing had changed. No lights were on. The shutters were still closed. He castigated himself. Why had he not asked how long she was staying?

He had spent a more than agreeable night with Keiko, that was the girl's name, the girl from the market. He had arranged to meet her again the following night, but then Natsumi began to play on his mind. So he had not gone.

The following week, he went to sit on the beach in the shade of one of the pines. He watched the holidaymakers playing in the backwash of the surf. In three days, his own time in Shirahama would be over. He would be returning not to Tokyo, but to Osaka, returning to he knew not what. Now that his new manuscript was almost complete, the future stretched out amorphously in front of him.

He sat watching a girl who had been concealed by the rise of the slope emerge from beneath her beach umbrella. She was wearing a light multicoloured summer dress which showed off her legs, a straw hat, and sunglasses. She walked indolently down to a group of children playing at the water's edge. She stood there talking to them.

The children were pointing at a blue-and-yellow beach ball bobbing in the waves not far from the shore. A little girl of about three was running back and forth, crouching, crying, stamping her foot, calling for the others to get her ball. The other two, a boy and a girl, older than her—perhaps five or six—stood silently watching. The ball seemed indifferent to the children's plight, neither floating further out, nor returning to them on the incoming waves.

He watched as the girl from beneath the beach umbrella kicked off her shoes. She turned slightly sideways as a wave broke just in front of her. Then she was wading out—one hand held up to her hat, her dress hitched up almost to her waist with the other—to retrieve the ball that was now, it seemed, waiting for her. Soon she was half-running, half-wading, back through the water in advance of the waves that followed her. She punched the ball over the children's heads onto the sand.

She crouched down to pick up her shoes. As she rose, she lifted the hem of her dress, inspected the wet arc that hung from her hand. Then she let her dress drop. She turned to look briefly back at the children playing happily again as she retraced her steps up the beach, then sat unseen once again beneath the umbrella, whose canopy blazed in the sun.

Ah, Katsuo thought. How pretty *she* is. Maybe here is the opportunity I've been waiting for.

He got to his feet. Went to stand on the slope behind her. He could see the girl now. She had her back to him and was half-sitting, half-kneeling on her heels. She was wearing sunglasses, but still she had her hand raised to shield her eyes. Something in this gesture tugged at his memory, reminded him of something. Or someone. And then he knew. This-*girl*-was-Natsumi. His heart leapt. Without thinking, he had already taken two or three steps in her direction. Could it be? This girl, in the summer dress and hat? He saw her wading out again through the swell, saw her girlish legs, her hand up to her head, her skirt hitched, saw her striding out towards the ball. But that girl had seemed so young.

And yet, it *was* Natsumi.

Instantly, he began to reconfigure his future. Three days. It was still possible. Just.

❀

Natsumi was so preoccupied watching the children on the beach that when she turned to reach for the book that lay at her side and saw the shadow on the sand advancing on her, she started, and looked up.

Oh, she said. It's you! You gave me such a fright.

She raised her hand once again to shield her eyes. He moved so that his shadow fell across her face and she took her glasses off. He saw her frown.

Yes, it's me, he said.

Oh, she said again.

I thought you'd gone.

Gone?

Yes. I went back to the house. But it was deserted. There was no one there.

No. I had to go back to Osaka for a few days, she said.

If only she would not frown. It was this, he thought later, her frown that undid him.

I thought you might have changed your mind, he said.

Changed my mind?

Yes, about meeting me. He fidgeted on his feet for a moment.

Yes, she said.

She turned to look down at the children.

Yes?

Yes. I will meet you.

He hesitated. She had got to her feet, and was now standing there, looking into his eyes.

When? she said, leaning down to pick up her shoes.

Tomorr...this evening, he said. What about this evening?

She did not answer. She looked up at him again.

At ten, he said.

Yes, ten. Ten would be perfect, she said. Just perfect.

Here, he said, I'll write down the address of the inn I am staying at. He got out his notebook. His pen. It's The Nine-Tailed Fox, he said as he wrote. It's small, just beneath the mountain—

I know where it is, she said. It's run by an old man whose name is Kenji, if I remember correctly. I've been there once before.

He searched her face. Did she already know that he was staying there? She bent down to pick up her mat. She folded it, placed it in her basket.

Well, Mr Ikeda. She smiled. Until this evening, then. She put out her hand.

Yes, this evening, he said, taking her hand in his.

She turned to go, then stopped. She must have seen him glance down to where the children were still playing.

Oh, I see, she said. No, goodness no.

She stood looking at the children for what seemed a long time, as if she were imagining some other, alternative life. The boy was chasing the girl. He had a bright red bucket in his hands. A transparent arm of water suddenly leapt out from it to seize her small arched back.

Oh no. Dear no, she said again. They're not mine. That's why I returned to Osaka, she said. I had to take the children back. Their father had called to say he wanted to take them on a holiday. To New York, can you imagine! How could I compete with that? Once they'd gone, there was nothing more for me to do in Osaka, so I came back here.

And then she was walking away from him, up the slope. He watched her disappearing against the sky. First her back, her shoulders, then her pale straw hat. It was almost as if she were sinking into the earth beneath the vacant blue sky. Then he too turned, and began walking away from the beach, away from the children still playing there.

❀

Once back at The Nine-Tailed Fox, he took out a sheet of his favourite paper: *My dear Tadashi,* he wrote. *She's back. Natsumi. We have arranged to meet. If only you could see her!*

Chapter 13

AFTERWARDS, he could barely remember her knocking on his door, she was so beautiful. This older woman. Natsumi.

Then they were out on the balcony, a cup of the finest saké in their hands. The moon was full. The light it shed glanced off the rooves of the houses below, out onto the sea. Frogs were calling. Fireflies in ones and twos dipped into the shadowed garden beneath them.

With Natsumi standing on the balcony in the lantern light, her back to the moon, Katsuo thought she could easily have been a woman from another age, someone he'd seen in a work by Utamaro, or Hokusai, or Kiyonaga. It made her seem all the more unreal, inaccessible.

What a beautiful view, she said.

It had always troubled him, this tricky terrain, this uncharted territory in which he often found himself, between the instant, as he was now, when he could be standing on a balcony with someone new, someone he wanted, and that later moment when the two of them would both be lying naked on a bed. This prelude to desire realised, this interregnum, he was no good at it. It *always* sent him to the brink.

And Natsumi, so calm, unhurried, so self-contained. Now leaning as she was against the balustrade, listening to the idle chatter of the couple on the balcony beneath them. Perhaps he had been mistaken. Perhaps Natsumi was here merely to pass a pleasant hour or two, chatting, sipping his saké, thinking about who knew what.

Newlyweds, she said.

She turned back to look at him.

We could always bring the futon out here, she said. Pull the mosquito net around the balcony.

❀

He could not recall carrying the bedding out to the dimly lit, transparent tented space. Natsumi standing, smiling. Then undressing. Themselves. Each other. The longed-for moment—seeing her naked for the first time. Her body more complex, more beautiful, than any he'd seen before. The echo of the girl she once was now made more ravishing by the history written on her skin.

He knew immediately he had crossed a threshold. That he'd never go back to being the Katsuo he'd been before he saw her.

Then he and Natsumi were lying on the bed. Her flesh against his flesh. Her lips on his lips. Moving as though they were one. He could see the bright scattered stars above her head. The pale, attentive moon. She was the centre of his universe, the one making love to *him*. He had found what he had not known he was looking for.

At some point, Natsumi pushed away from him, her hands on his shoulders. Her movements like small curling waves endlessly coming into shore. Below, he could hear the young couple chatting, laughing. Softly. Oblivious. But when Natsumi first cried out, they stopped. He and Natsumi stopped too. They floated there on the thin layer of words that still lingered in the night air around them. Natsumi smiled down at him. He heard a chair, or chairs, being moved. He imagined the young couple getting up and walking to the edge of their balcony. He pictured them looking up, wondering if anyone was really there, if they'd heard what they thought they'd heard. The first few tentative words of a conversation interrupted drifted back up to them.

Natsumi began to move once more. The brazenness of what she was doing seemed to arouse her. She began to whimper softly. All conversation below them instantly stopped. Then, all at once, Natsumi was like a force unleashed. Katsuo heard the couple's hurried footsteps, the screen doors close. Then, all he could hear were Natsumi's urgent murmurings mingling with the night sounds now returned.

❀

You know, she said later, I am twenty-eight years old, and my husband and I have not shared the same bed for almost three years.

In the lamplight, with her kimono only half-covering her, Katsuo saw for the second time what he had seen earlier, that her body had that strange beauty only experience brings, in which every cell knows what still good thing the next moment might bring.

This is a beautiful kimono, Natsumi said, picking up one of its deep-blue seams. She gathered up a flock of cranes in her hand. Just beautiful, she said.

You can keep it, he said. I bought it for you.

He sends me here, you know, my husband. To Shirahama. I'm sure he knows what I do. I'm sure that's why he does it.

She lay back on the bed. The kimono fell open. As she talked, she ran the tip of a finger around one of her nipples distractedly, as if he wasn't there.

I thought you were a governess, he said.

I am. At least, that's how I feel. Now. You know, she said, the first time I came here, I think my husband paid someone to seduce me. A young man, someone from his firm.

She reached for her cup of saké. Took a sip. A drop escaped her lips, curved down her chin and fell onto her breast.

Oh dear, she said.

She sat up a little. She dipped her finger into the tiny

tear-dropped pool on her skin.

It never occurred to me to have an affair with him. I was still too troubled by my husband's withdrawal. Trying to understand what had brought it about. I *had* had two children. But had my body not returned to its former youthfulness? I used to stand in front of the mirror, trying to discover what had changed. I wished I had kept a photograph of myself as I was when my husband first married me, so that I could see the difference. Had I changed that much? Hadn't I become more beautiful, not less?

Not that my husband was not good to me. He was. He had become successful. He provided for me. And our children. All my friends envy me. But they do not know how much I still long for him to see me. To speak to me. To fracture the silence with a single word.

I know it's not going to happen. Not now, she said. The time for that has passed. So now, each summer, I come here. And each summer I find someone who still finds me attractive. And we spend a few nights, sometimes a few weeks, together. And I will keep coming here until no one wants me. Until no one sees me. Until all I am is myself.

❀

In the morning, when he awoke, she was gone. The saké cup had been returned to its place in the cupboard. The half-empty bottle was back on the shelf.

He walked into the bathroom. It was as ordered as if he had only just arrived. The mosquito netting on the balcony was folded. He leaned over the balustrade. There were two half-full glasses of saké sitting on the table below. A piece of clothing was draped carelessly across one of the chairs, as if it had been thrown there. The garden below was still.

Chapter 14

LATER that same morning, he went to see Soseki again.

Master Ikeda, what can I bring you?

Soseki, my good friend. You know Mrs Kanzai?

Yes, Master Ikeda.

What more can you tell me about her? You said she's been coming here for years.

Yes, he said. Every year, she comes down from Tokyo.

Tokyo? he said. She told me she came from Osaka. That she was born there. She told me that she lived near the famous Hamada art store.

No, no. She comes from Tokyo. Her husband is a very well-known industrialist. What you're saying doesn't make sense, Katsuo. She doesn't have an Osakan accent. Not a trace.

Yes, Soseki, but neither do I.

Natsumi is not you, Master Ikeda.

Katsuo thought about what Soseki had said. That she

was not from Osaka. She was from Tokyo.

Do you know anything else about her?

Soseki looked away.

I am sorry, Master Katsuo, he said. But there is something I have not told you. You remember that first meeting—you pointed her out to me, asking if I knew her. And then you asked me if I could arrange for you to meet her.

Yes, Soseki.

Well, she asked me first.

Asked you what first?

Mrs Kanzai asked me to find a way to introduce her to you. She had seen you a number of times, at the markets, walking on the beach. I know why she comes here. It is an escape from the unhappiness of her life in Tokyo. She is not the only woman who comes here for the same reason. But Natsumi, Mrs Kanzai, seems so different. She seems…more lost. So she asked me to introduce her to you. And seeing you had asked me the same thing, I thought, how perfect. I would do what each of you had asked me to do.

Why didn't you tell me?

She asked me not to.

But we are friends, Soseki.

We are. But then, so too are Mrs Kanzai and myself. I have known her for a long time now.

She told me she was a governess!

A governess?

Yes.

Soseki let out a small owl-like laugh.

Ah, my dear friend, it seems that you are not the only one who can play this particular game.

So it would appear, Katsuo said.

He looked down to the beach, to where families with their children were already playing.

One last thing, Soseki, he said.

What is that, Katsuo-san?

Did Natsumi, Mrs Kanzai...did she know that I had asked you to introduce us?

She did, Master Katsuo. She did. She told me she wanted to see how determined you were. Whether you would persist if she made things difficult for you. And now she knows.

Chapter 15

THERE is a young woman here to see you, Mr Omura.

A year had passed since Katsuo had summoned me to Shirahama, Omura told Jovert late one afternoon. Katsuo had continued writing to me, telling me of the progress he was making, of the many conquests he had made, of the places he'd been, the people he'd met.

Does she have an appointment? I asked.

No, she doesn't. She seems very upset.

Upset?

Yes, very.

All right, I said. Just give me five minutes and I'll see her. What time is my next appointment?

Not till 10.30, she said.

I put what I had on my desk away. Then I picked up the phone: You can send her in now, I said.

Miss Nakamura came to the door.

Miss, she said. Mr Omura will see you now. She held out her hand and a well-dressed young woman in her early twenties came through the doorway.

I could see that she would have been very pretty if she had not looked so distressed. Her eyes, her nose, were red.

But I don't understand, she said, immediately on entering the room. *You're* not Tadashi Omura!

I'm sorry, I said, taken aback, but I *am* Tadashi Omura. At least, I am this Tadashi Omura. These are my offices.

But you're not the person I…I met. Last year, in Shirahama.

Shirahama.

You're not the Tadashi…

But the truth had already dawned on her. I could see her sifting through her memories: how she and this other Tadashi Omura had met, at a café, in the marketplace, on the beach. Had he offered to carry something for her, helped her with directions? Perhaps he'd made some comment about the shrine they were visiting. Permit me to introduce myself: my name is Tadashi, Tadashi Omura.

If, I thought, I went back through the letters Katsuo had sent me, would she be there somewhere, on one of those pages—this pretty young girl, that one, the one he had met in the forest, whose husband had followed her, who had chased him down the mountain?

All at once, she started sobbing, twisting her purse in her hands.

How could I have been so stupid? she was saying.

I got up, went to the door.

Could you come in here for a moment, Miss Nakamura, I said. Bring some tissues, please.

No wonder you weren't there that night, she said. I mean…I don't understand, she said. You…he, Tadashi, was so nice to me.

And this…Tadashi? I said. What did he look like?

She described him to me, his hair, how he was always brushing it back with his hand, his impeccable clothes, his shoes. She told me how he had described his legal practice. How, by chance—it had been lying under his coat—she had come across one of the documents he'd been working on. She had looked at it, seen the address. My name.

I'm sorry, Miss…?

Keiko Yam…She hesitated. I'm sorry, she said. I feel so foolish. It doesn't matter who I am. You know, that's why I went back to Shirahama this summer. I was hoping to see him again. But I see what has happened now. I've been misled. Made a fool of.

She dried her eyes, dabbed her nose.

I can't believe it, she said. He was *so* nice to me. So nice, she said again, as though remembering. Do you have any idea who he might be?

I signalled for Miss Nakamura to leave us. She bowed, turned and pulled the door to after her.

No, I said. I was in Shirahama last year myself. On business. Some of my papers were stolen. They had my name on them. This person must have taken them.

I see, she said. What a pity. I would so have liked to have seen you...to have seen him again.

She got up. Put the tissues in her purse. Brushed her skirt down.

Thank you, Mr...Mr Omura, she said. For being so kind.

I came out from behind my desk. She bowed a number of times, then looked up at me. I saw her scrutinising my face one last time, as if she were thinking, if only I could get behind this mask, then I might still find the real Tadashi hiding there.

You're welcome, Miss...Keiko, I said, bowing.

She turned and walked towards the door. I followed her.

Could you show Miss Keiko out, please, Miss Nakamura.

Certainly, Mr Omura.

I pulled the door closed. I went back to my desk. To think about what had just happened, and what to do about it.

❀

You can *not* do this, Katsuo, I said. These childish pranks. We are not at university anymore.

In the end, after much asking around, I had found his house, or the place where he was lodging, in one of Osaka's poorest suburbs. The house was shabby beyond belief.

The old woman who answered my knock at the door greeted me still holding a dirty tea towel. She was drying her hands with it.

I am looking for a Mr Katsuo Ikeda, I said. Is this where he lives?

Without speaking, but not before she had given me one last look, she flicked the towel over her shoulder and disappeared back down the corridor. I could hear her hollow footsteps retreating. Then I heard voices, a door close, more footsteps. Then nothing. I waited. Another set of footsteps came down the hallway.

Katsuo could not have been more surprised to see me than if I had waylaid him.

Tadashi! What are you doing here? How did you get this address?

Katsuo, I said.

We were like two sparring partners waiting for the bout to begin.

Aren't you going to invite me in?

He stood aside, gestured with his hand. He led me down to his room at the end of the corridor. In it, there was a narrow bed. An old wooden desk. Writing pens, paper. A small statue, incongruously beautiful. A piece of threadbare carpet, makeshift bookshelves overflowing with books. On the walls, a few woodblock prints.

He didn't waste any time.

So, Tadashi, what is it?

A young woman came to see me the week before last, I said.

He reached for his packet of cigarettes, held it out to me.

No, thanks, I said.

He took one out from the pack. Lit it.

Her name was Keiko, I said.

Keiko, he repeated.

Yes, Keiko.

Dear little Keiko, he said, exhaling. *Such* a pretty girl. Yes, I remember her. She reminded me of Mount Fuji. Mount Fujis.

She came to see me, I said. She thought I was you. You told her your name was Tadashi Omura.

He inhaled on his cigarette.

What did she say?

What do you mean, what did she say? She was upset.

And that was all?

I realised now what he was after. He wanted to know what she'd thought of him.

That was it, I said.

He stood there observing me as though I was an insect.

You can't keep using people, Katsuo. Keiko. Me. I have a career now, which I've worked hard for.

He still didn't say anything.

It *was* you, wasn't it, that time when I came to see you? You took one of my documents. One that had my name on it. To use. To impress someone, someone young, like Keiko. To get her to believe you were someone you weren't.

To impress her? he said.

He walked over to his bookshelf, retrieved a sheet of paper.

Here's your precious document, Tadashi, he said. I don't need it anymore. Not that I ever did. You have no idea how long it took her to find it.

He threw it across to me.

And just so you know, Tadashi, I could not care less about your career. Or your stupid, self-serving moral principles. Because you know what you are, Tadashi…

I could feel his anger building. He was speaking slowly now, with deliberate emphasis, as if he was explaining something to a dim-witted child, something he'd explained a thousand times before.

You-are-just-a-footnote, he said. A footnote. To-my-life. You-are-a-*nothing*, a zero, a meaningless cipher. He spat the words out. You're what happens when history blinks. Don't you see? You don't exist. Except as a function of me. You and your stupid, *stupid* career!

He seemed momentarily lost for words.

You have *no* idea, he said. None.

He turned to look at the bookshelves.

Oba-san! he shouted. Oba-san!

I heard footsteps hurrying.

He was still staring at the bookshelves. It was almost as if he didn't recognise what they were. He reached out with his hand. At first, I thought he was going to take something down, a particular volume, something to give me, as he had done in the past, something that would show me where I had gone wrong. Instead, with one powerful sweep of his arm, he swept a whole shelf of books to the floor.

None! he shouted. You stick to the law, Tadashi. You don't know it yet, but you and your principles are like cement. You're already set. Imagine what you'll be like when you're sixty!

Another row of books came crashing down. You won't be able to *move*! So don't you stand in judgement of me. I *choose* to do what I do.

He said these last words with pure rage. I, for my part, did what *I* had been trained to do. I stepped away, I removed myself, the better to understand what was happening. Calmly, with reason. I said to myself, just imagine that you are in the courtroom, that this *isn't* personal. If you don't, you won't be able to marshal your thoughts in the midst of this onslaught. This chaos. For the moment, observe, don't react.

O-ba-*san*!

I saw the handle move, but the door did not open.

Master? I heard the old woman say. Is everything all right?

You don't know, he kept saying. You just don't know.

But it wasn't clear to me if he was talking about me, or himself.

I went to the door. The old woman was waiting outside. She looked at me quizzically, then tried to see past me into Katsuo's room. But the door was already closing.

I walked down the long corridor with her following behind me. Then I was outside in the street again, listening to the silence which now surrounded me.

Part IV

MARIKO

❀

Chapter 16

TWO years after Mariko disappeared, Katsuo published a novel—his third—a semi-autobiographical work called *The Chameleon.*

Omura and Jovert were out smoking on Omura's balcony once again. Almost a month had passed since Jovert had seen him. The Paris skyline shimmered in the early autumn air.

Katsuo had already enjoyed successes before. *Spring Promise, The Dead of Winter*. But nothing, not even his own ambition, could have prepared him for the reception of *The Chameleon.* I remember the days immediately after it was published. I would see people reading it on the train, at the bus stop, in cafés. The park. It was amazing. As for Katsuo, well, overnight, Katsuo found himself lionised. Courted by everybody who was anybody in Osaka. He was feted wherever he went.

The Chameleon turned out to be everything he had said it was going to be. But then, barely had this outpouring of adulation reached its peak when he too disappeared. His grief over Mariko's loss had finally taken its toll. It was as if, in the midst of the grand party organised to celebrate his success, with all of Osaka's high society in attendance, someone—a young, exquisitely beautiful woman, no doubt, a glass of champagne raised to her lips—had paused to ask: Where's the guest of honour? Where's Katsuo? Only to find that no one could remember when they had last seen him.

And when I say disappeared, I mean exactly that. He vanished. Not for a day, not for a week, or a month. He was gone for years. And no one, not me or anyone else, knew where he was, or heard from him. The letters I used to so look forward to had dried up long ago.

Then, just as he was beginning to fade from people's memories, and just as suddenly, he reappeared.

A colleague came up to me one day on the courthouse steps. Have you heard, Tadashi? he said.

Heard what?

Katsuo Ikeda. He's back.

Naturally, I tried to contact him. I sent him messages. Phoned. But I got no reply. Then one day—I remember it exactly—I ran into him quite by accident in a side street in Osaka's textile district. I had gone there to pick up a suit I had ordered. I was about to enter the shop when there he was, coming towards me, deep in thought.

Katsuo? I said.

He looked up, surprised.

Tadashi.

I did not know what to say. That he had disappeared in the way he had, without telling anyone. That he had been away for so long, without contacting me. That he was back, and had been for some time. These questions all jostled for attention. He, for his part, appeared agitated, anxious to get away, as though the friendship that had been part of our lives for so long had ceased to exist, or indeed, had never existed in the first place. We exchanged a few awkward words. I was on the point of asking him where he had been, when he interrupted me.

I'm sorry, he said. I'm late. He looked at his watch. And then, as if by way of afterthought: Forgive me, he said. And he turned and walked quickly away.

Not, forgive me, Tadashi. Merely, forgive me.

I stood there, stunned. People had to step around me in the street. It wasn't until I got home that I realised I had forgotten to pick up my new suit.

Soon afterwards, all sorts of rumours began to circulate. About someone, a beautiful young woman from some obscure mountain village, who had come to live with him. Or, that he had gone mad, that he could be heard wandering about his garden late at night arguing with himself, that he rarely ventured out.

So, late one evening, it must have been a couple of months later, I decided to visit him. In the back of my mind, I think my intention was to confront him, to find out why he had been avoiding me.

I had heard that he had moved back into his old house high above the bay. It was midsummer, warm. I took a taxi. I remember getting out at the top of the hill and looking down at the thin capillaries of light that outlined the harbour below. I could just make out the sea beyond, its surface pale and flat and still.

I had not been to the house in years, but I could recall as if it were yesterday the day Katsuo had rung to tell me that, at last, he had found the perfect place. I can still hear him on the phone saying: You must see this house, Tadashi. You must see it.

At that time, we were both in our mid-twenties. My legal practice was beginning to flourish. Katsuo's new novel, *The Dead of Winter*, had done well. And after years of freedom, of philandering, he was finally on the verge of marrying Mariko. Mariko had turned out to be as tempestuous as she was beautiful. We all thought she was more than a match for Katsuo.

I remember that some days after Katsuo had called me about the house, the three of us—Katsuo, Mariko and I—went to inspect it late one afternoon. It was a wonderful old place, a former consulate, a mansion really, set high into the mountain-side overlooking the bay. When we got there, the estate agent opened the door for us. We walked from one radiant, weightless room to another. Katsuo had been ecstatic. Unstoppable. He could not believe his luck. Here, finally, was the perfect place, the place he had imagined owning for so long. We walked out onto the vast terrace. It seemed to reach seamlessly out to the still grey sea beyond, as if the house were just floating there.

I remember Mariko going to stand with her hands resting on the stone balustrade behind her. In the failing evening light, with the darkening sea at her back, she looked more ravishing than I had ever seen her before. Katsuo was standing beside her, his hand on her right shoulder, his fingers resting on her flawed but flawless skin.

Katsuo ended up buying the house. A few months later, at a glittering ceremony on the same balcony, with the sea again at their backs, he and Mariko were married.

Within a year, however, the marriage had begun to falter. Mariko had wanted a child. Desperately. Katsuo did not. He was too young; he wasn't ready; he had his career to think about; he could not see himself as a father. Not now, not ever. There were any number of excuses.

He and I spent long nights down by the harbour, going from one disreputable place to another, endlessly discussing this growing knot of unhappiness at the centre of his existence.

Sometimes, when it began to get late, I would point to my watch. Katsuo would nod, and we would get up to go, only to find ourselves sitting in some even more squalid place five minutes later, amongst the dock workers, the fishmongers, their tattooed women. And Katsuo would start again.

He loved Mariko, he said. More than that, he was obsessed with her. He knew that he could not live without her. That was his problem. He both loved and felt trapped by her. Particularly now that she wanted a child.

I would sit there wondering what Mariko was doing, alone in that beautiful house high up on the mountainside, the house he had bought for her. What did she make of his spectacular absences? How unhappy was she? And how ironic was her unhappiness. She seemed as much addicted to him as he was to her. I remembered how dazzling, how perfect they had seemed as a couple when they first met.

At some inevitable point during one of these endless nights, we would reach the same threshold, and I would bring the late hour to his attention once again. He would wave his hand dismissively in my face. I'm not *ready* to go, Tadashi, he would say. Just like I'm not ready to have a child. You go, my good and proper, my *principled* friend. You go. You have a child. And he would look me in the eye, and laugh his cruel laugh, as if this proposition were inconceivable, even to him. A child is the *last* thing I want, he would say. I have my work to do. Doesn't Mariko understand that? And yet, if you could be with her, he would say. If you could *see* how beautiful she is…

❀

Their arguments escalated. These two people, so favoured by the gods, began to tear each other apart. Without, it seemed, knowing why. We could all see it. We understood what lay at the heart of their unhappiness. But Katsuo and Mariko? They did not. Why, we asked ourselves, could they both not wait?

To avoid her wrath, he had an iron gate built into the garden wall. At night, after Mariko had fallen asleep, Katsuo would slip secretly out of the house, and through this gate. He would descend into the dissolute city in search of two or three of his more sordid friends, people who occupied the shadowy peripheries of his life, people whom I barely knew. He'd track them down to wherever they were lurking: the sleazy, lowlife bars, the choked gutters of the harbour slums; he would hunt them down in the wild and dangerous places he'd become addicted to, the places in which he could lose himself, and whatever else he had to lose. In the end, he did not care.

And then, suddenly, Mariko was gone. Where once this beautiful, radiant creature had been, there was nothing. While we waited for her to return, a return that never came, it was as if the world itself had stopped.

Six months later, in one of the bars we had so often gone to, when the years of heartache that followed had only just begun, Katsuo told me of their final confrontation.

What if I just went ahead, Katsuo? Mariko had said. Allowed myself to fall pregnant?

They were sitting opposite each other in the long room that overlooked the balcony. The temporary truce that had existed for some weeks between them was about to end.

I would not do that, Mariko, Katsuo had said with a menacing calm.

Why not? You couldn't really do anything about it.

You think so. I could always go and see old Eguchi, he said. Then you might wake up one morning and find that you were pregnant no longer.

She stared evenly at him across the low table.

You would do that, wouldn't you?

I would.

But why, Katsuo? It's just a child.

It's *not* just a child, Mariko, he said bitterly. It's a life. Mine.

And what if it's already too late?

Now it was his turn to look at her. At her beautiful face, at her eyes, which he could not live without.

Then, Mariko, please remember what I said.

He put his book down onto the table. Stood up.

I'm going up to the library, he said. And then I am going out.

She sat watching his retreating form.

Goodnight, Katsuo, she said.

Goodnight, Mariko.

When he returned home, in the early hours of the morning, washed out, full of remorse, he went up to their bedroom to rouse Mariko as he always did. To take her in his arms. Tell her how much he loved her. Tell her that he had changed his mind. If she so desperately wanted a child, he would not stand in her way. But their bed was empty, and she had gone.

❀

So, late that night, I found myself walking down the hill beside the stone wall surrounding Katsuo's garden. I was thinking about the house, about Mariko, about Katsuo's unbending will, and the breakdown of their marriage. It seemed so long ago. So much had happened in between.

Then I was standing by the iron gate, looking down into the garden, seeing it as though for the first time. The lanterns, the elaborate terraces planted with bamboo, the ferns, trees of all sorts. I could hear the sound of falling water. Here and there, the serpentine flagstone paths reflected the light as they wound their way up the mountainside. At the heart of the garden, barely visible, shrouded now by masses of faintly transparent leaves, was the house itself.

All about me I could hear the odd amplified sounds of summer. Frogs calling to each other. The endless thrumming of crickets. The slow tock, tock, tock of a water clock. From far below, I could hear the muted stirrings of a harbour city coming to life.

I reached through the grill, pressing myself against the wall as I tried to locate the latch pull I knew was concealed inside. The stone felt cool through my shirt. As I stretched my arm out, a tiny movement caught my eye. A small, vividly green lizard was clinging to an ivy leaf just centimetres above my head, its bulbous eye staring down into mine. I was so close I could see its fat padded toes, its thick-rimmed lips, in its side, the fluttering of its tiny heart.

The gate opened silently. A few metres in front of me there was a large ornamental pond. Plate-sized water-lilies hovered in clusters about its perimeter. From some, flowers cupped like white hands stood on stalks. Sour-faced fish floated through the limbs of trees.

I crossed the stepping stones. I saw my shadow flicker

from tree to tree. A breeze stirred, setting the leaves above me shimmering.

It was only then that I saw her. At the far end of the house, a young woman, sitting motionless with her back against a pillar. She was wearing a ceremonial kimono, its white dazzling against the surrounding darkness. Her hair had been intricately pinned. Muted light spilled from the lantern above her.

She was so still she could have been arranged there. I heard Katsuo's voice calling from inside the house.

Sachiko...Sachiko?

His tone sounded vaguely urgent.

I slipped back into the shadows. I saw his silhouette appear against the lighted doorway. He said something to the young woman, to Sachiko. Without replying, she slipped down from the wall, knelt to gather up something from the ground, a book, a small box. Light fell across her face. As she rose, she reached one hand up to Katsuo's face and kissed him. Then she disappeared into the house.

Katsuo remained in the doorway looking out into the garden for a few moments, listening. Waiting. Then, he too turned and disappeared inside.

I made my way back to the gate, silently released the catch. I looked up to where the lizard had been, but it was no longer there. Below me, I could see the brooding stillness of the harbour. The sound of a foghorn, long and mournful, seemingly without beginning or end, floated up to me. As it faded away, I started on the long, steep descent into the city beneath me, my head full of questions. Who was Sachiko; where had she come from; why was she dressed the way she was; how long had she been there; and, most of all, why was Katsuo keeping her hidden away from us, and the rest of the world?

❀

You know, Inspector, I wish I had never gone there that night. Sometimes I say to myself: Tadashi, if only you had never gone there. If only you had never gone.

Chapter 17

A MEMORY comes back to him.

Tell Mariko the story about your father, Katsuo says.

What story?

❀

And so Omura tells Jovert of this memory.

We, he says—Katsuo, Mariko and I—were standing out on the terrace of Katsuo's new house. Katsuo had just had it refurbished. He had arranged a huge party, to celebrate the fact that the work on the house was finally done.

While the other guests congregated outside, or sat in what he now called 'the long room'—the sitting room that looked out onto the terrace—Katsuo showed me his special creation, his 'study' as he called it, the secret room he had had constructed at one end of the house, a room with a one-way mirror which looked through to an elaborate bathroom. I knew immediately where this had come from, and what it would be used for. I had seen such a room many times before.

You know, he had said to me once, Utamaro, Shigenobu, Eisen, all the great artists did their best work from life. From careful observation. You should come down with me one night to The Peony. I could get you in. You could observe one of your favourite tableaux come to life. And see what you're missing out on.

❀

I have often wondered, Omura told Jovert, what it must have been like to be him, to be inside his skin, just for a few hours, a day, to experience the world that inhabited him. How extraordinary it must have been.

❀

You know the one, Katsuo said. The story about your father and the jigsaw puzzles.

Which jigsaw story? I said, even though I knew.

The one about your father...The one where he goes out and buys one of those western-style jigsaw puzzles.

I don't think so, I said.

Oh, come, come, Tadashi, my dear friend. Please. Mariko wants to hear it.

But I remained silent. I knew better than to trust Katsuo when he was drunk.

Katsuo started to tell Mariko the story himself. I had only told it to him once but was unsurprised to hear Katsuo using almost exactly the same words I had used. It was as if I was speaking. I thought again of how he used to observe us. How powerful his memory was. He even acted out the part of my father with uncanny accuracy.

And Tadashi, tell Mariko what you told your father when he saw that the half-completed image was the same as the image on the box in which the puzzle had come. What did you say to him? What words of pathetic encouragement did you give him? No? Okay, let me see. He pretended to think for a moment. Katsuo knew exactly what he was going to say. He raised himself momentarily on his toes. I had never realised that I did this until I saw him do it that day. I saw how foolish I must seem.

Imitating my slightly clipped way of speaking, he said: Perhaps there's another way of looking at it, Father. Perhaps it means something like this—that it doesn't matter where you start, if you keep going, you will always find…you will always… Now, what was it? Oh dear. You-will-always-find…

Completion, I said.

That's it. *Completion.*

He repeated the word slowly. Completion.

He started to laugh.

Ah Tadashi, he said. You are *such* a comedian.

Mariko had one arm around her waist. The other crooked

into her side, holding her cigarette up to her face. She was turning slightly from side to side, her body rippling with suppressed laughter. Katsuo had turned away from me, his arms outstretched on the balustrade. But I could see that he too was laughing uncontrollably. It was as if they were sharing some private, oft-repeated joke I knew nothing about.

Mariko inhaled deeply on her cigarette, blew the broken smoke up into the night.

Come on, Katsuo, Mariko said. Leave poor, sad Tadashi alone.

She looked around. At the people dancing on the far side of the terrace. At the lights. The orchestra. The cars that littered the enormous forecourt below. At the city twinkling in the distance. Mariko had clearly grown tired of this game. She must have heard this kind of thing a hundred times before, after they had left some gathering or other, after she had watched Katsuo play the magnanimous host, the habitual centre of attention.

I'm so, so, *so* bored, Mariko said to Katsuo. Let's go and find Kimiko. Almost immediately, she changed her mind. No, she said, her eyes wide. I have a better idea. Let's go down to the waterfront. Have some *real* fun.

She swirled the last of her drink in her glass, finished it with a flourish, set the glass down on the balustrade, flicked its rim with her fingernail.

Look around, Katsuo, no one's going to miss us.

As the two of them drifted through the glittering lights and jaunty music, the ragtime crowd parted and closed in their wake.

I knew if I looked down a few minutes later that I would see the sleek, phantom shape of Katsuo's great car edging its way past the line of lesser marques crowding the driveway, down towards the wrought-iron gates that were already opening. I would see it pull out onto the road that led to town. The sumptuous roar of its multi-valved engine accelerating down the hill would drift up to me. I would see its receding headlights twisting effortlessly through the trees. In my mind I could see the two of them sitting together in the back of the car, already doing who knew what to each other as they sped breathlessly on towards the sordid pleasures that lay waiting for them in the shadowy recesses of the city below.

❀

Katsuo was right. Once I had nurtured ambitions to be a writer. But that space was already taken. By Katsuo. In some mysterious way, he seemed to suck the light out of things. There was nothing left for anyone else. All of us came, in one way or another, to experience this. Ironically, however, in Katsuo's company, we also felt privileged. Things happened. You *never* knew what, or where things would go. But afterwards, when we returned home, we all felt like lesser beings. We knew that we'd been used, made fools of. But it didn't matter. We still waited, until next time. When Katsuo would crank the world up for us again.

Part V

SACHIKO

❀

Chapter 18

TALK to me, he says.

I'm so cold, Katsuo, so cold...

Talk, Sachiko. Just talk. It will help.

And so she starts to tell him once again what he already knows. Later, he will write it all down, so as not to forget.

❀

In the spring, just after my sixteenth birthday, my father takes me down to Osaka for the first time.

It is still dark when my grandmother comes to wake me. She doesn't know that I have been lying in my bed for hours waiting for her. Waiting, and listening. Until, at last, I hear her door slide open, hear the scuff of her slippered feet on the floor, like a dog panting, and I know that my great adventure is about to begin.

I hear her strike the match and, suddenly, there on the wall above me is her shadow, liquid in the toppling light. It leaps against the descending glass. Then steadies.

There is a small blue water bowl beside my lamp. I hear the match tip's extinguished hiss.

Then—silence.

I know my grandmother is standing there, looking down at me. Moments later she puts her hand on my shoulder. Her untried voice is husked with tenderness.

Sachiko, Sachiko, she is saying.

❀

Later, on the verandah, my grandmother brings me breakfast for the journey, a small feast she says will sustain me—chicken broth, rice cakes, fish, vegetables, things I don't even know the names of, things I have never tasted before—steaming in the cool morning air.

Behind me, the mountain peaks blaze like white teeth in the first rays of the sun. Darkness seeps back into the earth. The grey-tiled rooftops of the village, clustered together like sleeping cattle, begin to surface. Here and there, pale columns of smoke rise from chimneys. On the outskirts of the village, a solitary lantern, like a tiny stranded star, appears and disappears in the creviced streets.

Beyond the village, the valleys, still and undisclosed, lie waiting.

I hear my mother's shrill voice coming from inside the house. She is arguing with my father. Only fragments of what they say reach me.

But it's nothing, Hideo. You can barely see it. You must convince him.

I think they are talking about the kimono my mother and grandmother make, which, each spring, my father takes down to Osaka to sell. But they are not. They are talking about me.

❀

Then we are waiting outside our house. My friend Kimiko, who had gone the previous year to work in one of the Takaragawa houses, is there. She gives me a beautiful pearl hairpin. To remember her by. She puts it into my hair. She smiles. Write to me, she says. We hug each other. I feel her warm tears on my cheek.

The kimono have been folded, packed. Sealed into chests. Two men are loading them onto a hand cart. We are ready. My grandmother stands there silent. Her hands struggle to free themselves from each other. She comes to embrace me.

My mother does not. Instead, she says: Be careful, Sachiko. But she says it coldly, as if admonishing me for some wrong I have already committed. Kimiko and I embrace one last time. I say goodbye.

These trips are always fraught. Will my father sell all that my mother and grandmother have made? If he doesn't, we will not survive until the next year, my mother, my father, my grandmother and me.

Each year now, when my father returns, he returns exhausted. It was not always like this. He used to be proud to take what my grandmother and mother had made to Osaka to sell. But now, when he comes home, it is someone else who arrives on our doorstep. Someone I don't know. Someone who is withdrawn, defeated, unreachable. He will not speak to me. Or my mother. I never know why. For two or three days afterwards, he will go down to the village. To drink. To not come home. Eventually, one of his friends will bring him back to us, drunk, half-dead, muttering to himself: Forgive me, forgive me. But we never find out what it is that we have to forgive him for.

And then the storm abates. The memory of Osaka fades. My father begins to return to himself again. Until next year.

❀

My father and I are walking down the steep, winding path to the village, silently following the two men balancing on the cart in front of us.

The ancient bus is already waiting in the marketplace. It belongs to Mr Nakagawa, one of my father's friends. The engine covers are missing. The wheel arches are full of dirt. There are men scrambling around on top of it, as busy as ants. They are securing pieces of luggage, crates, lengths of timber, to the roof. I watch as our chests full of kimono are hauled up to them. My father paces up and down beside the bus, giving them instructions. Which the men ignore.

Hiroshi, the bus driver's son, is sitting in one of the front seats. Rocking. He is tethered there. Our eyes meet. He grins his idiot grin. I turn away. Hiroshi is a giant. He brims with slow-witted malevolence. No one trusts him. He is big, unpredictable.

The year before, I had had my own reason to fear him. The path behind our house leads to one of the springs above our village. It is famous for its huge red boulders poking out of the earth along its length. Each stone is like an enormous skull, round, perfectly smooth. When I was little, my grandmother told me how bald-headed giants had come down the mountain one day to take revenge on the village. When the villagers heard them coming, they prayed to the gods to save them. And the earth swallowed the giants up, leaving only the tops of their heads exposed.

At certain points along the path, it is possible to jump from one head to another. I used to run along them as quickly as I could, remaining on each for only an instant, fearing that if I lingered too long a giant pair of hands would reach up out of the earth and seize me. Even now, I have a vague sense of terror just thinking about them.

On either side of the path, there are bamboo thickets. In places they are twenty metres tall. The surface of the bamboo is hard, polished, as green as insects' legs. When there is a breeze, the bamboo sways back and forth in long, slow arcs. High up, two shafts sometimes rub against each other, producing an unearthly, melancholy sound, like a child crying. I sometimes lie in bed at night listening to this sound, wondering if in some way it is connected with these giants drowned in the earth.

The incident I remember with Hiroshi has nothing to do with the path. Or the crying bamboo. It has to do with children laughing. At least at first.

I have been running. I am out of breath. Perhaps I have been jumping from skull to skull, trying to see how many I can jump in a row. Each year I can add another one, or two, or three.

I am almost at the pool when I stop. It is summer. The sun filters through the trees. I hear a child's shout, then a splash. Then another. There is more laughter. High-pitched, piercing, intoxicated. I crouch down, slip out of my sandals. The stones beneath my feet are cool. I reach out to steady myself against a shaft of bamboo.

Even when most of the pool, and the smooth rock face at its far end, is visible, I can't see them. Then, high up, on one of the boulders, something moves. It is a child. A boy of about five or six. He is crouching, his hands on his knees. He looks into the water. I recognise him. His name is Ichiro. His father owns a trinket shop in the village. He is naked. He stands and runs back and forth on top of the boulder. Gestures. Yells. I can see his tiny sex bouncing as he runs. His wet hair lies flat against his forehead. A thin spray of water falls sparkling through the sunlight. Then he is gesturing again, to someone, an invisible companion, somewhere in the water below him.

I watch as he plucks the drops of water suspended from his

nose with the tips of his fingers. He spreads his arms in a low arc, bends his knees, draws his child's belly up into his chest. Then, with an inelegant leap, he launches himself off the rock. His little boy's outstretched arms rotate quickly in the air as he plummets. I hear a splash as he hits the water. Laughter.

Now, between the pillars of bamboo, I see his friend—another boy his age, whose name I do not know. He emerges from the shadowed edge of the pool, glides out into the sunlight. Only his head pokes out above the cool dark plane of water. Their clothes lie in disarray on the stones of the bank opposite.

Above the sighing wind, I think I hear a sound from somewhere behind me. I turn, half-expecting to see another child on the path down which I have just come. But it is empty. I think to myself how inviting the water looks. Then I, too, am standing half-naked on the bank, my clothes folded on the flat stones at my feet. I step into the sunlight at the edge of the pool.

It is Ichiro who sees me first. He must think I am an apparition. He has just surfaced from a shallow dive. Water is still flowing from his eyes. He shakes his head. One hand reaches up to his mouth. He looks across to his companion who is swimming back to shore.

He has probably never seen a half-naked girl before. A shiver passes through his body. He remains motionless in the water. I smile at him. He smiles shyly back, uncertain. He brushes the remaining water from his eyes.

Sachiko, he says.

I slip into the water. Its coolness sweeps up my legs and

along my body. I glide out into the centre of the pool. Ichiro has swum to the shore. He is standing with his companion on one of the topmost boulders. They are both looking at me. I float, looking up at them. The sound of insects fills the air above me.

I see Ichiro grasp his friend by the shoulder. He points at the bank behind me. He calls out something to me, waves, points. At first, I can't see what he is pointing at. But then I see Hiroshi emerge from the shadows of the path. In his half-stooped giant way, he staggers over to where my clothes are lying in the sun. He leans down, picks up my trousers. He has them by one leg. The other dangles in the water. He brings them up to his face. Smells them. Turns them over. Smells them again. Then he gathers both legs up in his hands, looks for the waist. He goes to put them on.

Hiroshi, I shout. No, Hiroshi, no!

He stops, locates me in the water. He holds the garment out to me.

No, I yell again.

Then he drops them into the water. He turns to look behind him, then turns back to me. Across the water, I see his face change, grow ugly. A chill runs through my body. His mouth has dropped open, and he has begun to bob up and down. I know what he is thinking. That I am alone. That there is no one here to see him. That no one will know. He looks around again, mouth gaping. Listening. Looking into the bamboo forest. Then his gaze sweeps back to me.

I have swum into the shadows at the far side of the pool, to where little Ichiro and his friend were jumping. The water is deep here. I keep my legs, my arms, moving. Hiroshi steps into the water fully clothed. He strides out towards me. Immediately a plume of water, like a ghostly white arm, shoots up out of the water in front of him. Then another. He stops, confused, unable to make out what is happening. He looks at the water around him, as though this is where the attack is coming from. He doesn't see the black stone curving down. It strikes him on the shoulder. He looks up. Another is on its way. It appears to have launched itself up over the boulders above the pool of its own accord. Hiroshi's hand goes up to catch it. But he misjudges, and the stone strikes him again. He bellows like an ox.

More stones begin to rain down. I can hear the two boys' demented laughter. Abruptly the stones stop. Hiroshi is waist-deep in the water staring open-mouthed into the silence above him. He looks at me. I have circled around to where I can feel the rocks on the bottom of the pool. I watch his eyes fall from my face to my breasts. I cover myself with my hands. His mouth closes. Still he does not move.

Out of the corner of my eye I see two small heads poke out over the top of a boulder behind him. Then their straining small-boy bodies appear. Their legs are bent. Between them they are carrying a rock the size of a man's head. Ichiro and his friend struggle to hoist the stone up to their chests. They are intoxicated by what they are doing. Their effort is heroic. But they must know it's futile. They could never reach Hiroshi from where they are. I càn hear their suppressed, grunting giggles. They steady themselves.

Just as the stone leaves their uncoiled arms, Hiroshi looks up. It hits the water with a loud smack. The rock seems to crack open the very surface of the pool. A thick column of water shoots into the air. Hiroshi is caught in the spray. Ichiro and his friend are running about triumphantly in the sunlight on top of the boulder. Hiroshi has seen them now. He lunges angrily after them. It is as if he believes he can step up directly out of the water and up into the air to get them. He stumbles. His head and body disappear beneath the surface. He comes up coughing, thrashing about. He turns, wades unsteadily back to shore, wipes his eyes. Then he lurches up the slope towards the boulder upon which the boys have been standing. But they have gone. The moment he disappears, Ichiro materialises from behind the bamboo thicket beside which my clothes are lying. He picks them up, gestures rapidly to me.

When I am before him, still soaked, half-naked, he reaches up with his small hand and gives my clothes to me. I can feel the water trickling off my body, the sun on my shoulders. His arm remains outstretched as I take my clothes from him.

I kneel and kiss him on his forehead, touching the small kernel of his shoulder.

Thank you, Ichiro, I say, for saving me.

Before turning to run back along the path through the bamboo, before disappearing, he reaches up to touch my face. Even now, I can still feel the tips of three small fingers on my cheek, and see the look of disbelief, of wonderment, in his young boy's eyes.

❀

Standing in the marketplace, I realise that this memory is not about me. Or Hiroshi. Or the pool. It is about Ichiro. About the night, a few months later, when Ichiro's father comes banging on our door.

It is well after dark. Perhaps ten or eleven o'clock. The tourist crowds have all gone home. We are asleep. And, all at once, someone is pounding on our door. I hear my father get up. He says something to my mother. Goes to the door. I hear voices. Men's voices. Then I hear my mother. I sneak down the hallway to listen. It is Ichiro's father.

Ichiro hasn't come home, he is saying. He hasn't come home.

My father says something, but Ichiro's father is still talking.

I left him on the mountain, he says. I wanted to teach him a lesson…and now he hasn't returned.

I peek around the door jamb.

My father and mother have their backs to me. Ichiro's father is between them, by the still-open door. His head is bowed. My father has one hand on his shoulder, trying to calm him. But he is swaying back and forth. Shaking. Wringing his hands. He keeps repeating the same words.

I left him on the mountain. I left him on the mountain.

Ichiro, his beloved son.

❀

My grandmother and I are on the verandah peering through the darkness at the lights gathering in the marketplace far below. Lanterns, torches, poles wrapped with burning oil-soaked cloth. We can see clotted groups of men forming and re-forming. Their fragmentary voices waft up to us on the warm night air.

The lights divide, separate into groups. Each to search a different part of the surrounding forest.

Later that night, lying in my bed, I can hear their distant voices calling: *I-chi-ro, I-chi-ro...I-chi-ro.*

❀

Of course, it is Ichiro's father who finds him. The men have all returned home after midnight without him.

His half-unhinged father gets up before dawn. I'm not supposed to know. But the next evening I hear my mother and father in the kitchen, and I creep down again to stand outside the door.

Ichiro's father has gone back to the cliff face high above the village, to walk its length. He thinks perhaps Ichiro has stumbled in the dark. Perhaps he has fallen onto the rocks below. A father's intuition drives him.

An hour after sunrise, in the cruel early morning light, he sees the crow. He is climbing up through the small rocky ravine when he comes upon it. This big, solitary, black bird. He sees it half-obscured between the rocks, ready to take flight.

He stops. The bird's hard, bright-yellow eye does not move. It is watching him. Calculating. Measuring. He sees the crow cock its head. It takes one last look at what lies beneath its feet. There is time enough. The gluttonous black beak plunges, plunges again. The tremulous swallowing quick. Pitiless.

Even as he is running, Ichiro's father knows. And even though he is now a madman, shouting, waving his arms, his booted feet pounding across the furrowed ground, the crow remains for a moment where it has been, on the boy's forehead, the perfect place from which to pierce the eyeless lidded skin.

❀

Ichiro isn't dead. He isn't badly injured. Just unconscious. Concussed. In a couple of hours, he will wake, and try to open eyes he no longer has.

I have often wondered what it must have been like for him, Ichiro's father, to have knelt down, scarcely able to breathe from running, to cradle his newly dark-worlded son, with the sound of the crow's scooping wings still echoing in his ears as it rises into the air and peels away across the yellow morning slope.

❀

I turn away from Hiroshi. I see Ichiro sitting outside under the eaves of his father's store. His head is moving back and forth.

I have seen where his eyes once were. Two pitted knots of sunken flesh. His father refuses to conceal what has happened to him. To remind himself of how he failed his son.

All expression has been erased from Ichiro's face. I go over to him.

Ichiro, I say.

Sachiko.

I came to say goodbye.

Where are you going? he says.

To Osaka, with my father.

To Osaka. He nods. He must be thinking about what that could mean.

Forever? he asks.

Perhaps. For a long time, in any case.

He is silent. His head is still. He could be looking out across the marketplace.

I remember, he says softly, almost to himself.

He raises his hand, searching for my face. I kneel and he touches my cheek. His hand drops. His head starts to move back and forth again, and I know he's no longer there.

Chapter 19

IT is my first time down the mountain. Down the narrow, treacherous roads. The bus is packed with people from our village, spring tourists returning to Osaka, merchants, a few businessmen, children with their governesses. There are chests in the aisles. Bags have been squashed into the overhead racks. Things hang from the roof. I have no idea what they are.

The road is potholed. The sun is flung about the horizon. We are descending into valleys full of mist. I am irrationally afraid. My father is slumped in the seat beside me, asleep. I have no way of telling him of my fear. He has hardly spoken to me since we left. Even when Kimiko came, he barely said hello. Kimiko, whom we have known all our lives.

Mist, dense, impenetrable, rises to meet us. Engulfs us. The sun is snatched away. It is almost impossible to see the road ahead. The bus could be wrapped in cloth. We begin to feel our way down the mountainside. The only way I know we are moving is the constant jolting. Otherwise we could be stopped.

I begin to feel as though I am suffocating. My heart is pounding. I look around. Most of the passengers are asleep. The rest are unconcerned. I lean back into my seat, close my eyes, concentrate on the rise and fall of the engine. When I open them, Hiroshi is staring at me. He is in the seat opposite his father, Mr Nakagawa, the driver. I realise that he has been staring at me since we left.

In the afternoon, it begins to rain. At first, on the dirty windscreen, a few splattering drops ringed with red. Soon it is streaming down. It is raining so hard that when I look outside it is as though we are underwater. The noise is so loud I'm afraid the roof is going to cave in. We are forced to pull over on the side of the road. Some of the passengers, including my father, are beginning to wake.

What's happening, he says.

There's a storm, I say.

My father gets up. Squeezes past me. He goes and squats down next to Mr Nakagawa. I can see them talking. They take turns, leaning into each other's ears. The windscreen looks as though it is molten.

My father comes back.

We can't stay here, he says. It's too dangerous. There's an inn not far ahead. We're going to stop there until the rain passes.

The engine comes to life. We pull back onto the road, creep slowly forward. Half an hour later we reach the inn. The rain continues unabated into the evening. We are forced to stay the night.

In the morning, it is still raining. I can hear it drumming on the roof when I wake. A dull, hard noise. Thunder rolls away down the valley.

I dress, have breakfast. Afterwards, I go out onto the verandah to sit under the eaves. The area in front of the inn looks like a shallow pockmarked lake. The bus stands morosely tethered on the other side.

Mr Nakagawa comes out onto the verandah with Hiroshi, who steps forward, stretches his hand out, slaps at the rain. Mr Nakagawa goes back inside. Hiroshi sees me, stops. I hear his father's voice calling him. Then again, louder this time: Hiroshi!

Twenty minutes later, my father comes out onto the verandah. He looks anxious, annoyed.

Where have you been, Sachiko? he says. I've been looking everywhere for you.

I haven't been anywhere, Father, I say. I've just been sitting out here, looking at the rain.

And then he says something strange, something that doesn't make sense to me.

But you must tell me, Sachiko, he says. You must tell me where you are. You have to be careful. You don't know what these places are like. People disappear.

But Father, I say again. I'm here.

But you must *tell* me, Sachiko. You must understand.

He looks across to the bus.

Why today? he says. Why rain today?

I go to sit in the inner gloom with the other passengers, some impatient, some resigned. Late in the afternoon, the rain begins to ease. Two men in suits, who have been sitting by the window, get up and go to Mr Nakagawa.

We can't wait, I hear them say. We *have* to go on.

The three of them walk out onto the verandah. Mr Nakagawa is listening to them. One is shaking his head. They come back. Mr Nakagawa beckons to my father.

They are right, Mr Nakagawa says. We have to go on. The rain has eased. If we don't leave now, we won't get there before dark.

He turns to the rest of the passengers, tells them to get their things. We are pressing on, he says.

The bus is waiting for us by the verandah when we return. Steam is rising from its exhaust. Mr Nakagawa and my father hold umbrellas above our heads as we begin to file on board.

Barely have we pulled away from the inn when it begins to rain again. Hard. Mercilessly. Wave after wave of rain beats down on the bus as though to punish us.

We are halfway down the mountain. The road is slippery, unsealed, with treacherous curves which double back on each other. Piles of fallen rock lean against the escarpment. We are forced to manoeuvre around them. We slow to a walking pace. There is no turning back.

Every few feet it seems there is another turn. Mr Nakagawa is half out of the driver's seat, almost standing, grappling with the wheel, turning this way, then that, hauling the bus back across the road. Away from the edge. Away from the valley that lies obscured below. I can see his feet working. He could be trying to kill something. Which won't die. Which keeps rising up, again and again, to strike at him.

Darkness begins to fall. The beams of light from the headlights swing alarmingly from embankment to embankment. They bounce wildly into the trees, over boulders. They disappear into the black void ahead of us. At times it seems it is only they that prevent us from plunging into the abyss. The bus moves strangely beneath us, as though it has become disconnected from the earth. Above the beating of the rain, I can hear the engine. Every now and then it snatches another breath, changes pitch. Then it falls back to the same monotonous throb. Until next time.

And so we go on.

Later, my father takes the seat behind Mr Nakagawa. He leans on the rail in front of him, talks to him. Mr Nakagawa shakes his head. He glances at Hiroshi, who is asleep in the seat opposite, then back at the road, at the rain, and the growing darkness ahead of us.

❀

I must have fallen asleep because, all at once, I am jolted awake. It feels like someone has kicked my seat violently from behind. I am shunted forward, then back. My head hits something metal.

The bus seems to be leaning at a crazy angle. Dazed, I pull myself forward. My father is not there. Bags have fallen out of the overhead racks. Somewhere at the back of the bus a child is crying. The man in front of me turns around. His forehead is bleeding. I watch blood trickle down into his eye. He blinks. Wipes his forehead with his hand, frowns.

The engine is roaring, but we aren't moving. Although the headlights are on, all I can see is the pitted darkness in front of us. There is no road. A prolonged burst of lightning flickers on and off. I sit up. Outside my window, inches from my face, a rocky embankment tilts fitfully away into the night. Above it, I can see the arched trunks of trees. I begin to think that we have had an accident, that we have plunged into the ravine. And yet we are still upright.

What's happening? someone at the back of the bus calls.

The engine dies away. People have begun to stand. I hear Mr Nakagawa's voice.

We have to get out.

In this rain?

I'm sorry, he says. Get your coats, and your umbrellas. We're stuck.

What did he say?

The message is relayed to those at the rear. I can hear people complaining.

And then my father is pushing his way through to me. He has his coat on. His hair is layered to his scalp in long, thin tentacles. His face is drenched. I hear Mr Nakagawa apologising to the passengers ahead of us.

Take your coat, my father says to me. Make sure you are warm.

What's happening?

We're stuck. We're going to have to pull the bus free. It's too heavy with us on board.

We begin filing out. Mr Nakagawa is standing at the foot of the steps, helping. Water is cascading down the hood of his jacket.

I'm sorry, he says to the woman in front of me.

He takes my hand as I step down into the mud. Most of the women and children, some of the old men, are sheltering in an uneven line on the far side of the road. One or two have lanterns. I can see their faces in the broken light. The rain bounces off their translucent umbrellas in tiny splinters. The mud pulls at my shoes as I wade across to join them.

Two men with gas lamps attached to long poles are already standing behind the bus. It is clear what has happened. Part of the road, the part nearest the embankment, has subsided. A large pool has formed. The water is the colour of straw. Only the tops of the rear wheels are visible. I watch as one of the men wades into the water. It comes up to his knees. He reaches up through the rain to grasp the rung of the ladder at the rear of the bus. Goes to pull himself up. But the water won't release him. Not at first. He pulls again, drags his legs free, then climbs up the ladder onto the roof of the bus. One of the men standing in the water hands the lantern pole up to him, then climbs up himself. The world seems to list, then right itself again, in the swinging lantern light.

The man on top of the bus kneels down beside two battered chests. He begins to undo their clasps. Crouched there in the light, in the rain, he looks like a ghostly spider trapped beneath a silvery net, trying to get free. He begins retrieving coils of rope. He throws the looped bundles down to the men waiting at the side of the bus. Amongst them is Hiroshi. He is staggering back and forth, watching what the man is doing. He moves to the rear. He half-stumbles into the widening pool, falls to his knees. He looks around, his wet, lunatic face ecstatic. His father is bending down, reaching into the muddy water, trying to attach a rope to something beneath the bus. Hiroshi wades in, begins to climb the ladder. His father sees what he is doing. Hiroshi! he yells. He reaches up, grabs the back of Hiroshi's jacket, pulls him brutally down. He slaps him across the head with his open hand, points to the side of the road. Hiroshi stands behind him. In the middle of the pool. In the rain and the pitching white light.

We are all looking at him.

He wades around to the side of the bus. He bends down to examine one of the trapped wheels. His hair is dangling in the water. He touches one of the tyres. Then he stands up, tries to kick it with his foot. He almost falls backwards into the water.

Mr Nakagawa comes to the side of the bus. Shouts at him again. Raises his fist.

The men have divided into two groups. One at the front of the bus where most of the ropes have been attached. One at the rear. One to push, one to pull. Everything is ready. We are all waiting. Mr Nakagawa moves to the door of the bus, goes to get in. Stops. Points to Hiroshi again and then to the side of the road where the rest of us are gathered. For a moment father and son stare at each other.

All this time, the sky is lit up by lightning. The embankment, the stranded bus, the tree canopies in the valley below, flicker in the darkness. The thunder echoes against the mountain. The pool has grown. Mr Nakagawa is in the driver's seat, his dimly lit silhouette just visible. The engine begins to turn. With a sudden churning beneath the water it comes to life. Steam rises from the far side of the bus. The headlights come on. Now we can see the men in front of the bus. They are stretched out in the rain, four or five to a rope. The ropes rise from this muddy plane, begin to go taut. A dozen men have gathered in the water behind the bus. In the reddish brake lights they appear to float there, like spectral half-men just risen from the mud.

The engine noise rises. The men at the front of the bus begin to pull. The road is now a river of mud. We see their feet slipping. The men at the rear have braced themselves, ready to push. The engine revs again. The bus seems to move. The wheels begin to churn. The bus falls back. The engine rises again. The two groups of men are shouting to one another. Trying to establish a rhythm. Forward, then back. Forward a little more. We can see their straining faces in the headlights.

The road is slippery, the ropes are wet. Forward, back. Forward, back. The bus begins to break free. The wheels begin to emerge. The engine noise is deafening.

The bus is almost out—all but one of the men behind it have stood back. Then the wheels begin to spin. For an instant, nothing happens. The men at the front, who have begun to relax, who have already seen themselves triumphant, brace themselves again. The wet ropes snap tight. It is as if something ugly has been lurking in the darkness above us. The bus begins to slip backwards. One of the men shouts a warning to his companion, who is still behind the bus. Inexplicably, he is still pushing. The brake lights come on. There is another shout. The man half-turns. And we all see who it is. It is Hiroshi.

Unobserved, he has joined the men at the rear of the bus. Now he stands there alone, open-mouthed, wild-eyed, looking back at us over his shoulder through the beating rain. The bus looms over him. Someone, a woman, cries out. But now the bus appears to rush, to lunge at him. It clubs him heartlessly backwards into the water. Which seems to open up and swallow him. The underside of the bus hits the water with a tremendous thump. A wall of water and mud bursts up over the semicircle of men at the pool's edge. Then it begins to settle, to drain back into the pool. We all think Hiroshi will just rise up out of the water, coughing and spluttering. Looking foolish. But he doesn't. Instead, a brief, inhuman cry erupts from beneath the bus. A single, strangled howl. Then nothing. The muddied surface begins to still.

It is clear that Hiroshi is trapped. The men at the rear leap forward, into the water. Two of them begin reaching around, arms deep in the water, searching for him. There is shouting. Some of the women drop their umbrellas. They rush to the front of the bus, yelling to the men: *Pull, pull!* One of them is pounding on the driver's door, screaming something up to Mr Nakagawa, who realises something terrible has happened. The engine roars again. The wheels begin to spin. The water churns. Steam from the exhaust billows up over the bus. The two men have found Hiroshi. They have him by one of his arms. They are pulling on it, trying to drag him free. I can see his wet and bloodied hand above the men's bent backs. It is opening and closing, as though it is some ghastly mouth able to suck air down into his drowning body. But it isn't. And the bus refuses to move.

❀

An hour or so after sunrise, we come around a bend in the road and there, sprawled below us, is Osaka. The city spills down the mountainside towards the bay which lies motionless in the early morning haze. Further south, along the coast, it is impossible to see where the city ends. It dissolves into the grey and indeterminate horizon beyond.

It took more than an hour to pull the bus free. In the rain. In the dark. The light from the lamps grown dim. With everyone shaken, silent, as if we were all already aware that each of us had been brought there for some obscure and terrible reason to witness what had unfolded. We all felt guilty. We could not look at each other. But we all understood one thing. We had escaped. Only Hiroshi had been made to pay. And his father.

When the bus was finally pulled clear, Hiroshi had bobbed to the surface like a cork. No one moved. At first. We all stared at his floating body, watching it turn slowly in the rain. Then his father, and one of the other men, waded into the pool to lift him free.

I can still see Mr Nakagawa kneeling at the rear of the bus, in the yellow mud, on his own, with his dead idiot son cradled in his lap, rocking him slowly back and forth, saying something over and over, which I cannot hear.

❀

How many times has Sachiko told Katsuo this story? How many times have they sat on the terrace at night looking down at the jewelled city, or in the darkness of the lit garden, listening to the frogs, the slow tock, tock, tock of the water clock, the strings of a shamisen?

Some nights, they would walk through the maze of narrow streets above the house, to find out where the music was coming from. As they walked the sound seemed to change location, echoing softly off the hillside, or a stone wall, or the air itself. Sometimes far off, sometimes near, it constantly circled around them, a kind of playful living thing. And yet so melancholy.

And all the time, at his urging, Sachiko would be talking to him.

Tell me again about helping your grandmother lay the kimono out on the snow, tell me about the horses, or Kimiko, he would say. Tell me about the night you stole away, about the lovers in the pool.

And he would see Sachiko's shadow darting through the trees as they walked. Once, on their way home, Sachiko stopped, grasped his sleeve.

Listen, she said. It sounds like the music is coming from our house.

They listened for a long time. She was right. It did sound like it was coming from their house. But, of course, it wasn't, and never could have been.

❀

In the garden, Katsuo pictures the anvilled clock's tipping. Slow, then quick, the water spilling from its bamboo lip. Then faster still, as if it too is hurrying back to its tock, tock, tock.

How many times had he listened to her voice in the darkness? Each time she added something new. Some just remembered thing. He kept having to go back, to change what he had written.

No longer. Now there is nothing more she can tell him.

Chapter 20

SHE hears them first. Their hooves, thundering up the slope. The sound hangs in the crystalline air. Two horses, black as night, rise up out of the snow like phantoms.

The mare stands still in the sharp morning light. Ears twitching. Vigilant. The stallion, wild-eyed, circles. His dark flanks steaming. Rippling with uncontained energy. Anticipation. Their shadows etching the radiant snow.

Sachiko lies hidden in her thicket, in the field above her house. She is a twelve-year-old girl watching two horses circle each other. Their shadows coupling, uncoupling, then coupling again. Their fogged breath. The steam clings to these apparitions in the snow, like spirits reluctant to depart.

She sees the tremors pass in waves along the stallion's flank. One after another after another, like a shadowed sea. He paws the snow-covered ground. Nuzzles the mare. Butts her haunches with his head, trying to turn her. She stands her ground.

He charges away from her, a sudden dark-hooved fury. Possessed by something he does not understand.

Sachiko waits.

She hears the echoes of his hooves. Circling, elusive. Then, from a different bearing altogether, the stallion rises up out of the snow again. He comes thundering back. He stops just short of the mare. Tosses his head. With a start he veers away from her again. Circles. She is his pivot. The locus about which his momentary being revolves. His breath comes now in short exhortations. He paws the ground, is still.

She has never seen anything like it before. It is like some new and unimagined life form, a creature as long and thick and smooth as her arm. That has come out to graze from some hidden place deep within the stallion's belly. It makes no sense. It hangs there, its dark weighted head swaying just centimetres above the snow, as if it is searching for something it has lost.

And then she understands.

The realisation is catastrophic. Her brain is reeling. This, she knows, has something to do with her. Her future.

She watches the horses intently now. The two are coiled. Every muscle tensed. The stallion so perfectly still he could be an artefact. Until his surface breaks. Without warning, he lunges. Tears viciously at the mare, her mane. He rears.

Sachiko watching.

Now he strikes at the mare's neck with his hooves. Again and again. He shies away, turns a tight pirouette. Returns. Lunges at her neck again. His eyes glazed. There is a kind of madness here.

She can see a dark trickle of blood issuing from the mare's torn flesh. On the white snow, a chain of blood-red looping drops. She, too, is locked in their trance.

The mare can no longer move. She is transfixed. Her bulging eyes waiting.

The stallion paws the ground again.

Their coupling is beyond imagination, beyond reasoning. Nothing has prepared Sachiko for this. The awkward, urgent, clumsy manoeuvring. Confused hooves jostling in the kicked-up snow. Their slow turning purposeful. They dance a dance to steps that only they know. It is impossible. What they want. But, at last, the desired union. Images from a grotesque dream. The stallion still bends to tear the mare's already bloodied neck, as if to anchor himself there.

Sachiko's first instinct is to run, to intervene. To stop this bloody onslaught. Now, watching, she cannot turn away.

Without warning, something white erupts against the stallion's flank. Another explosion, higher up, on the horse's neck. A white peony bursting from the horse's flesh. Then another.

Sachiko knows what these are. She sees the concealed stones falling. Sees them instantly swallowed by the snow.

Now they come in volleys. Their short arc brief against the perfect sky. As they fall, white against white, it is impossible to see them. It is only when they hit their mark that they are visible again. These snowballs packed with stone.

Then, miraculously, as though they too have risen up out

of the snow, half a dozen boys are charging. They have been lying in wait. Now they emerge from behind the snow-covered bushes. They are running, churning the soft snow, yelling, hurling their missiles at the rutting horses. Who stop, still united, in the face of this incomprehensible thing.

Sachiko emerges from her cover. Runs. Shouts: No! No! Don't hurt them. Leave them be.

But it is too late. The horses have broken apart. Another wave of snow-stones plummets down on them. Then, with the spell irrevocably broken, the horses return to their separate worlds. They pull away from each other. They turn, and plunge down the slope again, away from her, their phantom shapes absorbed once more into the morning snow.

Sachiko feels her anger rise. The boys too have watched the horses disappear.

Why, she yells at them.

The boys turn to her, this girl who has spoilt their fun. There is a strange hiatus, a recalibration. What to do to restore the equilibrium? One of the older boys steps forward. He wedges his feet into the snow, leans back with his arm outstretched. He is now a human catapult. He launches a snowball high into the air. It plummets down. Disappears into the snow a metre or two in front of her. Then there is another. Closer this time. Sachiko looks up to see each of the boys readying themselves. They are all human catapults now. She turns to run. But the soft snow impedes her. She can hear the thuk of snowballs landing around her. Unseen by her, one of the boys has found a piece of wood. He throws it after her. It turns end over end in the air. It strikes her, high on her shoulder. It pierces Sachiko's skin through her blouse. She stumbles. Falls. Then she feels the pain, like a knife blade in her back. The boys stop. They stand some distance away from her. This is not what they came here for.

It's Sachiko, one of them says.

She rolls onto her back. Lies dazed, looking up into the pure sky.

Fear decides the boys. They back away. Turn, run, in high looping bounds, down the slope.

Sachiko pushes herself to her feet. The pain has begun to ebb. She arches her shoulder, winces. Brushes herself down. She sees the piece of wood that struck her. Its sharp end bloodied. When she turns towards home, she sees the blood-red stain on the snow. Its magnitude alarming. She reaches over her shoulder, pulls at the fabric of her smock. Feels the sticky wetness, looks at her fingertips now painted red.

And knows there is no escaping the pain that now awaits her.

❀

Why did you go there, Sachiko? Why? Explain it to me again, how you fell?

It becomes her mother's constant lament. Sachiko sees it in her every look. It comes to occupy the space between them.

Her father was on the snow-covered slope above their house that day, doing what Sachiko should have done, laying out the new season's kimono in the snow. How dazzling white the white ones were. It hurt your eyes to look at them.

By chance he glanced up to see his distant daughter walking towards him. He knew instantly that his world had changed. And because he had been the one to run to her—exclaiming, broken-syllabled: *Sachiko, Sachiko*—he was held to blame. He had not been watching over her.

Chapter 21

THE bus terminal is deep within the vast and teeming square. Even at this early hour, traffic is jigsawed to a stop. Battered trucks, hand carts, buses, clog the interstitial spaces. Schools of ancient bicycles swim through the narrow fissures. All around them, a swirling tide of men ebbs and flows, shouldering their wares, heads bent. Near and far, horns bark, men shout. High-pitched whistles shred the air. The bus floats on a shallow sea of dust and diesel fumes. A smell as thick as fog seeps in through its carapace.

The bus creeps forward, stops.

Is this it, Father? Sachiko says.

Yes, he says. This is where we get out.

She looks at the tumult around them. The buildings on the square's far periphery are like a distant shore. She wonders how they will get from here to there.

Stand up, Sachiko, her father says. Get your things.

The doors of the bus open like floodgates. The brutal outside floods in—the noise, the pungent smell of rotting fish, the diesel fumes, the stench of men. Sachiko feels herself being swept back into the bus. Which begins to fill. She cannot breathe.

Her father is behind her. He leans into her ear. Take this, he says. He hands her his handkerchief.

Put this over your nose. You will get used to it. Here, hold on, step down.

Only a few passengers get off. Two or three exhausted businessmen, their suits dirty, crushed, their eyes drawn. One of the old women, who smiles at Sachiko in the stairwell, pats her arm.

Sachiko looks down at what awaits her. Then she steps into the swirling chaos. She and her father are by the bus, pinned against it by the noise, the smell. By the mass of bodies sweeping past them.

Wait here, her father says. I have to collect our luggage.

Here? she says. She can hear the panic in her voice.

I won't be long, he says.

Wave upon wave of fetid, choking air washes over her. She grasps the wheel well of the bus to stop herself from being dragged into the cross-currents. She is pulled this way, then that. Unseen things touch her. She imagines hands reaching for her from within this seething mass, tugging at her, touching her, sliding across her body. She cannot move. She is embossed into the side of the bus.

There are no women here. Just men. Men with their carts.

Men with their pieces of paper. Men with cigarettes. Men on their own, who stare.

You want to sell?

A hideous face looms up in front of her. One glaucous bulging eye faces skywards. The other, with its small dark pupil, fixes on her, then turns to someone perched above her. Someone Sachiko has not seen. It is one of the businessmen from the bus. He is standing in the stairwell. He has not heard what the man has said. Instead, he is looking out over the sea of heads, searching for something. Or someone.

You want to sell? the face repeats more loudly.

The sightless tallowed eye seems to move of its own accord. It scans the sky, as though still trying to pinpoint exactly where the previous danger had come from. Its owner tugs at the businessman's trouser leg. Attracts his attention. He rubs one stained finger against his thumb. Points to Sachiko.

What? the man in the suit says impatiently.

You sell?

The man indicates Sachiko again. He steps forward so that he is centimetres from her face. He looks at her sideways with his one unclouded eye. At her hair. Her eyes. Her mouth. Her skin. Assessing. Calculating. How old is she? Is she still fresh? Sachiko can smell the stench of stale tobacco and something else on his breath. He reaches out, grasps her arm. Tightly. He is pulling her away.

Father! she screams.

But the man in the stairwell has already leapt down from

the bus. He seizes her assailant by the throat. She sees his knuckles blanch. The fingered grip around her arm goes limp.

When she looks again to where the blind-eyed man should be, he has gone, swallowed up by the turmoil around them. The man in the suit turns back to her.

Thank you, Sachiko says. Her eyes well with tears. She rubs her arm. A small bruise has already begun to surface.

Her saviour barely glances at her. He is brushing down his coat. She pictures what he sees. She knows what he is thinking. She wants to tell him that he is mistaken. That she is here with her father. She is waiting for him. Surely he has seen her on the bus. But he is no longer interested in her. He has already resumed searching for the thing he has not yet seen.

She is shaking. Alone. The world is blurred. Her fingers find the tenderness in her arm again. She dare not look down. She is dizzy. She does not know how much longer she can stay afloat. And now the stranger is stepping down from the bus. He is leaving her. She sees his retreating back. It is too late to cry out to him. To plead with him to stay.

Miraculously, as she is watching, her father appears from the same void into which the stranger has disappeared, as though he has been transformed into him. She is overjoyed. Now her father has returned, she is safe.

But her ordeal is not yet over. A wagon laden with bamboo trunks passes between her and her father. Then another. She looks left, then right. Where has he gone? A sea of new faces sweeps up around her. It surges up against the bus, then cascades down on her again. Her panic returns. Where is he? Wave after wave of people crash over her. Nausea, hot and thick and viscous, rises in her throat. The noise and heat and fetid smells of the square press down on her, on her shoulders, her head. She feels her legs grow weak. Her knees begin to buckle. The earth gives way. She is forced under. Now she is drowning, struggling for breath.

Father, she cries out.

But there is no answer. Instead she feels a hand closing around her arm once again. She sees the sickly clouded eye, how it turns in its socket. The buyer of young girls has returned. She struggles to get free. But can't.

❀

Sachiko, Sachiko…

She hears her father's voice calling. From a distance. As though from a dream. Sachiko…

When she opens her eyes, her father is crouched beside her. Is it night? Shadow figures swim past her in the darkness. Pale spectral faces turn her way.

Sachiko…

She is lying in a sheltered doorway. They are no longer in the square. They are in some kind of dim arcaded alley.

Are you all right, daughter? her father's voice says.

Her heart is still pounding. Her eyes fill with tears.

Here, drink this, her father says.

He cups her head. She sips the water he has offered. Then he says to her the same thing he said to her at the inn.

You must be careful, Sachiko, he says.

She remembers.

You must be careful.

Chapter 22

TO her, he is always the man without a face. Mr Ishiguro.

She recalled lying on a cold stone step in a darkened doorway. Hearing her father's voice, the dull-edged tumult of the square now distant. Faces turning her way.

Then her father is saying: Sachiko, we're here…Sachiko.

Memories of a hand waylaying her, malevolent. Meaning her no good. Swirling around her, a nightmare noise. She is tumbling beneath the waves. Trapped in a tangled mass of limbs. Shadows close over her. She cannot breathe.

Sachiko?

Then she is awake.

Where are we? she says.

We're here. You fell asleep.

She lies curled on the soft leather seat. Her father's coat is folded under her head. The pleated grey sky above her is horizoned with blue. She begins to surface. Leans up on one elbow. She and her father are encased in a car that is coming to a stop so gradually it could be an ocean liner.

Outside, above the door sill, a smiling, hatted face, as round and full as a festival balloon, bobs up and down. She imagines a small child, a tiny clenched fist tugging on a string. When her father opens the door, the mask rises abruptly into the sky, and is checked there. The light outside is blinding.

Ah, Yamaguchi, a voice says. Finally, you are here.

She sees that the smiling face is invisibly stitched to a suit. Her father is still sitting beside her in the car. A hand reaches in. Takes her father's hand. Shakes it for a long time. It seems it will never let him go.

Ishiguro, her father says.

So this is the Ishiguro her father has spoken of. Whose name her father sometimes calls out in his sleep. The Ishiguro about whom her mother endlessly complains. Whose spirit has occupied their house for longer than she can remember.

Please, Mr Ishiguro says. He holds his other arm out, half-stepping aside to make room for her father. He still has her father's hand in his.

What happened? Ishiguro says.

I'm sorry, Ishiguro. We were trapped by the storm on the mountain last night. The bus broke down.

Her father turns to Sachiko. Who is now sitting up. He reaches in, takes her hand. Helps her slide along the seat. Then she too is standing beside the long black car, its roof gleaming in the splintered sun.

Sachiko, her father says, this is Mr Ishiguro. I have told you about him. It is he who buys the kimono your grandmother and mother make.

Miss Sachiko, Mr Ishiguro says.

He extends his hand, bows deeply. The gesture surprises her. This is not what a man would normally do. Not with a girl her age.

His hand still waits. Her moment of hesitation passes. Her father is here. She is safe.

Mr Ishiguro is smiling. Sachiko can see the fold of skin that encircles his face. She thinks of the plump crease that separates a newborn's hand from its wrist, as though this is just a temporary hand, not yet permanently attached. The final choice is yet to be made. She feels sure that, if Mr Ishiguro took off his hat, the mask would come with it, and the something completely different that lies beneath would be revealed.

❀

Your father, Miss Sachiko, is a truly valued customer.

They are in an unfurnished room. Against the walls, hanging on horizontal bars, are bolts of cloth. They are arranged to mirror the changing day, from dawn to noon, late afternoon to dusk. And, finally, night.

Beside each array stands a young woman dressed in a kimono made from one of the samples. Seven girls. Seven kimono. All different. All exquisite.

Each of the girls is painstakingly made-up, her face powdered, her hair tied up, pinned. Each arrangement coded. Each face porcelain-perfect. Their lacquer rosebud lips glistening, as though, just now, they had sipped from a water cup, the memory of which still clings to their lips.

To one side, two women tend a brazier on a wheeled cabinet. An ancient iron kettle, two squat cups, a bamboo whisk. Rows of small stoppered jars arrayed on shelves. They are preparing tea for her father and Mr Ishiguro. She can smell the faintly perfumed burning coals.

Negotiations, she knows, will not begin until this ritual is complete. She will not be allowed to stay.

A girl not much older than her comes in. She bows to Mr Ishiguro, goes to stand inside the door. She too is meticulously made-up.

As though Mr Ishiguro has read Sachiko's thoughts, he nods to the new girl.

The girl comes over to Sachiko, takes her arm. Mr Ishiguro has asked me to show you the mills, she says, sliding the door closed behind her. I am Misako. And you are Sachiko, are you not?

Misako leads her down a long corridor. There is a wooden door at its far end. She pushes it open. When they step through the opening, Sachiko is momentarily disoriented.

I know, Misako says. I had the same feeling when I first stepped out here. The corridor is so long, you think you're walking the building's length, but you're not, you're walking through it.

They have emerged along one side of an enclosed square, parts of which are open, designed to trap the light. Other parts are shaded, with carefully tended gardens, oases of tranquillity where Sachiko imagines one might sit and read. Or think. Or meet at night. In the centre of the square there is a lotus pond, so large she cannot see its outer limits.

What a beautiful garden, she says.

Yes, it is, isn't it.

Misako too stands there for a moment surveying the gardens, the lotus pool, the trees, the discrete areas of sun-filled light, as though for the first time. Then she breaks free of her reverie.

They walk across to the shaded verge of the pond. Leading away from the edge, into the water, is a pathway of flat stones.

I know, it looks like they're floating, Misako says. But they're not. See. And she steps impossibly out onto the first stone.

❀

The stepping stones did not lead directly across the pond. Instead, at certain points, they branched off. As Sachiko and Misako made their way across the water, a brightly coloured comet's tail of red and gold and silver koi trailed after them.

When they stepped off the last stone onto the edge at the far side of the pool, they stood facing the building opposite. There was a door in the wall in front of them, the mirror image of the door through which they had just come. Misako opened it to a deafening clatter and they both stepped inside.

❀

In the semi-darkness, rows of women sit at looms. Each loom is lit by a narrow, overhead light. From each, cloth spills into wooden troughs below. The cloth looks like brilliantly coloured, viscous liquid.

Some of the women glance up when they enter the room. None of them stops what they are doing. There are a number of girls her own age sitting at the tables with the older women. They too look up.

She sees the unasked question: Is this the new girl who will soon be joining them?

A luminous white cloth catches Sachiko's eye. In the overhead light, it is as if the cloth has been spun from newly sunlit snow. She recognises the fabric instantly, its pattern—tall thin stems of still-budding orchids pushing up through freshly fallen snow.

Oh, she says, leaning into Misako, her voice alive with surprise. This fabric was one of my grandmother's favourites. I remember helping her lay the kimono she made from it out in the snow, so that the cold could fix its colours.

Yes, it's beautiful, Misako says. We've only just begun making it again.

So, Sachiko says, is this where I will be working?

Misako takes a step back, frowns, then looks into the vast room again; at the rows of women working there, the young girls, the looms, the shuttles, the bolts of freshly woven cloth.

She turns to Sachiko. Says something. But Sachiko cannot hear what it is over the noise of the machines. Misako points to the door.

❀

They went to sit in the sunlit courtyard.

You know, Sachiko, Mr Ishiguro was right, Misako said eventually.

What do you mean?

Mr Ishiguro told us all you were coming. He said you were beautiful. And he was right. You are very, very beautiful, Sachiko.

Sachiko felt the heat rise to her face.

You don't believe me?

I don't know, she said. You are beautiful yourself, Misako. And besides, Mr Ishiguro does not know me. He has never met me before.

Misako laughed, a short, soft, not unfriendly laugh.

Oh, Mr Ishiguro knows a great many things about you, Sachiko. A great many things. And you are mistaken. He *has* met you before.

When? she said.

Years ago. When you were young. And a number of times since.

She wanted to ask Misako what she meant. But Misako was now sitting on the stone wall, leaning back on her arms, swinging her legs, warming her face in the sun. Her eyes were closed.

How do you bear it? Sachiko said.

What? Misako asked.

That, in there, being tied to it all day.

Misako's laugh seemed to well up from within her again. She was shaking her head, smiling.

Oh no, Sachiko, she said. I don't think you understand.

And she laughed her strange, full-bodied laugh once again.

Chapter 23

SO, Hideo, Mr Ishiguro said, the car will come for you at nine.

Sachiko and Misako were still sitting in the courtyard. Mr Ishiguro and her father were standing in the open doorway behind them.

Agreed? he asked.

Sachiko's father looked across to her, then back to Mr Ishiguro. He nodded.

Agreed, he said.

Nine o'clock then, Mr Ishiguro repeated. Don't look so worried, Hideo. I assure you, everything will work out for the best. You will see.

Mr Ishiguro turned to glance at Sachiko across the stone expanse that separated them.

What had Misako said? *Mr Ishiguro knows a great many things about you, Sachiko.*

The two men bowed to each other. Mr Ishiguro turned

again and bowed to Sachiko. His hand was resting on her father's shoulder.

Are you ready to go, daughter? her father called to her.

Yes, she said.

Thank you, Misako, for showing me the looms, she said. I hope that one day we will meet again.

I am sure we will, Sachiko, Misako said.

Sachiko stood up.

Mr Ishiguro was now walking alongside her father, guiding him towards the stone archway at the far end of the courtyard. They both stopped to wait for her.

Miss Sachiko, Mr Ishiguro said.

Mr Ishiguro.

I hope Misako has looked after you, he said.

Yes, she said. She was extremely...She searched for a word. Kind, she said, when what she really meant was free.

❀

The archway led down to the stone terrace overlooking the forecourt. At the far end of the driveway, the car sat half-hidden in the shadows of the trees.

The three of them—Mr Ishiguro, her father and Sachiko—walked down the steps onto the driveway. She could hear the crunch of their footsteps on the gravel.

I have arranged a car to take you to Ikeda's, Mr Ishiguro was saying to her father.

Sachiko saw that the car had already begun to glide silently out from its shadows towards them.

The same car will pick you up tonight at nine, Hideo. Remember, at nine. Not eight as usual. Miss Sachiko can make herself at home. Ikeda-san will be there. Everything has been arranged. Ume will take care of her.

The car came to a stop beside them.

Mr Ishiguro turned back to her father. Don't *worry*, Hideo, he was saying. You will see. You have made the right choice. He grasped her father high on his shoulder once again. I promise you. A man like Ikeda comes along only once in a lifetime.

A uniformed driver got out of the car. He stood waiting. Mr Ishiguro bowed to her father.

He turned to Sachiko. Reached out, took her fingers lightly between his, bowed.

You are a beautiful young woman, Miss Sachiko, he said. Your father must be very proud of you.

Sachiko thought again of what Misako had told her: *Mr Ishiguro said you were beautiful.*

It has been a pleasure to meet you, he said.

Then the uniformed driver was opening the door.

Miss, he said.

As they pulled away, Sachiko looked out the side window. Mr Ishiguro had gone to stand at the top of the stairs. Their eyes met for an instant as the big car wheeled around to face the gates through which they had come. Then the car swept him from view. She felt sure, however, that if she turned to look out the rear window he would still be there, immutable, silent, his long shadow spilling down the dark stairs towards them, as if he was a stone custodian positioned there to see who came, and who went.

Chapter 24

THE journey took them half an hour. With them slumped back in the car's plush interior, the world passed by outside as though they were in a high-sided boat.

They began the slow climb up the mountainside. Sachiko could hear the dull sound of the engine effortlessly rising and falling as the great black machine pulled itself up and around each bend. Trees floated past them outside. It was late afternoon. The light was already beginning to fall.

Eventually, the car turned into a small side road. They pulled up in front of two wrought-iron gates set into a high stone wall. The gates began to open. They entered a tall, winding hedgerow.

A minute later, without warning, the car emerged onto an open forecourt. Mr Ikeda's house loomed over them. Against the afternoon light, the house appeared as though it had been made from an enormous transparent ledge hammered into the side of the mountain. The light seemed to pass directly through it to illuminate the forecourt below. She saw now that this ledge was, in fact, a huge terrace. The house itself was set further back.

Then the driver was standing by her door.

Miss, he said, reaching in for her hand.

When she and her father alighted, Sachiko stood looking up to the house. It was even more imposing than she had at first thought. The terrace now seemed to soar out into the air above them, at once both impossibly light and impossibly heavy, as if it was only the tension between the two that held it there.

The shadow of the mountain had already begun to spill down towards them. The interior lights of the house were on. A long seamless wall of glass looked out onto the terrace. Sachiko thought she could see someone standing against the window. It was no more than a shadow on the glass. And then it was gone.

Her father, too, was gazing up at the house.

Mr Yamaguchi. Miss.

The driver had their bags in his hands. He turned towards the house.

They followed him up the stairs. When they reached the portico, the driver pressed the button beside the door. They waited. The door opened and an old woman appeared. She was small, her face thin, her sallow skin crumpled like paper. She had a smattering of small dark sunspots on her cheeks and forehead.

Miss Sachiko, the old woman said. Welcome. We have been waiting for you. Mr Yamaguchi. Please, come in.

She bowed a number of times, stepped aside, held her arm out.

My name is Ume, she said to Sachiko. But you can call me Ume-san. I will be attending to you and your father.

She turned to the driver.

Did Mr Ishiguro tell you? she said.

Tell me what, Ume-san? the driver said.

That the Master has been called away unexpectedly. He will not be back until later this evening.

Ume turned to Sachiko and her father.

I am so sorry, Mr Yamaguchi, Miss Sachiko, she said. Unfortunately, Master Ikeda is not here to welcome you himself. He was called away at the last minute. He has asked me to give you his apologies. I have prepared your rooms for you. If you would follow me.

They followed the old woman through the long rectangular room that ran the length of the terrace. Sachiko glanced across to where the figure she thought she had seen earlier had been standing. But there was no one there.

In the middle of the room an island of armchairs floated silently on the polished floorboards. Sachiko stopped to look out through the glass onto the terrace outside. It was impossible to see the city below. Instead, in the muted afternoon light, beyond the half-shadowed edge of the terrace, all she could distinguish, stretching endlessly along the horizon, was a narrow band of sea, a band so dark and still it could have been made of stone. Beyond this was the sky, vast and pale and empty.

She heard her father's voice calling her from the far end of the room.

Sachiko? he was saying.

And she turned to follow him.

❀

This is your room, Miss Sachiko, Ume said.

Ume switched on a lamp. A soft light revealed the room's sparse furnishings. The bedding had already been laid out. On each side of it were two old side tables. On one, a shaded lamp. A low cabinet against the wall adjacent to the bed. White orchids on a stone plinth.

Ume walked over to two screen doors opposite the bed. She slid these open.

Here, unexpectedly, was the garden. It stretched up the mountainside, the ragged edge of which towered above them. The sky had turned a deep late-afternoon blue. In the evening breeze, against the darkening silhouette of the mountain, the canopies of the trees looked like masses of cloud drifting through the garden. She could hear frogs calling. Near, then far. Running water. Somewhere, the repeated hollow tock-tock-tock of a water clock.

It's beautiful, Sachiko said.

Ume was watching her. Their eyes met. The old woman bowed, acknowledging what Sachiko had said.

Do you have any questions for me, Miss Sachiko? Ume said.

No, I don't think so, Ume-san, she said.

If you want anything, do not hesitate to call me, the old

woman said. All you need do is press the buzzer. She indicated a bone-coloured button set into the wall beside the door.

Thank you, Ume-san, she said.

I will leave you to recover from your journey, she said.

Then Ume turned to her father. Mr Yamaguchi, she said, if you would be so kind, I will show you to your room.

Her father was still standing in the doorway to the garden. He seemed nervous, uncomfortable. His suit seemed shabbier now, older than Sachiko remembered it.

When Ume went to the door and slid it open, her father followed her. He did not say goodbye.

She heard their footsteps retreating on the polished floor-boards. She heard another door open, then close. Then she was alone, in the silence of her room, looking into the darkening garden outside.

❀

The long, slow sound of a foghorn, a sound so solid, so thick, that she seemed to be suspended in it, reached out to Sachiko in her sleep.

Then she was awake, disoriented, confused.

She found herself sitting in a wicker chair on a stone terrace. It took her a moment to recall where she was. Fragments from her day began to resurface. Ume-san. Being shown her room. The car door opening. Standing on the gravel driveway looking up at the house. The figure at the window. She and her father floating through the trees in Mr Ishiguro's plush, unhurried car.

She must have gone out onto the terrace. Fallen asleep. The sky was a deep indigo now. Beyond the balustrade, she could see the reflected sky-glow bloom of the invisible city below. The distant growl of evening traffic washed intermittently up over the balcony to her. She could hear the burred rumble of a truck braking; car horns sounding; the quick gear-changing gulps of a departing lorry, like a swimmer swimming.

The sound of the foghorn returned to fill the air. The terrace reverberated beneath her feet. She sat watching the light changing, feeling the air grow colder. She pulled her cotton kimono more tightly around her.

She stood up. Walked to the balustrade. She looked out over the bay. In that strange crepuscular light, the horizon line, so darkly distinct when she and her father had walked through the long room, had disappeared. The sea and the sky had fused, were now one. Looking down, she felt as though she was peering over the broken edge of the world. Tiny toy boats hung suspended in the void. The vast white bow of a freighter hovered impossibly above them. She watched it ascending into the sky. All at once, the terrace, the house, and the mountain behind her seemed to pitch forward. She had the dizzying impression that the world was about to topple over the balcony into the abyss below. She reached out for the cold stone balustrade. The long, mournful call of a foghorn reached up to her again.

Then came another sound, a voice, calling her name.

Sachiko...Sachiko?

She turned back to the house. In the long empty room, the lamps were already lit. It took her a moment to locate her father standing at the far end. He was searching for her.

Sachiko, he called again. There was a note of urgency in his voice.

I'm here, Father, she called.

He looked about as if her voice had come to him out of the air itself.

Here! she said again.

She stepped away from the balcony and ran to open the sliding glass door to the sitting room.

Father, I'm here. I was out on the terrace.

I thought you'd gone, her father said.

But where would I go, Father?

He did not answer. He just stood there looking at her.

I went out onto the terrace, she said. I must have fallen asleep. I'm sorry.

She wanted to tell him about the changing light, about the horizon line disappearing, about the boats floating in the sky. But the sun had moved on. The dark horizon line had returned. The world had been cantilevered back into place.

Ume is looking for you, her father said. To prepare you for this evening.

Has Mr Ikeda returned? she asked.

I don't know, he said. But it doesn't matter. You must still get ready. Ume will help you.

❀

She found Ume waiting for her in her room.

I'm sorry, Ume. I did not mean to inconvenience you.

Do not concern yourself, Miss Sachiko, she said. I understand. Everything is so new, so different. You will get used to it.

There was warmth now in the old woman's voice. She was carrying a simple white bathrobe on one arm.

The Master asked me to prepare your bath, she said.

Ume went to a column of drawers set into the wall. She pulled one open and lifted out a dazzling white kimono. She laid it on the bed. Light undulated across its surface as though it was a thing alive.

Sachiko recognised the material at once. It was the snow fabric she had seen at Ishiguro's, the one with the budding orchids poking through. She went over to the bed, picked up one of the kimono's sleeves. Felt its richness between her fingers.

Ume watched her turn back one of the cuffs.

Is this the kimono I'll be wearing? she said.

Yes, Ume replied.

How strange, she said. My grandmother made this. She raised a sleeve to her face. I remember this material from when I was a little girl. My grandmother loved it. I can still see us spreading it out in the snow above our house. And then I saw it again this afternoon, at Mr Ishiguro's. They have only just started making it again.

She ran her fingers down the inner lining, across its perfect close stitching.

I don't understand, Ume-san, she said. How did you...how did Mr Ikeda come to have this? This particular kimono? You see, I'm sure this is a snow kimono my grandmother made. Years ago. I would recognise her stitching anywhere, she said. Look at this. Only my grandmother closes off like this. It is her signature.

You are right, Miss Sachiko, the old woman said. Your grandmother did make this. Katsuo-san, Mr Ikeda, bought it a long time ago. When you were still young. He has kept it in this drawer for you ever since.

What do you mean, Ume-san? Sachiko said. He kept it for me?

But now the old woman would not look at her.

Ume-san? What do you mean—he kept it for me?

The old woman still did not answer her. Instead, she bent and refolded the garment on the bed.

Ume-san?

I cannot say, she said. Master Katsuo will explain. But you must promise me you will never tell him what I just told you.

Ume looked up at her. Sachiko saw the anguish on the old woman's face.

I won't, Ume-san. I promise you, I will never betray you. Never.

Ume, who had been expecting her, who had greeted her

and her father at the top of the stairs, who had shown them to their rooms. How subtly their relationship had changed in a matter of hours. It was as though, Sachiko thought, she had emerged from a chrysalis, had left its empty husk behind.

Chapter 25

IT was not Ume who saw the scar first. It was Mizuki, her assistant. She was towelling Sachiko's wet hair, drying the last thin rills of water from her neck and shoulders. She had eased the bath wrap away from Sachiko's back with her fingertips and reached into the crevice with the cloth to dry the last drops of water stranded there.

Oh, she said, pulling away.

Ume saw Mizuki recoil, her hand to her mouth.

What is it? she said.

Mizuki leaned tentatively closer.

It's a scar, she said. On Sachiko's shoulder. It's like a...

But she hesitated, glanced at Ume.

Ume stepped forward to see what Mizuki had seen.

Sachiko thought of that day in the blazing snow, how she had lain hidden, watching the two horses. How the boys had turned on her. Her dull legs trapped in the nightmare snow.

The sudden piercing pain. Her falling. Afterwards, when she stood, the circle of blood so distinct, so red, she could have picked it up.

Ume leaned down. Pulled back the collar of Sachiko's bath wrap. Sachiko felt her trace the curled outline of the scar with her fingertip.

How curious, Ume said. It's like a small scorpion.

Hearing what Ume had said, Sachiko flinched. Ume's nail caught briefly in her flesh. Instantly, Sachiko felt the echo of that stinging pain she had felt years ago. She cried out. She stood so abruptly her bathrobe fell to the floor.

The thought that there was a scorpion crawling in her flesh filled her with horror. She pictured the scrabbling crescent claws, the upturned tail, the tiny, beaded eyes. Watching. Waiting. Ready to strike.

Oh, she said, trying to look over her shoulder.

Ume was already at the basin, moistening the twisted tip of the towel with cold water.

Sit down, Sachiko, she said. You're bleeding.

Ume faced her away from the mirror so that she could moisten the towel with ease. Sachiko felt the cold, wet cloth on her shoulder blade. She sat hunched over, her arms clasped about her breasts. She was sobbing quietly. Now she understood why her parents, her mother, had been so angry when she had returned that day, dishevelled and bleeding, from the upper fields.

She recalled her parent's conversation on the verandah when she and her father had set out. When was that? Could it have been just yesterday? She could still hear her mother's voice coming to her from within the house: But it's nothing, Hideo. You can barely see it. You must convince him.

❀

Seen from another vantage point, in the muted light, with her bent over like this, Katsuo thought Sachiko's back looked pale and vulnerable. And extraordinarily beautiful.

How many times had he gazed upon her like this since? How many times, with her bent before him, had he seen her scar? Only to feel the same longing in his heart. It was as though, in Sachiko, Mariko had returned to him.

He saw, high on her arched shoulder blade, where Ume's nail had pierced her skin, a tiny blood-red drop begin to pearl. It seemed to issue precisely from the tip of the scorpion's tail. He watched its sudden breaching, saw the thin trail of blood spill down Sachiko's back.

Later, Sachiko remembered Ume stepping away from the mirror, remembered her waiting, then dabbing again at the blood with her wetted towel. Its coldness had made her flinch again. She imagined the scorpion tensing its body, tightening its claws, as though it would not be willingly plucked from her skin.

Is it gone? she said. Ume?

Ume pressed the cool cloth to Sachiko's back, waited to see if any more blood would surface.

There, Ume said. The bleeding's stopped. I'm so sorry,

Sachiko. I did not mean to hurt you.

I know, Sachiko said. She took two deep breaths, clenched and unclenched her fists, sat up.

I want to see it, she said. I want to see what it looks like.

She twisted her head to look back over her shoulder. It took her a few moments to locate the scar. It was higher up than she had imagined, right on the ridge of her shoulder blade. A pale silhouette against her paler skin.

Ume and Mizuki were right. It did look like a scorpion. Sitting there. Still. Vigilant. Her shoulder blade its permanent lair. As she pulled her arm around in front of her the better to see it, the scorpion seemed to scuttle up her shoulder a short distance, and stop. Sachiko shivered. A faint arc of blood appeared again where Ume's nail had broken her skin. When she relaxed, let her arm go, the scorpion moved again.

Oh, it's horrible, Sachiko cried. Horrible.

She turned away from the mirror again, hid her face in her hands.

It's horrible, horrible, she kept saying.

Ume dabbed the towel on her back once more. When she had finished, she looked at the scar again. Sachiko's skin was flushed from rubbing. The scar appeared oddly fainter now, less scorpion-like, more benign, more, Ume thought, like the character 毛, which meant fur.

It's nothing, Ume said. Nothing. I should not have said anything. You can barely see it, Sachiko. She patted her shoulder. If I had not said it looked like a scorpion, you would not have thought so yourself. It could be anything. Anything, she said.

But I saw it move, Sachiko said.

It's just a scar, Ume said. It doesn't mean anything. There, the bleeding's stopped.

Sachiko looked over her shoulder once again. All trace of blood had been sponged from her back. Now she could barely see the scar. She turned her back from left to right. It was only when lit from one particular angle that she could see it clearly. And when she did, Ume was right—it could have been anything, a meaningless piece of calligraphy; a small, delicate flourish etched into her skin; some other, less sinister image. Or, what it was—a small, barely perceptible scar, of no consequence to anyone, least of all to her.

❀

When Ume and Mizuki had finished, when they had powdered her face, tied her hair up, helped her into the snow kimono, Sachiko barely recognised herself in the mirror. She had been transformed. It seemed to her now that there were two of her, each inhabiting a different world—the one from which she watched, and the one she was watching.

❀

In the end, Mr Ikeda, Katsuo, did not join them. He had sent a message. He was yet delayed.

Sachiko sat opposite her father at the low table. From time to time, two young women knelt into the silence between them to place a steaming new dish of food onto the table, and remove the tepid, barely touched remains of the one that preceded.

Her father did not speak. He made no comment. Not on the beauty of the kimono she was wearing. Not on the fact that it had been made by her grandmother, which he must have known. Not on her hair. Her face. Even when she had entered the room, and he was already there, he did not speak. He had stood, bowed, but he had done so as though to a stranger.

Now her father sat pushing pieces of food around his plate. The sound of a shamisen came from somewhere in the garden.

Are you all right, Father? she said, when she could stand the silence no longer. You're not eating.

He seemed to weigh up how rude it would be not to reply to a direct question from his own daughter.

Yes, Sachiko, he said, picking up his cup. I am just not hungry. It has been a long day and I have much to think about.

Sachiko.

Her father rarely used her name. He only used it when he was calling her. Or talking about her. But almost never in her presence. It had always been Daughter this, Daughter that.

She heard footsteps approaching along the corridor, and then Ume was standing in the doorway.

Mr Ikeda is ready for you, Mr Yamaguchi.

Ready?

Sachiko looked at her father. What did ready mean? But she

did not have time to ask. Her father was already on his feet, wiping his mouth roughly with the back of his hand. Again, he did not say goodbye. Sachiko watched him leave.

The two young women detached themselves from the wall and came to collect his plate.

How long has Mr Ikeda been home? Sachiko asked them.

They glanced at her, each other.

I am sorry, Miss Sachiko, one of them said. We do not know.

Chapter 26

SACHIKO takes a breath.

Has Ume returned? she asks him.

Not yet, he tells her.

It is dark now, still snowing. Katsuo is kneeling beside her. Sachiko marshals what little strength she has left; then, despite the cold which has begun to invade her, she continues to tell him of that first night.

They are just two intermittent voices talking in the darkness. In the cold, cold night.

❀

After my father left me, she tells him between breaths, I went to lie on my bed. You did not come down for the meal after all. I wondered why. So much had been made of my coming here. Being presented to you. Ume had already told me about the snow kimono, the one you wanted me to wear...which I am wearing now.

❀

How strange life is.

Katsuo waits.

She told me you had saved it for me...How it rippled in the light when Ume laid it out!

Sachiko pushes herself up on her elbows. Katsuo cradles her head in his lap. Her forehead is burning.

Oh, Katsuo, Katsuo...I'm so sorry. I cannot bear the pain. When will they come for us?

Soon, he says. I am here with you. Just keep talking to me. It will help to take away the pain.

He looks about. At the now moonlit sky. The attendant trees. Their ghostly blue shadows. How quiet they all are. The snow silent all around them. Then he looks down at Sachiko. At her swollen belly. Her snow kimono. Which has begun to bleed.

Now that he has seen this, his heart has ceased to beat.

Oh, my beloved Sachiko, he says to her. Talk to me. Talk to me. Please, he begs her. Do not go to sleep.

After a moment in which the universe itself seems to hold its breath, she begins to speak again. Her words weave themselves around the many already woven into his memory. In the moonlight he can see her lips moving, he can see her fitful, cooling breath, but he no longer knows whether she is speaking to him or not.

Chapter 27

SHE is a bird above the garden.

Ume has shown her the viewing platform. There are things up here that cannot be seen from anywhere else. Twisted tree trunks reach up through the penumbral light. Boulders, stone seats, small waterfalls, bridges. Pathways across the water. Small swarms of tiny white camellia buds move about the garden like fireflies. She watches them disappear. Moments later, further up the slope, another group appears. Then another, lit by invisible beams of light. Here and there, she can see the reflected surfaces of the flagstone paths. Elsewhere, half-hidden statues watch from the shadows.

The sound of a car engine drifts up to her. From its rise and fall she knows that it is making its way slowly up the mountain road, the same one she and her father drove up earlier that day. She recalls what Mr Ishiguro had said.

A car will come to pick you up at nine, Hideo.

She glimpses headlights through the trees. They disappear, reappear, disappear. She waits. Then she sees them sweep around the last tight curve leading up to the driveway. She hears the engine change pitch, and change pitch again. She sees the probing headlights dip as the car comes to a stop. She watches the twin beams dim, dim, dim, as the wrought-iron gates open. The car is now a glow advancing between the deeply creviced hedgerows. Then its low dark form appears in the lights either side of the driveway. A door to the house closes beneath her. The headlights disappear beneath the unseen terrace.

She stands, her hands on the platform railing, listening. The garden fidgets below her. Then, in quick succession, the sound of two car doors closing. A moment later, a third. Headlights sweep across the tree tops at the far end of the house. A patch of driveway lights up, begins to move. The outline of the great car follows in its wake. Two small red lights gather in the road behind.

As it moves away from her, she can see that the car's interior lights are on. Its two almond-shaped rear windows are illuminated dimly. In them, like the pupils of two eyes looking back up at her, she can see the silhouettes of two heads. The car floats down the driveway. Out through the gates. Then it turns onto the road, towards the beckoning city.

Chapter 28

IN her room, Sachiko stands looking out into the garden. She holds her breath, listens. There is no breeze. No movement. No leaf stirs. The surface of the pond is mirror-still. The lunar edges of the water-lilies lie flat and snug against their reflections.

She goes to the door. Opens it quietly. Looks out into the corridor. She tiptoes barefooted into the half-darkened sitting room. The vast uncurtained windows look out onto the terrace. Its shadowed surface is waiting.

She pulls the sliding glass doors aside and half-runs to the balustrade. How cold the stone is on her feet. The sea unmoving. The glittering city lies suspended below her. At its furthest ends, denser webs of light shimmer in the cool air.

The moon, huge and red, begins to rise above the horizon. Part-hoisted, it seems to pause. A ribbon of light unfurls across the sea's dark mass. It zigzags up to her across the flat tiled rooves of the houses below.

Sachiko imagines herself scaling the balustrade, skipping down across these rooftop stepping stones to the waiting sea. She sees herself dashing, barefooted, across this glowing ribbon of light, plunging into the safe embrace of the moon. But she is already too late. She has missed her chance. The moon has begun to move again. With one last heft, it pushes itself free of the horizon. It hovers there unsteadily for a moment, like a weightlifter lifting a weight, then rises effortlessly into the sky.

She hears her father's voice. He is calling her again.

Sachiko, Sachiko…

She goes to the sliding door, tries to open it. But it is locked. She pulls on the handle.

Who would lock me out? she thinks.

Her father is standing inside the half-lit room, pacing back and forth. She realises that he isn't calling her after all. He is merely calling her name: Sachiko, Sachiko, he is saying again and again.

Sachiko…

How was it that a name could contain so much sorrow, so much pain?

Father? she calls out.

But he does not answer. He seems deaf to her. She pounds on the glass with her fists, runs closer to where he is standing. She pounds again. She waves her arms. Still he does not see her. Instead, he keeps pacing.

Father!

She looks for a side door. But there isn't one. A solid sheet of glass now extends seamlessly from one side of the terrace to the other. Keeping her out. She runs back to where the handle was. It too has disappeared.

Father! she calls again, more urgently.

The moon is now high overhead. She is a tiny figure poised on the teetering horizon, imploring the moon to return, to come back, to save her.

❀

She awakes in the darkness of her room to voices. At first she thinks they are part of her dream. But they come again. A man, two, and a woman. She hears the woman laugh, her laughter like a ball bouncing down a staircase. She cannot place where they are. Something crashes to the ground. Shatters. She hears a man's voice, entreating his companions to be quiet.

❀

I thought that, at last, you had come home, she says. I pictured you raising a finger to your lips.

❀

The house returns to stillness. But now Sachiko is awake. She will not go back to sleep.

She reaches for the lamp, turns it on. She is lying on her

still-made bed. She is no longer wearing the snow kimono. Instead, she is wearing a loose night wrap. She imagines Ume finding her in her room, asleep. Still dressed. She pictures Ume undoing her kimono, rolling her gently to one side, then scooping up the armfuls of snow. She sees her laying the night wrap out.

But surely she would have woken.

The snow kimono hangs against the wall like a sentinel. She lies there on the bed, thinking about the voices she has heard. It is after midnight. The events of the day jostle in her head. They settle for a moment. Then, like a flock of birds at dusk, they take to the air, whirling round and round in the sky above her.

She sits up, rises, pulls her night wrap tightly around her. She goes to the door, slides it open. The cool floor of the corridor on her bare feet reminds her again of her dream. She makes her way down the darkened hallway. She stops outside her father's room. Listens. No sound comes from within.

Halfway down the corridor, a skewed lozenge of light floats on the floor. Vague aquatic shadows are circulating there. In the darkness, she waits for her eyes to adjust. She can see a fissure of light at the corridor's far end. She can just make out the panelled shadows of the door above it.

Then she hears their voices. A muffled exchange. A man's voice, then a woman's.

She stays standing in the corridor like this, listening. Barely breathing. A faint shadow passes fleetingly through the bar of light beneath the door. She starts to walk towards it.

She stands in the pool of light on the corridor floor, looking up through the window. Tier after tier of half-illuminated tree limbs are etched against the night sky. The tops of the trees are swaying. The whole garden seems to be moving. And yet there is no sound. No frogs calling, no crickets. Even the water clock has stopped. It is as though she is tethered to the ocean floor and is gazing up through the thick and vitreous water, at a forest of strange and exotic sea plants undulating silently above her. The voices come again.

❀

I thought it was you, she tells Katsuo. I thought that you had come home. Then I am outside the door, waiting, listening, my toes lit by the light coming from under the door. I can feel my heart beating.

What if you open the door? I think. How will I explain my presence here? What will I say? I am a guest in your house, someone whom you have not yet met. Or seen. Could I lie? Could I say that I had become disoriented, that I was looking for my father's room?

I hear another noise. Like a mattress settling, or a floorboard creaking. I hear a voice, a woman's voice, something low, guttural, repeated. As if she is in pain.

I feel the heat rising to my face.

How shameful it would be to be discovered here, I think again. Outside your door, listening.

Then I hear your laugh. Except that it isn't your laugh. It is someone else's. Someone I know well.

It is my father's.

❀

Suddenly the world is all turmoil. All the roosting birds have taken flight. The dark-limbed trees have erupted into the sky. Now all the birds are wheeling about, screaming. I am the crouched heart at the centre of this swirling mass. I raise my hands to protect myself. To block the noise out. But a thousand wings beat at my face.

My father, I think. What is he doing here?

As if to answer my question, I hear the woman's laugh.

And then I understand the history of my father's visits. I see how pathetic, how old, how out of place he is. I see Mr Ishiguro's fixed smiling face. I see my father led astray. I see his tormented homecomings. The days that follow. His silences. His inward-falling.

I recall his absences on the nights that follow his return. His descent into town. To get drunk. To seek oblivion. I see his penitent returns. His pitiful remorse. How he cannot look at me.

Does my mother know?

I see her face, resigned, bitter, defeated. And I know she knows.

Now that I understand, I know that there is no going back. I can never forgive my father.

I have left my childhood behind. It has been wrenched from me. I am on my own.

❀

Ume has told me something she should not have. She begs me not to tell you. You kept the snow kimono for me. Petals are falling from the sky. The bath has tiny red boats floating in it. Ume stirs them in with a wooden paddle. When I open my eyes, someone is staring back at me. She has a white face. Red lips. It is raining again. The rain beats down like stones. I think the roof is caving in. Who amongst them did they want to punish? Ichiro has not come home. My beloved son is lost. You still have not returned. Whose words are these?

I start to piece things together. Although not in the way things turned out. I had no idea, then, that I was coming here to be with you. But I had already guessed that I had not journeyed down to Osaka with my father merely to accompany him, or to work for Mr Ishiguro.

This is not now. In the snow. Not anymore. This is memory.

Sachiko is sitting on the ledge in the garden, swinging her bare, hypnotic feet; she is standing on the terrace, looking down into the rain-cleansed city; she is walking with him in the quiet streets above the house. She never tires of answering his questions. And he never tires of asking them.

❀

Sachiko has stopped talking. The trees have edged closer. Terror has finally found him out. The long journey is over. There is nowhere to go. No one to help him. He leans down into the sorrowing snow. To see if she is still breathing.

Part VI

JOVERT

❀

Chapter 29

WHAT had Professor Omura said? *We can only see our lives through the eyes of another.* Did this include history? Hindsight?

Jovert went to the Bibliothèque Nationale. He phoned ahead, to arrange to see their maps of Algiers.

All of them? the woman on the other end of the line asked.

He pictured her with the phone tucked under her chin—prim, efficient, glasses, early fifties. Her hair tied up. The type to tap her bundles of paper on the top of her pristine desk. Line them up. Tap, tap, tap. Squeeze the straightened pile in the middle.

How many of them are there?

Just a moment. He heard her fingernails skittering on the keyboard. She was talking to herself.

Let-me-see...No, no, I won't be a minute. I'm-on-the-phone. The exasperated 'o' arched like a playing card. *Merde.* Ask Gilles...I don't know. What time is it? For God's sake, under her breath. Here we go. Hmm...There are—eight hundred and seventy-nine. Yes. Now a tiny three-point rapier flash: 8–7–9... Inspector?

That many?

Merde? Okay. Younger. Early thirties? Yes, definitely, he could hear it in her voice now. Maybe even younger.

Yes, that many. What, precisely, are you after?

He told her. He was looking for maps of the inner city. The Kasbah. The streets just east of it. The harbour. Preferably from the fifties. And, if they had any, something more recent. From the eighties—1985. Or last year, perhaps. To compare.

❀

Algeria: 1958–59

That March morning, the light in the harbour had been blinding. Madeleine had lain in their cabin. Still sick. Or sick again. She had spent the last twenty-six hours crouched over the toilet, her head on her arm, throwing up.

Oh God, she had said. More than once. And he had knelt down beside her. His hand on her back, rubbing her shoulders.

Oh God, oh God.

And her back would arch again.

It's okay, Auguste. You should try and get some sleep. I'll be all right.

His knees ached from kneeling. He thought of his six months training in Dien Bien Phu. What it felt like to be tortured.

You have to *know*, their commander had said. Kneeling forward. Bent over, hands tied behind their backs. The weighted helmet on their heads. Another kilogram. The sharpened twin-tined bamboo spikes beneath their necks mercifully capped. But it hurt. It hurt so badly you screamed. You wanted to die. Until, in the end, your muscles—there were so many you didn't know you had—collapsed. You begged. Help me. Help me. Oh God, please, please. Get me *up*!

The competition between them fierce. How long could each of them last before they gave up their secret word?

Or suspended upside down. Hands tied behind their backs. The madness set in train. Their manacled ankles ratcheted apart. Until they were sure they were going to be torn in two. Because this time they didn't stop, even when you begged. Instead, they left you alone. To think: Had something ghastly happened? Had they forgotten you? Accidents did happen. They all knew that.

Later, you would see the film.

It was worse if you'd had breakfast first. With its tasteless supplement undeclared. Today's exercise is...Without telling you. That took half an hour before it took effect, before your guts began to churn.

No, you don't need to change. Yet.

The laughter nervous.

God, what now?

Only five got through to the next phase.

Some didn't last. Were *never* the same.

Oh God, she says again.

The ship's doctor came to see her, twice.

Madame Jovert, Capitaine.

How many months pregnant was she? Five. The middle of the second trimester. Had she ever been seasick before? Jovert noted the assumption. He meant, on her previous trips home.

Was it obvious she was not French, but French-Algerian? She didn't have an accent. If she did, he'd know. He was an expert in that kind of thing. The best in his class. Madeleine had lived in Marseille most of her life, had studied there. Her skin was no darker than anyone else's from the south. The epidermal texture no different.

Maybe it was her eyes. The thing about her he loved most. Some tiny genetic inflection. Their shape? Colour? Their deep aquatic green? But you had to be close to her to see that.

The afternoon on their first day was the worst. The storm that had been building all morning finally delivered up its wrath. The ferry began to heave, to make its endlessly repeated slow ascent up the face of each oncoming wave, each one steeper than the last, to balance briefly at the top, before the apex sideways-twisting roll, the vertiginous descent. Into the next trough. A tiny calm. Then, the same slow climb again.

The doctor would not prescribe her anything. A palliative. Which only made her worse.

He heard the toilet flush again.

The night before they left, he imagined them standing on the deck together, his arm on her shoulder, the sea air fresh, watching the approaching city. But now it was only him.

He remembered the morning calm on deck, Algiers on the horizon, raising his hand to shade his eyes. The whitewashed walls of the houses impastoed onto the surrounding hills concentrated the light like a lens, pinning the ferry to the coruscated sea like a tiny upturned beetle. Exhausted, half-dead, still struggling on its back. The reflected light an invisible membrane, keeping the tiny ferry at bay. He felt the slow harmonic rise and fall of the engines beneath his feet. They were yet to find their way in.

A departing tanker passed so closely it was like a moving wall. It loomed over him, blocking out the sun. He watched the repeated pattern of its welded plates, the twin hemline of rivets above the surging waterline a racing blur. He felt dizzy, the churning water reaching out to pull him in. He pushed against the railing with his hands. He saw the broken line of tankers stretching dreamlike out behind him towards the horizon. All escaping back to Marseille.

And then they were there. An invisible wave of harbour stench washed over him: diesel fumes, sea-ditched refuse, rotting fish, vegetables, sweat, excrement—donkey, human, who knew what else; the smell of burning rubber. All concentrated by the governing sun into its lush constituents, pungent, caustic, inescapable. It would seep down the gangways now, and into the corridors, the passageways; it would seep under every closed door, into the holds, the engine room, into every cavity, every blameless empty space.

And there was something else, a delicate hint of something sweet, like an aftertaste floating on the air. A note from somewhere past. A memory. Bastille Day. The night sky twitching. Fireworks exploding. The echoing scent of cordite.

Madeleine came up from her cabin to find him. She saw him at the rail. She went to stand with him. Leant unsteadily against his arm, strands of her long hair twisting about her face in the breeze.

I heard the engines slow, she said. I knew we must be here. Then I smelt the harbour.

How are you feeling now? he said. He put his hand up to her face.

I think there's nothing left, she said. But the memory of her night turned her away. She dry-retched over the side.

Oh dear, she said. She wiped her mouth with the back of her hand, inspected the thin moist smear.

See, there's nothing left.

Maybe you shouldn't have come up. Why don't you go back down? We'll be there in ten minutes.

No, she said. The cabin's unbearable now.

She looked pale, exhausted. He glanced down to where the breeze was circling her body. He could see the impress of her dress, the small bow of her growing belly.

You're beginning to show, he said.

I know.

She held the fabric against her stomach with her splayed fingers.

There's no going back, is there? she said, half-smiling.

She put a hand up to shield her eyes. Didn't you say that

there would be someone waiting for us?

Yes, he said. After we've been through passport control.

I don't see anyone, she said.

He had already scanned the wharf himself. There will be, he said. We should go down and pack.

I've already done it, she said.

He turned towards her.

What else was I to do?

And then she said something he would never forget: Home, she said, looking up at the looming city. I can hardly wait.

The engines gave one last fitful rumble, churned briefly, then died away. The deck stilled with a half-hearted heave.

So, this is it, he said.

This is it, Madeleine said. She took a breath. This is it.

❀

Passport. The French civil service—they had forgotten how uncivil it could be. But who knew where allegiances lay these days, now the war had begun. The black-capped face looked at Madeleine's passport, her photograph, at her. Tapped the folded passport on his palm. Handed it back. Took Jovert's. Jovert saw him hesitate. The registering of his name. Thank you. Sir. But the cap did not look up, its uniformed arm was already reaching out for the passport behind him.

It was young Thibaud who had been assigned to him. He was, as had been arranged, waiting for them on the wharf, standing by the car. Jovert carried their two suitcases.

God, I can't believe how much it's changed, she said. She took his arm unsteadily. So, *mon capitaine*, what do you think?

He surveyed the white arc of houses that stretched up the hillside around him.

It's not Marseille, he said. But I can see what people mean, about the light.

They were almost at the car.

Thibaud stepped forward, his hand out.

Good to see you again, sir, he said.

But when he saw the look on Jovert's face, his hand dropped. Jovert reached out. Took Thibaud's hand in his.

Good to see you, Corporal Thibaud. Permit me to introduce you. Thibaud, this is my wife—Madeleine, *ma chère*, Corporal Thibaud.

Madame. Thibaud inclined his head. Jovert could almost hear the faint click of his heels.

Thibaud had already read the unexpected news the breeze brought with it. At least he was thinking now.

Here, let me take your bag, Madame.

No, it's fine. Thank you, Corporal, she said. I'm happy to keep this one with me.

You can help me with these, Corporal, Jovert said.

He was at the rear of the car. He was smiling. Two suitcases at his feet.

Thibaud went to open the boot. Picked up the bags. *Merci*. You're welcome, sir.

Then they were on their way, across the clattering wooden wharf, and up through the maze of streets to the house which awaited them, the one he had inspected, the one he had prepared for them, three months before.

❀

In the library, Jovert begins to retrace the route they had taken from the wharf, or, at least, the one he thinks they took, up through the tangle of the streets to the house they had shared, worked in, lived in, made love in, died in, during those fateful fifteen months, thirty years earlier.

And so begins the process of prompting, probing, of resisted stimulation, to force his memory to surrender what he has spent decades trying to forget.

He knows what he has to do. Even if it breaks him.

Memory, he had once believed, was our real refuge. It was who we were. What we returned to. A somehow sacred place. Our cells might die, be replaced, but not their secret synaptic codes. That was the paradox. Memories were our sanctuary. What bound us to each other. But he knew now that that was an illusion. Memories could change, be destroyed, be rewritten.

Now, in the library, he *would* remember. He would force himself to recall *all* the pain, to give up those things he wished he could have left buried. He would overcome his own resistance. After all, how many nameless people had he helped in the past to do just this? How many people, struggling against inescapable odds, had he helped to see clearly? To recall things they might have otherwise forgotten. Or said they had.

No, he knew he could do this. He had always had this gift. He knew every trick in the book. Had invented some. It was why they had chosen him. So he sat there, in the vast space of the Bibliothèque, looking at the maps spread in front of him. Two from 1955. One from 1988.

She was even younger than he had imagined, the woman on the other end of the phone. Twenty-four, maybe. Six. Welcoming—Ah, Inspector. The smile friendly. Her teeth perfect, dazzling. Helpful. Even her glasses were chic.

❀

Not far now, Thibaud says. Down the narrow worn-stepped alleyway. Thibaud behind them, carrying one of their suitcases.

Here, this is it.

The house lay hidden behind a high white wall. An arched wooden gate painted blue. Thibaud's hand on the black wrought-iron latch. Convolvulus. The portico blue. His memory hurries him through to the balcony off their bedroom where the two of them, he and Madeleine, are standing, looking down over the flat white rooves that lie before them, a pile of fallen white dominoes, to the still, blue harbour below. To the north, the naval docks; to the south, the Terre-plein spit; the squat lighthouse in between.

He pulled the map closer. Where exactly had the house been?

Young Thibaud, who would be killed in an ambush a month after Jovert left, had stopped the car…here.

He marked the position with his finger. Drew an imaginary line towards the spit.

Later their luggage would arrive. Four shrouded Arabs suddenly in the courtyard, sitting there as quiet as assassins. Smoking. The gate still open.

From the balcony, the dockyards. Nearby, the Villa les Tourelles. He holds his fingers out. A reverse trigonometry. He draws a small circle on the map with his fingertip. He leans down. Tries to prise the streets apart. But the map resists. It won't give up its secrets that easily to him.

He remembers the hundreds of aerial-surveillance photographs he had had at his disposal at the Villa les Tourelles, where his best work was done. If only he now had access to these. But that was impossible. Even if he had still been with the Special Operations Branch, he could never have got to them. That part of his life had been wiped clean. What had his contact said to him when he had asked after Haifa, the warning clear? *I thought that was ancient history*.

❀

The house is off rue des Oiseaux, Thibaud says. They are in the car again. Thibaud. Madeleine. Driving up from the port.

You're lucky, the house faces east. You can see the old port from the balcony. He pulls the car up around another bend.

Only to be trapped by a truck on the narrow broken cobblestoned street in front of them. The truck—old, blue-canopied, dirty—almost stops. The gear change makes him wince. A river of half-dreamed men appears about the car. Sleeping, sun-drugged dogs. Children staring.

It's about a fifteen-minute walk to the harbour. There are gardens nearby.

He is standing on the balcony with Thibaud. The sound of retching comes to him from the bathroom.

Your wife might find them comforting. There is a small viaduct off rue St Augustin. A pharmacy on Place Randon, run by an Arab who trained in Paris. Here, here it is. Just above his crescent-fingered nail. Place Randon! Perhaps you should see him—get something for your wife.

Memories, shuffled, reshuffled from his past.

❀

The first night, after their frugal meal, untouched by Madeleine, he told her.

I have to go out, he said. I don't know what time I'll be back.

Already?

Already. There is something I have to attend to.

He leaned down, kissed her on the forehead.

Will you be all right?

I'll be fine, Auguste. Don't worry. Fatima's here. Tilde is calling by later.

Fatima, their live-in housekeeper. Mathilde, Madeleine's teaching colleague, both of whom she was watching over.

I'll see you in the morning, she said.

If I'm back.

And he turned to leave her, to think again about the new baby that would soon be with her, with him. And the new lives that awaited them.

Chapter 30

HE went downstairs into the basement. Through the concealed corridor that led underground to the house below. It looked as lived-in as his own. He changed. Madeleine knew about the house, but not about this other him. Out into the small courtyard. Through its gated archway. And onto the street, where Thibaud was waiting for him in another car.

He tapped on the passenger-side window.

Thibaud stubbed out his cigarette, leaned across, unlocked the door.

It's good, Thibaud said, looking at his unruly hair, his glasses, his elbow-patched jacket. You could be a prof. He bent forward to see his shoes. Yes, very good, he said again, nodding. Unrecognisable.

Thibaud checked the rear-view mirror, put the car into gear, pulled out. Down the narrow street. A few streetlamps coming on. The paling sky.

I'm sorry, Thibaud said, when the air began to thicken.

Jovert did not reply. Silence, he knew, was a useful tool. People didn't like silences. They waited for them to fill. Or filled them for you. What had General Saressault said? *In an empty set, everything is possible.* One's worst imaginings. The death of a loved one. A child. Your own. The as-yet-unuttered truth.

An empty set—an occupied cell.

Yes, there was something exquisite about silence. Which now began to fill the car, until it began to suffocate them. Or one of them. Thibaud wound his window down.

Then they were turning into the street, the one he was not meant to know about, that led down to the harbour. It was already busy. The shops reopening. People beginning to re-emerge. Thibaud slowed the car.

Again? Jovert said. Nice to see you, again.

I know, sir. I know. It was stupid.

Thibaud raised his hand from the steering wheel, pale palm up, as if the answer to his dilemma lay out there on the street.

But Jovert was watching the men walking ahead of them. Walking as though the car weren't there. As though it were invisible. As though they were invisible.

Do you think she knows?

Madeleine's not stupid, Thibaud. It was the first thing she asked.

And?

Slow down, he said.

He leaned forward, scanned the buildings to his right.

A nondescript, dust-covered Citroën crawling down the broken street. The wake of men behind them seemingly what propelled the car forward. Shops, cafés, hole-in-the-wall shoe-repair places, tobacconists, car clutch-plates, glass wares, coffee beans, dust-filled kitchen utensils—most with their owners sitting on stools outside, studying the broken pavement at their feet.

Is this it? Up ahead?

Yes.

Thibaud slowed almost to a stop. The car rose and fell now on the potholed roadway like a tiny barque.

Okay. Pull over.

Thibaud pulled the car up onto the cracked pavement. Men spilled out around them. It was quiet now. Jovert had experienced this before, many times. An oasis of newly minted silence in an otherwise swirling street. No one talking. No one looking their way. The men streaming past them might come close to the car, but not one of them would touch it. Everybody knew.

Jovert could see the burnt-out shop front. The blown-out brickwork. The neatly circular black after-image stamped on the surrounding walls. The footpath. A few fragments of uncollected glass still glinting in the afternoon sun.

How many dead?

The owner. Hamid. Two customers. Two children playing outside. His. Seven injured. One still critical.

Hamid. Didn't I recruit him? Two years ago. A bit more. Just before GS left. Didn't we bring him in?

GS?

General Saressault.

Okay.

And Hamid?

Yes, we did. We brought him in. Once. In July '57.

And?

Useful. Very useful.

Jovert sat in silence. You could read an explosion, its blast trajectory, its detonation pattern, distribution, the way its haloed scorch-mark radiated out: all perfect, a textbook example—this explosion 'roseate'. Professional, perfectly judged, beautiful.

He did the calculations. No more than 120 grams of the new *plastique*. The 'drop', the 'gift', the 'visitor', whatever you wanted to call it, placed just inside the door. The blast crater shallow. The sphere of influence—out, up, and in. It was this that killed, the compression echo: being hit first from the front, then, a millisecond later, from behind. In an enclosed space the shock wave shredded whatever was in between. You didn't need shrapnel, just physics, to kill.

He looked up through the windscreen, at the wall above them, then leaned across to scan the surface of the adjacent wall. The pit marks high up on the façades, the pits not deep—glass fragments, rubble, nothing significant. The lower wall clean. But you could see where the damage started. A kind of low-tide line about a metre up. Scatter marks above this. There must have been a car parked where they were. And one just outside the shop. Theirs? To concentrate the blast.

He could see it now: cars parked either side of the street;

the drop, two couriers, one a customer, asking for something, directions, the cost of a repair; the other, a friend, waiting just inside the door, one hand in his pocket, smoking. At the counter—thank you, thank you, you have been most helpful. The double handshake. Then the quick, stiff-bodied bow. Did they see the two children? Would it have mattered? The collateral benefit immeasurable. Pragmatic. The message unambiguous.

He was sure he knew who did this. He recognised the signature. Its unsentimental precision. Its telltale logic. He'd seen this perfection before. Not that he would ever find out. Their mantra: don't ask what you don't need to know.

But Hamid had been one of his. What had happened in the time he'd been away? Why wasn't he told?

Do they know I'm here?

No, this is just between you and me.

Which is the way it will stay.

A car horn sounded behind them. Jovert turned to look back through the rear window. But it wasn't for them. A waiting hand cart. A car behind it. Who had not seen them.

He turned back to watch the faces of the Arabs walking up towards them. How some were caught by surprise by the sudden blockage in front of them. He saw how they looked unthinkingly up. How they saw first the car, then the men in it. Then quickly looked away. This endless flow of men passing unimpeded around them, an invisible boulder in an uphill stream.

And this *wasn't* one of ours?

No, sir. Not that I know. Paris is worried—about later. If any of this gets out.

You wouldn't tell me if you knew, would you?

No, sir.

It looks like one of ours.

No response.

I guess what Paris doesn't know, Paris doesn't know…And the *plastique*, where is that coming from?

Tunisia. Morocco. The FLN.

You mean, if it's them.

Who knows? You saw how easy it was to bring something in.

What about the widow?

She says she doesn't know us.

Jovert took one last look out the window.

Okay, he said. I've seen enough.

Thibaud released the handbrake. The car rolled forward. The men in front of them, in their ancient robes, with their walking staffs, did not move aside. It was as though the car, with the two of them inside, were some recently captured exotic animal they were leading down to God knows what at the foot of this stinking hill.

He hated to think of what would happen if everything really got out of control. To date, it hadn't been a war. Not really. That was why they were there, to make sure that that kind of chaos never took hold.

Does she know that you were here? Thibaud asked.

Madeleine?

Yes.

I don't think so. I told her I knew your father, that you were one of my star pupils.

I didn't know that, Thibaud said.

What?

That you knew my father.

Didn't he tell you?

No.

Jovert was looking through the windscreen at the men again, at how their dark heads seemed to float on a strange, undulating wave in front of them.

Well, I did, Jovert said. I knew him well.

A small van blocked the roadway ahead. The space was tight. Thibaud manoeuvred the car up onto the footpath. Two old men playing cards gathered up their stools, went inside. Jovert felt the small resistance of the abandoned coffee glass against the tyre, heard the tiny splintering detonation.

Merde.

They could have got out. Seen what had happened. But what was the point? The tyre was either punctured, or it wasn't. They'd soon know. And the two old men would have long since disappeared.

I'm sorry, sir, Thibaud says again after a while. It was stupid of me.

Don't worry, Thibaud, he says. It's not a problem. You and I have never had this conversation. And I have never been here.

The car bumps down the uneven pavement. There is no one walking towards them now. It is only backs you see. You had to admire these people, how efficient their communication systems were, how quickly bad news spread.

Chapter 31

THEY said the city was a labyrinth. But it wasn't true. If it had been, it would have been easy. No, it was a maze, a confusing series of cross streets, folded-back laneways, cul-de-sacs, blind alleys, dead ends. There was a time he could have walked to his 'office' in the Villa les Tourelles from the house blindfolded without missing a step. But not now. It had changed. Or perhaps his memory had changed it for him. Whatever the case, now, in the library, once he stepped inadvertently off the beaten track he was lost. The unremembered was so much more vast than the remembered ever was.

They sat, in the beginning, in the evening, at the small wooden table on the balcony, each with their glass of wine, reading their papers, writing their reports, the music from the old city insinuating its way up through the night, curling lovingly around the pencilled minarets, through the snippets of half-heard conversation, up and over the high, white walls, to them, like the smoke rising from the mosquito coil in front of them. From time to time, they watched the intermittent progress of a freighter entering the harbour. Another. The fitful, distant reverberations of exploding shells oddly comforting. Sometimes, a helicopter would sweep up over them, impossibly low, impossibly fast, the urgent hollow thwop-thwop-thwop of its rotors slicing the music into ribboned pieces.

They're busy tonight, Madeleine would say. Did you know?

Hmm? Noncommittal. Still reading.

I'm only joking. And she would nudge his leg gently under the table.

Sometimes, when he knew in which direction to look, what time, when he remembered, he would wait for the first far-off night-sky glow. He always counted. Could not help himself. The time it took for the faint reverberation to reach them. One, sometimes two. Three hundred and forty metres a second. Three seconds a kilometre. Forty-five seconds—fifteen kilometres. A minute—twenty. Each soft boom a piece of history already written. By soldiers he knew. Sometimes commanded. It was like looking into the clear night sky, at the thousands and thousands of other tiny beating worlds that surrounded them. Except that what was written out there was written millions of years ago.

He'd glance up at Madeleine, at her lamp-lit frowning face. Her chin hunched on one bent-back hand, a pen in the other. Her eyes reading.

They're busy tonight, he would hear her say.

Now, then, a long time ago.

❀

See, he *was* good at this. He *had* been there. On the balcony. With Madeleine again. In the Bibliothèque Nationale. Except that the chair opposite him was empty.

Chapter 32

LATER, much later, he realised he had married her because she had somebody else's laugh.

She'd called him Jo-Jo when he was eight. His uncle's mistress. His father's brother. The younger son, who had done so well.

My little Jo-Jo. How's my little Jo-Jo today? *Mon petit beau*. My beautiful, beautiful boy.

He'd met her in Paris. Once or twice. She talked to him. She took the time.

Or at his uncle's summer house.

I saw you this morning, Jo-Jo. Kicking the ball. Fixing the firewood stack. Lying on the timber table. Staring up at the sky. What were you thinking, Jo-Jo? Come on, you can tell me.

Crouching down, her two hands on his two knees. She would look into his eyes as though something was swimming there. He remembered her mouth. Her lovely, slow-breathing summer dress. Her skin. How he ached for her.

Sometimes she called him Gusto. Augusto. *Our* Gusto? *Mi* Gusto. And she'd cuff him on the chin.

When she got bored, she'd say, Come on, Jo-Jo. Let's go. Get out of here. Won't you, please?

As if there was any doubt.

I'm off, she'd say. *Con mucho Gusto*. Or, *Con mi muchacho, Gusto*. With my gorgeous gallant beau. We're going for a walk.

And she'd get up. She would leave with him, hand in hand, his family's tabled faces turned towards the door. Her laugh as sharp as darting swallows, as if it was she who had set them free.

Once. A sun-filled, insect afternoon: Tell me what you think, Jo-Jo.

He thought of his uncle. His father's brother. Who had done so well. Of his ant-heap balding patch descending the stairs. Who was older. A lot older than she. Whose first wife had nailed him to a cross, when she found out. Although he'd seen his hands.

His uncle—who never spoke to him.

Do you think I should? He loved her voice, when she talked to him. When she was this close.

Marry him, she meant.

Not everybody was happy. About the wedding. His grandmother: She's not even French. She's from Madrid! Her grandmother was a seamstress! Thank God she's not here. At least *she* did the right thing. Last year.

He so, so liked her. And her name. Lina. Carolina—semiquavered, like her laughter. He lay on his back on the outside bench. Ca-ro-li-na. Carolina. The faster he said it, the faster it slipped off his pebbled tongue.

He fought them off. In her absence. Standing at the top of the table. When she wasn't there to defend herself. When cruel things crawled out of his grandmother's mouth. Slid down her chin.

No, don't say that! That's not true! Why are you so mean? She's *nice*. She's beautiful. She talks to me. She sees me. I love her.

❀

He went out to see the tables in the sun. Thirteen of them. Under the olive trees. The cicadas already thrumming. Thick white linen tablecloths hanging to the ground. The complex coded silverware all laid out. Face all the little tadpole spoons towards the edge. There, that's better. Flowers on the biggest table. The magic space underneath a long-tunnelled tent. He lay on the ground in his new white world. The white cloth sides undulating like gills. Like sails. They could be moving. A little kick or two just to keep up.

In the corner of his newfound ceiling, a blue-pen love heart, an arrow: *Céline loves Jules*. Up on his elbows. A closer look. No, not Jules. Julie. *Céline loves Julie.* He wondered what it meant. Now voices from the house. Coming. What's happened here? These spoons. Two polished black-leather shoes under each white hem. Moving in step. The glasses clinking. This one's chipped. Here, let me see. The flat black cockroaches stopping. Then on their sideways march again. Towards him. Lie quickly on his side. Here they come. Here-they-come! Their beetle-belly laces done up tight. A sprinkle of grass on each black toe. Past him now.

Okay, that's it. One to go.

The screen door slams.

Jo-Jo. Jo—Jo? Have either of you seen Jo-Jo?

Who's that?

The boy, my fiancé's nephew.

No.

Did she look around, did she look his way?

Jo-Jo. Jo—Jo.

Through the creviced flap. Carolina. In her white, held-up wedding dress. Her feet bare. Returning to the house. The wooden steps.

He sees the screen door close, and close, and close.

He never got to ask her. Why she came out. What she wanted. What she had to say. She was gone forever when he went inside, to all those silent faces turned his way.

❀

Later, he told himself he would never make the same mistake. How, he wondered, even then, had it happened? How did you end up leaving someone you must once have loved? Loved!

What had to happen in between?

When he was nine, they told him. It was the jack-in-a-box that never went away. Here, Auguste, open this. But what were these words he found inside? Separation. Divorce. Unhappiness. He had thought that all parents just fell silent.

For a long time he kept a box of photographs of them beneath his bed. He would get them out, sit cross-legged on his bedroom floor, go through them one by one. Take them in his hands. There was one he kept coming back to—his parents on their wedding day. His father's hand guiding his mother's, holding the polished knife blade just above the untouched cake. His parents laughing, his mother, in her wedding dress, bent forward, her pearl necklace reaching up to her like a tiny tender arm, her left hand on the table, her face lit by an iced ellipse.

There were other photographs of them: on the beach at La Baule, photos he had taken, photos of them at his uncle's, his father's brother, who had done so well, who never remarried; photos of them around an oval dining-room table, with their friends, in an apartment he'd never seen.

Once, when he was older, he went to La Baule. He took a photograph with him. Sought out the same rocky outcrop. Stood there himself, in exactly the same spot. In order to inhabit them. Feel them. But they weren't there. Time had erased all trace of them. It was a conceit to think that he could have found them in this way. 'Them'—the empty, two-word word he used for them.

In the end, he had to put the box away. This is what photographs did to you, he thought. This was their paradox. Their melancholy truth. He knew these permanently smiling faces, but not them.

He could not remember one word of tenderness his father had said to his mother. Not one. They must have talked. In the beginning. But, in the end, their marriage had outlasted the finite number of words that contained it. Perhaps they had exhausted what they had to say to each other long before they had gone their separated ways. He himself had never had a single serious conversation with his father.

After his father left, he never saw him again. Never heard from him. Not a word. Years later, when he could, he had searched the police database. Ludovic Emile Jovert.

His father had died in Santiago in 1970. Santiago! Had life been so unbearable that he had to seek refuge in the furthest corner of the earth? Vow never to see his son again?

And what had his father's other life been like? Did he have another son? One he loved?

Chapter 33

THE new girl's laughter spoke to him from out of his past. Not that he could place it at first. Or her. Amongst the new recruits. But he soon did.

He used his training. To cut her out. To let biology do its work. His status. His impossible height. His useful smile.

Sometimes he hated this. How easily people could be led. How little he had to do.

In the beginning, he loved only her laugh. Then found he loved her. This smart, lean-limbed girl, with her green eyes and dark skin. Her tripping laugh as sharp as swallows. He loved her name—Madeleine. Sweet-sounding. Unforgettable. She wasn't Carolina, whose ghost had come back to him. But it didn't matter. Not now. After the pieces had fallen into place.

❀

He would sometimes be gone a week. Sometimes longer.

In the beginning: Are you sure you will be all right?

Yes, I'm sure, Auguste. Don't worry. Fatima's here to help me.

But when he returned home, after the first absence, he found Madeleine lying on her bed, her face to the wall, her eyes closed. He sat on the bed, put his hand on her shoulder.

Is everything all right, my love, *ma chère*?

Yes, she said. Don't worry, Auguste. I'm sorry. I'm just so tired. I'll be glad when all of this is over. All I want to do is sleep.

It won't be long now, he said.

But when he squeezed her shoulder, he felt her body tremble. He leaned over her, to see her face. There were tears, not just one, but a river of them, spilling from her cheeks. He lay down beside her, pulled her close to him. But it was a long time before she settled into sleep.

❀

The first, soft knock nervous. A young corporal had come down from the barracks, down through the twisted, late-night, blacked-out streets, to his house, his two houses, at the centre of the village, its core.

Who is it?

Corporal Dumas, sir.

Just a moment.

From his bedroom window. The curtain cleft permanently

pinned. A solitary, shadowed figure at his door. He saw the shadow man look down at his shoes, then into the silent street. Corporal Dumas.

Then he was standing in the open doorway. They were not supposed to know. But they knew it anyway. Half of it. Why he was here. His special gifts. It was he who interrogated the prisoners they took in. Who got *so* much out of them.

He saw his reputation written on the young man's face. Knew what uneasy thoughts had kept him company as he walked down the hill to him through the empty curfewed streets. Twenty minutes rehearsing in the walking dark, his only companion a formidable ghost. What would he have thought if he knew there were two of him?

Capitaine Jovert. Have you met him yet?

There's a message for you, sir. A telegram. Personal. The rules infringed.

He handed him the piece of paper.

Thank you, Corporal.

Madeleine in hospital. Mother and baby both well. Tilde. A handwritten message scrawled at the base: *Jovert—Congratulations. See me in the morning*. The signature illegible.

He re-read the message.

Tell the colonel I'll be there at six. Thank you, Corporal.

Now, the thrust-out chest salute. Sir.

Both well.

But they weren't both well. Madeleine hadn't been well for months. That first night crack was now an abyss.

❀

He thought he'd had a son. At first. But after a while, when he had returned for the sixth or seventh time, he saw that he was wrong. It was Madeleine who'd had a son. Not him. After that, she had begun to drift away. Taking him, his son, with her.

This was how he came to see it. When he lay on his bed, in the almost darkness of the requisitioned house, a house that was not his own, listening to that night's operation unfolding. The windows lit up sporadically, the house trembling, the windows chattering, wondering how many interrogations he would have to do the next day, how far he would have to go. Sometimes they died, so badly injured were they, before they gave up anything. Had he had enough of this?

He returned every ten days, three weeks, to see her, and her child. To the house they occupied. Only to find that she had drifted still further from him. So far now that he could not reach her.

And it was not just her. The baby, his son, momentarily in his arms. But the look of panic, of fear, on his child's face, almost instant, not recognising him. How strong, how alarming his need to escape. The alien, swaddling body twisting, elongating in his hands, stretching out for its mother. Even though he might fall. He saw the fear in his own son's eyes: Where is she? The panic pulling at the corners of his mouth. No choice but to surrender him. Now rescued, the tumult subsides, his primal howl forestalled. There was no room for him.

He thought of his parents. The silent photographs. The empty, hollow clock-ticking evenings of his childhood. His summer afternoons alone.

❀

Jovert had not got back until three weeks after his son's birth.

The morning after Dumas' note, talking to Colonel Lemoine: I'm sorry, Auguste, we need you here. We've put too much into this. Madeleine is being taken care of.

Afterwards, when she had recovered, Madeleine went back to teaching—I'm fine, Auguste, I'm better now, I need to do this.

Perhaps, he thought at first, it was the cause, what they had come to do, that she had begun to doubt. A place for her, her forebears. For him. Their children. Instead, she had grown close to her teaching friends. To Mathilde, Khalid. These people she was supposed to be watching over.

Some evenings, they would be there when he came home. As if they were waiting for him. Already quietened by his footsteps echoing in the corridor. Their fidgeting scrutiny always awkward. Their leave-taking brief.

Auguste.

Tilde. Khalid.

Was Madeleine still reporting? He wondered if she knew, if they knew, about his other self.

He still went to her. In the beginning. Embraced her. But then—the first, almost imperceptible rebuff, a tiny seismic shock. A momentary freezing. So minute, so barely there, he needed to verify it.

It was over then.

Yet he wore an indentation in her bed. From where he came to sit. To uncomfort her.

Please, Auguste. Don't. I will be all right. Just leave me be.

Then: No don't, Auguste.

The turning away almost complete. Now the slow undoing of all the ties. Unspoken.

The time that passed.

Chapter 34

IN those four months: the village census complete. The families' names on each house. In white paint. The number of occupants. Here, what's this? Your identity papers. Keep them on you. Then the random late-night checks. Come with me. No, not you—you. Take the youngest son. Next day, show the father what's in the lattice-covered ditch. Trussed, bent over. Returned to him the *following* evening. The curfew unbreakable. The cost too great. A sheep. Two. From someone else. It helped them think.

The schoolhouse built. Attendance compulsory. Ages six to twelve. Including girls. The notices distributed. For each class, a morning roll. *No* exemptions. Every school day. Otherwise they risked a soldier's heavy rap. A lesser fine. But still too much. Where's Fatima? She's sick. Let me see.

A village council elected. You, you and you. Publicly paid, in the village square. Every Wednesday. And well. They either stayed or left. Most stayed. They had family here. They were compromised. They pay you! Where else could they go?

In six months: the village now contained. The checkpoints manned. The soldiers armed. No one in. No one out. Not without a pass. They had seen the consequences. An accident. A lost leg. One would usually suffice.

A dispensary. See Mr Valedire. A doctor—twice a week. The soldier's own. For them. For free. But *his* heart unhealed.

❀

A conversation half-remembered. When was this? In the library he tries to fold time back. Reorder it. But it's futile. This memory has been cast adrift.

I can't do this, Auguste. Not any longer. What if we're wrong?

We're *not* wrong.

But don't you see? We're being used. They don't want to save this country. Look what we've done. How could we have been so stupid? We'll be outcasts if we go back.

No, Madeleine, that's not right. Half of France wants this.

Now. What about later? People forget. Then someone remembers. Starts digging. Asks questions. How careful have we been?

That's not true. What we're doing is right.

No, it isn't. They lied to us. They've sold us out. Those traitors back home, those *cons*. Can't you see that?

He looked at her across the table. Her ravaged face still

beautiful. That's when his own first doubts crept in. How careful had he been?

It'll be okay for you. They'll just shut you up. Give you a promotion. Two. Inspector Jovert. Of the Special Interrogations Bureau.

Her laughter bitter now.

Inspector!

The cigarette in her shaking hand. Had she exhaled then? Brushed the smoke away?

But what about our son? What will happen to him? When they find out what we've done? In ten years. Twenty. He'll be the one who pays.

He went to her.

No, don't. Her hand held up. *Don't* touch me, Auguste. Not now.

And the final barriers went up.

❀

There was still so much to do. He stayed away. In Ighouna. In Sétif, twenty kilometres away. When he did come home, he came home to a house asleep. To his own room, his own bed. To the two sleeping strangers who lived there now. To his son, who looked at him as though he was an unknown thing. But the aching memory of him still imprinted on his hands.

At night, he would hear him crying, endlessly. As if he already knew what misfortune had befallen him. Madeleine would sleep on. He could not go to him, his child. Could not comfort him. For fear of stirring his tearful, infant raging once again.

❀

The second knock, six months later: Colonel Lemoine himself standing in the doorway. The urgent call to return. Surely he knew—he must have done. Thibaud waiting in the car. The high-speed night drive home. The car's bucking headlights quickly reeling Algiers in.

He sees them hurtling through the labyrinthine darkness, his arm outstretched against the dashboard. He can see figures running. Cars overturned. Buildings on fire. A man reaches out to them as they speed past; his face is imprinted on Jovert's brain. Beseeching them to stop. His splayed hands burst up in front of them like two white pigeons. Thibaud swerves to avoid him. All around them, there is artillery fire.

Thibaud is saying: What if she's not there? What if she's already left?

He strikes the steering wheel with the palm of his hand.

This is crazy, crazy. *Merde*.

This final syllable hangs in the air.

But Madeleine *is* there. She's sitting at the kitchen table when he bursts in. Her head in her hands, her pale, tear-stained face blank. She won't look at him. A woman he does not know sits across from her.

His child's not there.

Where's my son? he says.

He's in his crib, thank God. Asleep. Unscathed. Still innocent.

His heart still beating.

Mathilde Benhamou was killed today, the woman says. With her brother-in-law, Ahmed, and three of her students. A bomb explosion in town. At Les Trois Bleus, their favourite café.

How many thousands of times had he replayed this sentence since: Mathilde was killed today…Mathilde was killed today… Until he had to close it down, bury it. So deep he could not hear it anymore. Tilde.

Is that why it had been Lemoine? He saw his face looking into his. Don't ask what you don't need to know.

I was supposed to be there, Madeleine says. I was supposed to be there. With them. With Mathilde.

❀

He remembered one evening, an operation unexpectedly postponed, he had returned to Algiers. Madeleine had been surprised to see him. Tilde had been there. Tilde, whose husband had been killed in the riots of '57.

Tilde.

Auguste.

How are you, the children?

They're well, and how…

And Salima, how old is she now? She must be what, five, six?

Six. She's at school already.

It never hurt to let them know.

And Ahmed?

Ahmed, her brother-in-law, her sister Haifa's husband, whom she depended on.

He's well. Busy.

Busy, he said.

Afterwards, when he heard her leave, he slipped out, followed her down the dim-lit street.

Mathilde!

Tilde turned back, anxious, not knowing who it was.

It's me. Auguste.

He caught up with her. She was not unfriendly. Her fine-featured hijabed face handsome.

Auguste. What are you doing here?

I wanted to talk to you. About Madeleine.

She looked away.

Is she all right? he asked.

I don't know, Auguste. None of us knows. Since the baby was born, she has not been herself. She won't tell us why. I told her I was going to talk to you. But she begged me not to. I forbid you to tell him, Mathilde. It's got nothing to do with him. It's me. Just me.

That's why we come here. We take turns. To look after her. To make sure she gets some sleep, to see the baby's fed, settled, that he's all right.

She comes to school. The nurse is there. She teaches. But then, sometimes I'll find her in her empty classroom. She tells me then. She says she can't go home. She's afraid. I ask her why. And she says that that's where the fear is waiting for her.

What fear?

The fear that she is lost. The fear she can't find herself. At night, she goes looking. But she's no longer there.

Chapter 35

HE had not meant it to happen. Of course he'd had open briefs before. Infiltrate a cell. Do what you needed to do. For him it had been a commonplace. He had slept with targets before.

He was good at this. Better than good. He had that special intuition, that unique insight. Into the vulnerable. A woman with children. A woman with nowhere to live—now. A woman without money. Talk to the person next to her. Let someone else do the work for you. Let the subject *hear* of your kindness. Your generosity. The purity of your heart. Stay back. Volunteer. *Ask* for help, don't offer. Not yet. Something trivial. The envelopes you can't find. Directions to somewhere. If you wait, I'll take you. Talk to her then. While you search. While you walk. Not about politics, ideology. About school, her ailing parents, the death of a brother, the difficulty of finding a doctor—all the intimate things. Things you will be able to use. Discreetly. Take your time. Go slowly. Tick off the list—one, two, three.

Haifa was none of these. Her family was well educated. She had a sister, Mathilde; a husband, Ahmed, who was 'away'. And Jovert knew what that meant. Where that meant. He had a photograph of him—just in case. She didn't have children. She didn't need money. She had a place to live. He'd already been there. Been inside. Picked up her things. Her jewellery. Her earrings. Put them back again. She was strong. Independent. Intelligent. She'd studied jurisprudence in Marseille. By the time he'd made contact, he had followed her, watched her in the street. Observed her routine. Had seen her organising groups. Women, men. Seen how articulate she was, organised, revered. Loved.

Vulnerable.

Still, it would not be easy. She would be a challenge. Haifa was not your usual mark. He would have to clear the way. Be patient. Careful.

❀

His recollection, sitting in the library, was more vivid now than ever before. The sun more intense. The shadows sharper on the crevassed white walls. The cut blue sky more vivid, more angular. He *felt* the cicadas' serrated whirrings on his skin.

He was walking up the chipped stone stairs. Thinking of something else, someone else. Madeleine. Something was wrong. Something had changed. She had begun to push him away.

Then, suddenly, the air erupted around him. Some blinding

thing, a woman, emerged from the wall in front of him, her dress so white, so dazzling in the blazing light that it was like a disturbance in the air itself. She was already past him, a barely apprehended incandescent shape. But her after-image lingered. A dark-skinned crescent floating against her white dress. She was gone before he could look back. To the empty street. The air beginning to reassemble. Then he was knocking on the same blue door in front of him.

A young woman opened it. Alminah, the youngest recruit, prettier than her photograph.

My name is Philippe Valedire, he says. Yves sent me. He looks at the piece of paper in his hand: Is Haifa here?

No, she isn't. You've just missed her. She's gone to meet her husband. We weren't expecting you until tomorrow.

His look of surprise.

Please, won't you come in?

The door quickly closed.

I'm sorry, she says. You can never be too careful. My name is Alminah.

She shakes his hand. The grip is firm. Haifa has trained her well.

Haifa's just left. Brightness, warmth, admiration, in her voice. Just a minute ago. Yves's not here. I'm afraid it's just me.

I'm sorry, Almira.

Alminah.

Alminah. I will come back. I didn't mean to take you by surprise.

No, it's all right. Don't worry. We know who you are.

Here it comes: Would you like a coffee? He smiles at her.

Would you like a coffee? Yves will be here any minute.

It had been easy. Talking to her, Alminah. The coffee cup's length of conversation just enough.

He apologises again. Asks after Yves. How is he? His brother? No, no, we met in Paris. We were students together. Oh, and did they get the paper? The Roneo machine? Is it still working? Ah, yes, there it is. A half-turn of the drum. Lift the flap. Run one expert finger along its printing edge. Still dry. The coffee's good. We had to fix it, you know. It was leaking. But these old machines—unstoppable! Yes, Yves told us. Yves, who is late. A glance at his watch. Who's been delayed. Permanently. Yves is never coming back.

Oh, is that the time? I'm sorry, Alminah. I've got to go. I'll come back. No, no, it's no problem. No problem at all. At least we've met. One last quick sip. Thank you for the coffee, Alminah. You've been most helpful.

You're welcome.

Could you tell Haifa I was here? That I'll come back tomorrow. When I'm expected.

A small, shared laugh.

It's fine...Philippe. Don't worry. I'm pleased to have met you.

Tell her I'm looking forward to working with her.

I will.

Thank you, Alminah. Till tomorrow.

Steps one and two *and* three.

Tick.

Tick.

Tick.

It was always like this. He had once enjoyed the intricate preparation. The deft manoeuvrings. Now he found it slow. If only Alminah knew—trustworthy, dedicated, hard-working Alminah—just how many of her there were.

How focused had been his pursuit of her. Haifa. Yet how carelessly he had set the trap. Stood back.

Only to ensnare himself.

My name is Philippe Valedire. Yves sent me. Is Haifa here?

❀

They found they liked each other. Philippe Valedire and Haifa.

How long have you known Yves?

Oh, a long time. We were students together. Years ago. My father knew his father.

Yves was so helpful. He did so much for us. Do you know where he is now?

Philippe was not Yves. Yves was always joking. He was loud. But a gifted propagandist. If not always reliable. He'd sometimes disappear for weeks. This Philippe was quieter. More thoughtful. Committed. Fantastically tall. He *knew* Algeria. Its people. Us.

She liked his unruly hair, which he constantly brushed back. His round glasses. They made him look like a professor. Which he could have been. And yet he could fix her car. He knew how to build an irrigation ditch. Repair shelled walls. He read. One, two, three.

❀

He found himself thinking about her. At night, the lamp lit, the windows blacked out. A book in his lap. The thump of artillery shells not too far distant. And in the next quadrant. Not his. No need to worry. About her eyes, how luminous they were. Her mouth, her skin, so different from the French. From Madeleine. Although he no longer knew.

And he had seen the subtle signs—the changing colours that she wore. The blue against her skin. And then, from time to time, she wore that dress.

He thought of her lean body, when the wind blew, or she reached out to pay. For a piece of fruit, a loaf of bread. Fresh coffee beans. His body ached. Bodies. It happened to both of him.

He began thinking less of Algiers. Of the loss that inhabited him there. And more of coming home. Here. To Ighouna, this nothing nowhere village. And to Sétif. Where Haifa was. Although they still were just colleagues.

Then the news had come. The news he would remember. That small something he had forgotten to do. He walked up the stone chipped steps again. He no longer needed to knock. He had a key. For when he worked back late.

They were all there when he walked in. Except Haifa. All looking up at him.

Ahmed is dead. And Mathilde, Haifa's sister, Alminah said. They were killed in a bomb blast in Algiers last night. With three of Mathilde's students.

Ahmed Soukhane, Haifa's husband. Mathilde, Haifa's sister...Madeleine's friend. Whom she was watching.

She's at her parents'.

Had they just not told him?

Later that evening, at the outpost: Ahmed Soukhane was finally neutralised last night. Some collateral damage, but all in all, a good result. Thank you, Jovert, for your good work.

That was the truth. Now. And the truth could not be undone. There *was* no going back.

❀

Memory is a savage editor. It cuts time's throat. It concertinas life's slow unfolding into time-less event, sifting the significant from the insignificant in a heartless, hurried way. It unlinks the chain. But how did you know what counted unless you let time pass?

Haifa returned a month later. Not in mourning. She refused to be bowed. But the wound was there. Just like his own.

Now he sat looking across the library table into that moment when Haifa knocked on his door. A month, or two, later. Sent down at night from the checkpoint to see him, even though it was late. The sentry call. The long minutes waiting.

He had not slept with Madeleine for so long he could not

remember how beautiful a woman could be. Theirs had not been a union consummated in lust. They had sought each other out in sorrow. This one time. There would, they knew, be no tomorrow.

❀

I was supposed to be there. I was supposed to be there.

It drove her mad. The Madeleine that was lost to him.

They put her in the military hospital.

Where's my son? I want my son.

Colonel Lemoine came to see him. In Algiers. In the empty house.

She needs to go home, Auguste. She's not well. You understand. We'll provide a nurse. Someone to go with her. To look after her, and your child. To make sure she's safe.

He saw her to the ferry. But she did not see him. She stood there with the child in her arms, twisting in the wind. She seemed so thin. So alone. Then she was leaving, with no farewell. She had brushed his arm away.

He went back, to the emptier house. To where time stopped.

You should go too, Auguste. Your work is done. It's over now. Just pack your things. You know what I mean. Make sure you leave no trace.

❀

He had read accounts of people who had nearly drowned. How many said that they had seen a strange white light, that they had not been afraid, that they had felt a state of transcendent serenity, of acceptance, before they lost consciousness.

Perhaps this was true. Perhaps they did.

But all he could think of, when the third knock came, when Colonel Lemoine stood unexpectedly in front of him again, and gave him the brutal news, was of his son being ripped from his mother's arms by the impact of the water as they hit. During the night, unseen, the nurse asleep, Madeleine had fallen—or jumped, he would never know—from the ferry that had come to take her home.

He sees his son beneath the water, sees his startled eyes looking uncomprehendingly at his mother's sorrowing face as she sinks unstruggling away. He sees the child's first impulse is to swim after her, but she is already lost to him. And his thin-ribbed chest is already bursting, ballooning him up towards the surface, to the one slender hope he has of hanging on to everything that this life has to give. But the surface is no solace. It is all darkness. The boat is gone. No bright, twinkling lights. He is alone. He bobs in the sea for a moment before the primal urge to kick kicks in. Swim, it says. But swim to where? His child's brain already knows it's too late. There is no one there. Nothing to hold on to. Nothing to save him. Not his mother. Nor his father. Who was never there.

Part VII

MARTINE

❀

Chapter 36

WHEN Jovert had finished telling Omura about his dead young son, Omura was sitting by the window, with the first hint of dawn just registering on the curtains behind him. He imagined Omura doing what he had sometimes done, closing his eyes as he listened, so that his voice was the only thing that came to him.

He could see Omura's profile. How the outer edge of his glasses caught the dawn's first glow.

Omura looked old now, insubstantial, as though he too were already just a memory. No longer there.

Omura turned away from him. He reached up for his glasses. Took them off. He rubbed his eyes. In the now pale light, against the window, Jovert saw what he was not meant to see—a single teardrop momentarily meniscussed on the downward curve of Omura's glasses. He saw it holding on unsteadily in the early morning light, as though all of Omura's grief were concentrated there. Then the drop let go. It fell slowly through the air, slowly, slowly, until it disappeared back into him. Still Omura did not speak.

❀

This is her—Mathilde, he said.

How long had he waited before he handed Omura the crumpled photograph, after he had told him not everything—there was never any point in confessing everything—but enough to balance the ledger?

Omura pushed his glasses up onto his forehead, held the photograph up to the light. Squinted. His hand was shaking, as if the photograph, this almost insubstantial thing, was made of some newly discovered element of indescribable atomic weight, something so heavy it could barely be held aloft.

This is her? Omura said. This is your daughter?

He looked at Jovert.

Yes, he said. That's her.

And you will find her?

I'm not sure, he began to answer.

Of what?

Well, of many things. But I'm not sure that I want to go digging up the—

But she is your daughter, Omura interrupted. How could you not? How could you leave this question unanswered?

Which question?

This one, he said.

Omura gestured around the room. Then he understood. Omura's shaking hand meant *all* of this: in here, out there, out on the balcony, the streets. He meant every time Jovert opened his door. He meant rue St Antoine, the newsstand, the Metro, Le Bar l'Anise, the cold, mailbox-filled foyer, the lift. Everything that wasn't him.

And he saw that Omura was right. This question had encircled him from the moment he had opened the envelope. Like her photograph, he'd carried it with him wherever he went. And it would be with him now, when he got up out of his chair. It would follow him to Omura's door. It would come with him up the stairs. It would be there as he walked down the corridor to his apartment. And it would be waiting for him, just inside his door.

She is your *daughter*, Omura said. Your daughter.

Chapter 37

YEARS later, Omura told him, long after my father had died, I went to visit his village.

They were sitting at Le Cormoran in Place des Vosges, catching the last of autumn's late-afternoon sun. Earlier they had gone to look at the plaque outside Victor Hugo's door.

We had moved to Osaka when I was a boy, and I had only been back two or three times since.

My father's village was famous for its forests, which spread up the sides of the mountains that encircled it. In October and November it was possible to do a daylong walk, a kind of pilgrimage, circling from west to east along the mountain rim, to see the maple leaves, how they changed colour at different times of the day. Halfway up the highest mountain was a shrine dedicated to the people from the village who were killed in Hiroshima on the day the bomb was dropped.

I went in December, he said. Not having been to the shrine

since I was a child, I decided to visit it again. I went late in the afternoon, the best time to see the last leaves falling. To me, it was these falling leaves that were the most beautiful, more beautiful than those that remained on the trees.

There were few people making the climb at that hour, and only a trickle making their way back. The path was steep and I kept my eyes focused on the ground in front of me, so that I did not lose my footing. I was about a third of the way up when I heard a voice call my name.

Master Omura?

I looked up to see old Professor Todo standing on the stone landing just ahead of me. He was leaning on a walking stick, taking a moment to catch his breath. He had hardly changed. It was almost as if he himself had been preserved in stone.

I can see from the expression on your face, he said, that you have heard the news.

What news?

That I am dead. That I committed suicide years ago. I myself am not so sure that that is the case. He was smiling at me.

I would have expected Professor Todo to be a bent and broken old man. Instead, he seemed happy, happy in a way I had never seen him before.

He spoke of Katsuo.

I hear he has made a name for himself, he said. That he is now a famous writer. Ah, Katsuo. Such an interesting boy. Always watching. Always observing. He nodded to himself. Yes, Katsuo. Still the most brilliant student I ever had. I am pleased that he has done well. He shook his head. *Such* a brilliant boy. It is not always the case.

But Professor Todo, I said, taking the opportunity to ask the question I had always wanted to ask. With respect, Katsuo betrayed you. After all you did for him, he still betrayed you!

Yes, yes, he said, as if what I was saying was of no consequence whatsoever. But Katsuo was like a son to me, the son I never had. I knew his father well, you know. Very well. I've just been up there, chatting to him. He pointed with his stick up the mountainside. When we were young, we were like brothers. And, well, Katsuo. It was the least I could do. The money meant nothing to me.

The money?

But as soon as I said it, I knew. How stupid could I have been? The anonymous benefactor, the person who had provided for Katsuo's education, who had supported him from the time he was a boy. The money had come from Professor Todo.

Did he know?

Did he know what?

Where the money came from?

Oh, I don't think so. I had sworn his uncle to secrecy. No, I doubt that he knew.

And forgive me once again, Professor Todo, but you say you were just up there, chatting to his father? At the shrine?

Yes, he said. Didn't you know? His father was in Hiroshima on the day they dropped the bomb. With his wife, Ayumi. Except that she had stayed on the outskirts of the city, with relatives.

Only Haruki had gone into the city centre. They never found his body. Ayumi died almost a year later, of radiation sickness. You know, Master Omura, I once asked Ayumi to marry me, but she refused. She was already secretly betrothed to Katsuo's father. If only I had known. If only I had asked first. Life could have been so different...So, on the first Monday of each month, I go up there to say hello to him, and to Ayumi.

I could hear Katsuo's voice: My father was killed in a bomb explosion. A bomb explosion! I thought.

And you, Tadashi? What about you? I hear you have a legal practice in Osaka.

And I thought: How would he know that? I was only ever on the periphery of things. Perhaps I frowned, looked away. When I turned back to him, his old grey eyes were still fixed on mine. Something passed between us then, a moment of understanding. I am not a fool, Tadashi, his eyes said. And I have never been a fool.

I stood there observing Professor Todo, his face. Never have I seen a face so tranquil, so unburdened by the past.

You are a good person, Tadashi, he said. An honourable person. Say hello to Katsuo for me when you next see him.

And then he was walking away, as if we had never met, as if we had never encountered each other on this deserted mountain path one cold and wintry afternoon, years ago.

Chapter 38

INSPECTOR Jovert!

He was on his way home. He had stopped off at the Monoprix opposite the newsstand to pick up a few things.

He turned to see a young woman facing him. The world folded in on itself. She was standing on the other side of a bank of cold-storage units. Her face was narrow, olive-skinned, dark-haired; half-Algerian, he knew instantly—how many hundreds of these faces had he seen in his life. Luminous, blue-green eyes.

I knew I recognised you, she said. She was coming around the display units to him. We met at Le Bar l'Anise, she said. On Bastille Day. Actually, it was that night, at the fireworks. Don't you remember—I bumped into your table, spilt your wine?

Ah yes, now he remembered. She was the girl he'd looked through, the one in the black dress. But that'd been July, and here it was, already October.

Yes, of course, he said.

But where to go after this?

I *knew* I knew you, she said. But the light was so poor in the café. I remembered later—Inspector Jovert. You *are* Inspector Jovert, aren't you?

Yes, he said. I am.

You testified at my brother's trial, she said. Mehdi Lambert.

Of course, Mehdi. How could he forget? He looked at her again. He could see the family resemblance. She had Mehdi's dark hair. His thin face. His lean build. Different eyes, though. His were glacial.

I've cut my hair, she said. She reached up, pulled at a dark strand. Her hair was short now, as short as a boy's. And I'm not wearing my glasses, she said.

But he wasn't thinking about her. He was thinking about Mehdi. He could still have given Mehdi's height and weight if someone had asked. Mehdi Lambert, the seventeen-year-old boy who had stabbed his stepfather to death in one of those godforsaken socialist-experiments-gone-wrong high-rises on the outskirts of Paris. How long ago was that? Six, maybe seven years?

It was one of the worst cases he'd ever had to deal with. The stepfather, a violent alcoholic, a petty criminal, had abused his young children, Mehdi's half-brother and half-sister, for years. He was well known to police. Petty theft, burglary, assault with a weapon, grievous bodily harm. He had even, Jovert knew from the police files, assaulted the young woman—what *was* her name?—who now stood before him.

But if her stepfather had mistreated her, and her brother, it was to their youngest half-sibling, a boy of four, that their stepfather devoted his most vicious attention. The police files showed the boy had been hospitalised four times in his short life—a fractured skull, he'd fallen off his tricycle; a broken nose, he'd fallen down the concrete stairs to their apartment; two severely burnt hands, this had been when the boy was two. According to the boy's father, the child had been standing on a stool watching him cook when he had fallen forward, onto the stove. But the father could not explain how it was that the blistered burns on both his son's hands, now infected, were so concentric. It looked, from the photographs, said the prosecutor, as though the child's open hands had been held there.

The mother—their mother—had been too frightened to testify.

On the night their stepfather died, so too did their half-brother.

Jovert remembered how the father, unemployed, had come home in a drunken rage. The mother had been working the night shift at the nearby food-processing factory.

Mehdi had come home at around 8.30, perhaps a little later—he had been at his girlfriend's—to hear his stepfather's raised voice coming from their apartment.

I could hear it the moment the door buzzed open, he said. And as I came up the stairs, my stepfather's voice had got louder and louder. By the time I got to the top of the stairs I realised that he was screaming at Luc.

You fucking son of a bitch, I could hear him saying. You piece of Algerian shit. What did I tell you? What did I tell you? Answer me, he screamed.

Mehdi told the court that his stepfather had it in for the boy. He was darker than the rest of them. He accused his wife, their mother, of screwing around.

Look at him, he'd say. Just look at him—he's as dark as a fucking Arab's arsehole. Aren't you, Luc. And he'd slap him across the head. Hard.

Their mother said it wasn't true: she had *never* cheated on him.

It happens, she said. Some children are naturally darker. Please, Michel, don't hurt him.

I'll tell you what happens, he said. When I'm out, you cock-sucking whore, you fuck other men. You think I don't know. I see them come and go.

But no one comes and goes, Michel. No one.

Don't *lie* to me! I *see* them, you fucking lying bitch. I'm *not* stupid, you know. I have eyes, I can see.

One of his neighbours, an elderly Iranian woman, had been waiting on the next landing when Mehdi reached the door.

Pauvre petit, she said as he searched for his keys in his satchel. This no good, Mehdi. One day he kill him.

You fucking bitch. I'll show you, you fucking piss-drinking fucking whore.

Something crashed to the floor. There was the sound of breaking glass.

I will *kill* you, you cunt.

For a moment, Mehdi thought his mother must be home. That the two of them were arguing.

Allah, Allah. I sorry, Mehdi. I call police.

What did I tell you? his father was screaming when he entered the kitchen. Don't-make-sad, Luc. You make sad again and I swear, I'll fucking...

Mehdi found Luc and his stepfather in the kitchen. Luc was in his pyjamas. He was standing on one of the kitchen chairs. Mehdi wondered how long he had been standing there. The boy had been crying. But now he was silent. Pieces of a broken chair lay scattered on the kitchen floor. Half a wooden seat. The broken bentwood back. One piece, a slat or something, was in the kitchen sink. It appeared as though the chair had exploded. His stepfather was standing opposite the boy. He had a broken chair leg in his hand.

Luc hadn't even glanced at Mehdi when he came in. He stood looking down at the floor. Mehdi could see that there was something wrong with his left arm—it was hanging at an odd angle. An autopsy would later show that it had been broken in three places.

His father was still shouting at him: Don't make sad, don't make sad, Luc. Luc...I'm not going to ask again.

Luc, what's happening here? Mehdi asked. Why are you up on a chair?

My stepfather, he said, glanced at me in the doorway. I saw his rage intensify. It was as if he refused to allow himself to be judged by me, someone who meant *nothing* to him. I was not *his* son. I saw my stepfather turn the broken chair leg slowly in his fist so that one of its hard edges faced in. And...and then he struck Luc a blow to the side of his head with all the force he could muster.

Luc, Mehdi said, had teetered on the chair for an instant. But then it was like the air had gone out of him, as though he was one of those stovepipe men you sometimes see waving their arms about outside those places that sell cheap furniture and somebody had turned the compressor off. Luc collapsed onto the chair. Just like that. Then he slipped onto the floor.

And he didn't move. Not once. He just lay there, Mehdi said. I couldn't believe it. There was so little of him. Luc. So little. A moment ago he'd been alive. And now...My stepfather was standing over him, except that it didn't look like him, like Luc, anymore. The bloodied chair leg was still in my step-father's hand, and there was a look of indescribable hatred on his face.

What have you done? I screamed at him. Oh my god, what have you done? But before he could answer, I grabbed the kitchen knife that was lying on the bench, and I just started stabbing, stabbing, stabbing, saying: Never, never, *never* again.

❀

Martine, that was her name. Martine. It had surfaced now. He remembered her testifying. She'd been in her early twenties then, had had long dark hair, glasses. He remembered how quiet she was, how articulate, studious. She could have been the prosecutor herself.

She had testified that she'd moved back to Algiers a couple of years previously. To escape her stepfather.

Jovert looked at her again. How much more informed her face was now. How much more subtle. Stronger. He thought of the chasm of time that separated them. They were several lives apart. But for this temporal accident, had things, life, been otherwise, he knew he could have fallen for a girl like Martine.

Martine, he said.

Yes, she said, surprised. So you do remember?

I remember, he said. And Mehdi. How is he?

Mehdi had been convicted of manslaughter. Justifiable homicide. His teachers had testified on his behalf. He was a good student at the *lycée*. He worked hard. His mother depended on him. Despite this, he was sentenced to jail. Six years, to serve a minimum of three. There was an appeal. The sentence was too harsh. There had been mitigating circumstances. The judgment was flawed, it was racist. Mehdi was a half-half. His mother Algerian. His father French. There had been an outcry. No French boy would have been jailed under similar circumstances. Mehdi was released from jail, pending the appeal. But he didn't wait. He didn't trust the French justice system. It was too polluted by history. Instead, he took off for Algiers, where his sister, Martine, was.

❀

When he thought about it later, it seemed to Jovert that he had spent most of his life listening to people, sifting through what they said, weighing, assessing. Trying to fit things together. But life, unlike crime, was not something you could *solve*. What people told you was not always the truth; the truth was what you found out, eventually, by putting all the pieces together. And sometimes not even then.

But where did that leave his life? Perhaps, he thought, his life didn't matter in the end. It was life itself that mattered. It wasn't personal. Life just rolled through you. And then moved on.

❀

Martine told him that she had come back to revive the appeal process, to get help. But Mehdi had gone into hiding in Algiers. She could not find him.

Now, she thought, she might have found someone who could help her. He was standing right in front of her.

PART VIII

OMURA

Chapter 39

IT starts as a normal day. Tadashi Omura steps out of his apartment and pulls the door closed. He takes the lift downstairs. Then he sets out on the ten-minute walk to his office. The air is clear. The sun is shining.

He has no presentiment that truth is circling overhead. That it will be waiting for him when he arrives at his office.

Then he is sitting at his desk. He takes the document he has been working on out of his briefcase and opens it. Sees the isolated pools of red. His many emendations. There is still so much to do.

His left hand rests on the page. The fingers of his right hand reach expertly up for his glasses, snug in his coat top pocket. His detailed revisions are suddenly as sharp as barbed wire. His handwriting meticulous, dense, inescapable.

The document is a family will. It is the territory he hates most. The will is complex, an old Osaka family. They are well known, wealthy. Once, they were happy.

For reasons he will not disclose, the father, a former friend, wants his only son excised. His word—excised.

Omura remembers him, the boy, as a young child. Shy, smiling, well-mannered.

But now things must be watertight.

Where did this new bitterness come from? What transgressions did it conceal? He could not ask. The father unbending.

Watertight. No loopholes. No gaps. To ensure the carnage continues.

❀

Later—three soft knocks. He is still at his desk. His ashtray has begun to fill. He waits, glances at his open diary. The low reverberation of a departing freighter rolls across the city. Eleven thirty.

Mrs Akimoto, his secretary, knocks again. He imagines her leaning in towards the door, her small clenched fist still raised.

Come in, he says.

Mrs Akimoto is older, old-fashioned. She has been with him for years. From before she was married. She bows, as she always does.

Forgive me, Mr Omura, but there is someone here to see you.

He looks at his diary again. Perhaps he has missed something.

It's a lady, Mrs Akimoto says. She does not have an appointment.

I suggested she make one, but she said she would wait. All day, if necessary. Until you come out.

Tadashi hears what his secretary has said.

She says it's important.

Did she tell you what it's about?

No, she wouldn't say.

Did she give you her name?

She said her name was Yamaguchi.

Yamaguchi?

Yes, Mrs Yamaguchi.

He frowns.

The name Yamaguchi doesn't mean anything to me, he says. Do we have anything on file?

No, Mrs Akimoto says. I looked.

He turns back to the document on his desk.

Thank you, Mrs Akimoto. Ask Mrs Yamaguchi to give me ten minutes. I will see her then. Please bring some tea with you when you come.

❀

Mrs Yamaguchi is perhaps fifty. Perhaps older. Her face resolute. Her mouth a mere uneven crease in her face. But her eyes are steady. He can hear her saying: I will wait here until he comes out.

She sits in the chair opposite him.

I need your help, she says.

She has an accent. Now he knows she is not from Osaka.

Or Tokyo. She comes from one of the northern provinces. He has heard this accent before. The rural mud has stuck. And yet her clothing is beautifully made. The cloth expensive.

The bridge of his nose hurts. He takes his glasses off. Retrieves a soft cloth from his drawer. He polishes the thick round lenses.

Help in what way? he says, holding his glasses up to the light.

A little over a year ago, she says, my husband died. One evening, the police came knocking on my door. They told me my husband's body had been found at the base of the walking bridge at Akiyama. Amongst the rocks. His skull had been fractured. His neck was broken. They told me he had committed suicide. They told me...They told me Hideo had jumped.

I'm sorry, Mrs Yamaguchi, he says. He is about to go on.

That was a year ago, she says. I now know that my husband did not jump. He was killed.

Killed?

Yes, killed. Murdered.

The moment has arrived. Does he feel the fluttering of wings about his head?

Mr Ishiguro said to come and see you, she says.

Here it is.

Mr Ishiguro said to come and see you. The wings are beating now. *Mr Ishiguro said...*

He said it wasn't anything to do with him.

Mr Ishiguro? he says.

Yes?

Which Mr Ishiguro?

But he already knows.

Mr Ishiguro, the cloth maker. She touches the sleeve of her kimono. His factory is on the outskirts of the city.

And what else did Mr Ishiguro say?

She looks perplexed.

That you would know what to do, she says.

He sees the determination in her eyes. She is not going to go away.

And why do you think your husband was murdered? he asks.

Because I found his diary, she says. I have it here.

Chapter 40

I WILL pay you what you paid me, Hideo says.

Three months after he had surrendered Sachiko, Hideo returned. To get his daughter back.

How?

They were sitting in the long room. Hideo did not answer.

It's too late, Hideo, Katsuo said.

Why?

I cannot explain.

It did not take long for Hideo to produce his ultimatum.

If you do not return Sachiko to me, he said, I will tell her that I sold her to you. I will tell her that, from the age of twelve, every time I came down to Osaka, you paid me for her.

Sold her? Katsuo said. We entered into an agreement, Hideo. Sachiko would come to work for me, in exchange for which I would take care of her future. In the meantime, as you say, I paid you. Handsomely. We had an agreement.

Hideo said nothing.

And tell me Hideo, which is worse? That you sold her? Or that I bought her?

That you bought her.

Why?

Because of what you bought her for.

You took my money. You knew then what our contract meant. Or did you lie to yourself about that?

He waited for Hideo to reply.

Perhaps, he said.

Perhaps which?

Hideo hesitated.

Yes, I knew, he said.

You knew. And I waited. Sachiko is sixteen. You know I could have taken her much earlier. In the eyes of the law, I have done nothing wrong.

Both men remained silent, each watching the other.

I made a mistake, Katsuo-san, Hideo said. I cannot live with what I have done. That I sold her to you haunts me. I feel her loss every day. I have always felt it.

Katsuo knew of what Hideo spoke. The pain of losing someone. Had he not spent years mourning Mariko's loss after she had left? Years. And had he not known how much he loved Mariko until she was gone? What had Hideo just said: I feel her loss every day.

❀

In those first desperate weeks, after Mariko disappeared, Katsuo had searched and searched for her. Later, in his years of self-imposed exile, his longing had grown more unbearable every day. How could he have made such a mistake? Not to have recognised that he could not live without her. To have let her slip through his fingers.

Then, years later, not long after his return, he had been leafing through an old magazine, passing time while he waited to be shaved, and there, when he turned a page, was a photograph of her. It had been a shock to see her eyes again, eyes that he had not seen for so long, looking up at him. There had been a clutching at his heart, a momentary glimpse of hope reborn. And then the caption: *Consort of wealthy industrialist found dead.* He had read and re-read it.

She had changed her name. Why had he never thought of that? It had been so cruel to have discovered her death this way. So unexpected. So without warning. Mariko, the woman whose laughter he could still hear, whose face he could still see, who had walked his balcony by his side, had died alone, in a cheap room in a cheap hotel, of an overdose, the former consort of a man convicted of fraud. A man who refused to speak to him.

He had gone there, to that room, to that empty space, to be with her.

But it had been beyond him to envisage her sitting alone on the still-made bed, pausing that brief moment before she took the irrevocable step. His brain refused to imagine her lovely hands reaching for the bottle of pills, refused to see her pale eyes dulled with tears. And she still wondering—how had life come to this?

The room had been empty. No unearned forgiveness was waiting for him there. No shrine. She was gone.

He had kept the photo. Looked at it from time to time. So the wound would not heal. Life could have been so different.

Had she come looking for him?

In the years that followed, he isolated himself, became a prisoner to his own grief. He gave up hope of ever finding someone else. He no longer cared.

Then his friend Ishiguro started talking about a girl he had seen, the daughter of one of his clients, who lived in a mountain village hundreds of kilometres away.

She reminds me of Mariko, he said. Or what Mariko must have been like when she was young.

But Katsuo had dismissed him.

A year later, Ishiguro called.

I saw her again, he said.

Who?

The girl. The one that reminds me of Mariko. I tell you, Katsuo, she *is* beautiful. Her name is Sachiko. When you finish what you're working on, you should come with me. To see her.

Eventually, when *The Woman on the Beach* was done, he agreed to go. He was still not sure, however, that he wanted to be reminded of Mariko.

But Ishiguro had been right. The girl *was* beautiful. And

there *was* something Mariko-like about her. It was as if she were Mariko's echo.

Afterwards, back in Osaka, the thought of her lingered. He kept seeing Sachiko emerging onto her parent's lit verandah wearing kimonos made from Ishiguro's exquisite cloths. She was tall. Slender. Pale-skinned. He was struck by her poise, her reserve. Her extraordinary face. By the end of the evening, after he had continued waiting unrewarded for her to reappear, she had begun to inhabit him.

Sachiko.

It had been easy for Ishiguro to ask after her on her father's next visit; what his plans for his daughter were, her education, her future. Easy for him to mention a wealthy benefactor who was looking for a young girl to tend to his house, to become his secretary, his assistant—his current housekeeper being old—in exchange for furthering her education. A benefactor who was prepared to enter into a contract with him, but who was also prepared to wait.

Hideo had been flattered when Ishiguro introduced him to Sachiko's prospective employer. Ishiguro had not told him who this might be, and he would never have guessed. Katsuo Ikeda? The writer? Who was already famous. And Ume, who was indeed already old, who would oversee Sachiko's training, nodding to him, as if he were important.

Hideo could see Sachiko in this beautiful house. With its vast terrace, its view over the city. He could see her exploring its beautiful garden, which stretched endlessly up the mountain.

He could see her reading the books in Mr Ikeda's beautiful library. Being driven down to her lessons in Mr Ikeda's gleaming new car, with her own personal driver, her future assured.

As for Katsuo, Sachiko, the girl he had almost not bothered going to see, had indeed turned into a beautiful young woman. Who, from the moment her father left her with him, reminded him of Mariko almost more than he could bear. Apart from her face, her translucent pale eyes, she also had the same clear, bell-like laugh, so light it seemed to float on air. When he first heard it coming from the garden again, his heart had skipped a beat. He thought Mariko had returned to him.

And then there was Sachiko's scar. Something he could never have foreseen. Or hoped for. On *her* shoulder blade.

Mariko's scar, that tiny island-like map embossed on her skin, had, in the end, come to obsess him. It was the thing he looked for first. The thing he reached for. It was the first thing his eyes fell to whenever she turned away from him. It had been what he had missed most when he was with someone else. What he longed for. That nobody else had. This tiny flaw. Until Sachiko came to him.

No, much had changed in three months. He had already begun to love this girl whom fate had delivered him. His heart had begun to heal. It was as if he had been given a second chance. And he was not about to let her go. Not this time. He had made that mistake once before.

Hideo, Hideo, he said, his tone conciliatory, I understand how you must feel. He stopped, as if to consider what he was about to say. I know what it means not to be able to live without someone. He paused for his words to take effect. Give me some time to think about what you have said. Perhaps there is a solution that neither of us has considered. One that would satisfy us both. When do you return home?

Tomorrow, he said.

As soon as that?

Katsuo raised the arched fingers of both hands to his chin.

I'm not sure that that gives me enough time, he said, to think about what would be best for both of us.

How much time do you need?

Katsuo waited.

A week, Hideo. If I let you know then, one way or another, what my decision is, would you be agreeable to that?

For the first time since Hideo had arrived at Katsuo's, a faint shadow of hope registered on his face.

And you give me your word that you will not disappear, as you have done in the past? You will not take Sachiko with you?

You have my word, Hideo. As a man of honour, I will not disappear. Sachiko and I will be here.

All right then, he said. I will wait.

Thank you, Hideo.

The two men stood.

Can I get my driver to take you back to town? Katsuo said.

Yes, thank you, Katsuo-san. I would be grateful.

Katsuo went to the phone. Picked it up. Spoke into it.

Then he led Hideo out into the foyer. Ume was already waiting there for him. She bowed to him.

Mr Yamaguchi, she said.

So, Hideo, Katsuo said. It's all arranged. Ume will attend to you.

He opened the door, inclined his head. Reached out to shake Hideo's hand.

Until we meet again, Hideo, he said.

Until we meet again, Katsuo-san.

Ume held out her hand for Hideo to precede her. Katsuo watched Hideo step into the darkness outside. Then he reached for the door and closed it softly behind him.

After Hideo left him, Katsuo sat for some time in the semi-darkness of the long room. Then he went out onto the terrace and stood at the balustrade. Forty-five minutes later, when he saw the car headlights returning through the trees, when he saw the car turn into the driveway and stop at the gates, he went back into the long room, got his coat, and went downstairs.

He was waiting for the car as it emerged onto the forecourt. He was seating himself comfortably in the soft upholstery even before the car had rolled to a stop.

Ishiguro's, he said. And he pulled the door closed after him.

Chapter 41

DARKNESS slips into the valleys. Hideo is returning from his evening walk. The air is cold; there is no one else on the path.

On the other side of the river, the lights of the inn beckon. The ghost of the parked bus is just visible through the trees.

Hideo is thinking about what Katsuo said to him the night before. Perhaps there *is* another way. Perhaps all is not yet lost.

A solitary figure stands huddled in the middle of the bridge. Leaning on the rail. Smoking. The tip of his cigarette glows brighter. Then the butt is flicked spinning into the abyss—a tiny catherine wheel arcing into the darkness. A bat zigzags down after it. The lingering smell of burning tobacco faintly familiar.

It happens quickly. When he reaches the centre of the bridge, the figure steps purposefully away from the railing and stands in front of him, blocking his way.

Hideo.

❀

Did he wait long enough? Did Hideo see his face? Was 'Katsuo' the last word on the tip of his tongue?

Death is swift. Two brutal blows to the skull. An ancient samurai club in Katsuo's hand. The first, a slanting blow from above, so violent it severs the top of Hideo's earlobe. The other, a side blow, hits him even as he is crumbling, unconscious, to the ground.

The old man's body is lighter than Katsuo imagined. He holds him briefly over the rail. Lets go. There is no splash. Just one dull thud.

Has he done enough? He leans over the side of the bridge. Grasps the rail. He can hear the river. But he cannot see it. The world below is only darkness. Presumed. He stands still, listening. The lights of the inn glinting through the trees alarmingly close. No human voice comes to him. No cry.

The swirling waters will not remove Hideo Yamaguchi. His pale old-man's body will not be trapped forever beneath a submerged tree root as he had hoped. Katsuo has miscalculated. Hideo's body bounces once, skids to the water's edge, stops. Life is already abandoning him. A thin red stain weeps into the river bank. His disordered brain is no longer able to piece together the fractured truth. There will be no final accounting. No protest. No time to ask why? Just the darkness growing.

Katsuo is already making his way back to the inn. He does not look back. If he had, he would have seen the owl swoop down out of the shadows. Swift, intent, it glides silently just centimetres above the wooden treads. It lands, its black clawed feet outstretched, its great wings beating soundlessly. It sits motionless in the centre of the bridge. Its eyes serious in its white, dahlia-perfect face. A perfect, perfect thing.

The owl watches Katsuo's retreating form. The intermittent pinpoint glow of another cigarette. Katsuo has almost reached the inn. He is oblivious. Soon he will be back in the safety of his room.

The owl turns back to what it has come for. It hops stiff-legged towards something lying in the shadows. Something pale, curved. Something as thick as a child's finger. A caterpillar, perhaps. Except that this caterpillar does not move. Does not try to escape. The great bird looks down. Pauses. Then snatches up the piece of severed ear in its beak. It beats it against the wooden cross beam, hard, making sure it is properly dead. Then it stops.

Katsuo steps up onto the lit verandah. The owl turns to watch him once again. They are connected now, by what it has retrieved.

Who knows what small detail it sees. The hand that reaches for the door is spattered with blood.

The bird crouches, hops up onto the wooden foot rail. The piece of severed flesh still in its beak. Takes one last look. Then leans into the abyss and is gone.

❀

In the crisp morning light, on the bridge, the chattering school children. Half-walking, half-skipping. Holding hands. Unsuspecting.

One small cry and twenty small heads are at the railing. Looking down. Hushed. Fingers pointing. Quickly sifting doubts. It *is* a man. His body strangely twisted. The water licking at his cheek. Then they are running.

Chapter 42

THE photographs are black and white.

Why don't you leave it with me? he had said to Mrs Yamaguchi. The diary. I will have a look at it and get back to you.

After she had left, Omura sat back in his chair. He had not intended to start reading immediately.

Why, then, did he open it? And once it was open, why did he glance down and see the name Katsuo floating so prominently within its black morass?

She had called it a diary. But it wasn't, not really. It was a mere twenty pages. Stapled together. Handwritten. The writing tightly packed. Twenty pages!

Twenty pages. Fifteen minutes was all it took. And now, in that time, how the world had changed. A caterpillar turned into a butterfly in less. But this? How monstrous was this? Surely it took longer than that.

He spoke into the phone.

When he came out of his office, he had the diary in his hands. He did not look at Mrs Akimoto as he left.

Now he was standing in the court archives. Between the endless airless shelves. A file lay skewed on the shelf above his head. A box of forensic photographs, ticket stubs, a half-pack of cigarettes, a pearl hairpin, leaned against his chest.

Two of the photographs, those taken from the bridge, are slightly out of focus. Hideo's body is in the bottom right-hand corner. His legs face one way, as though he is running on his side, his arms the other. His right hand is in the water.

Three more photographs, from different angles, show Hideo's head. One is grotesquely sharp. Omura's throat constricts. His hand begins to shake. Hideo's open eyes look down in disbelief at the stain leading to the water's edge. A discoloured dark wisp still circulates in the water, as if his blood is still flowing. Perhaps his life has not yet fully left him. There may still be hope. A clump of matted hair. Half an earlobe is missing. What's left is pale, unearthly, incomprehensible. An ant is sampling its still-moist edge. Another is on its way to tell their friends of this good fortune.

Then there are the X-rays. He holds one up to the light. The primitive shadowed skull always faintly shocking. Two longitudinal fractures. Like the broken hulls of two broken boats. Transparent. Strangely beautiful. He takes his glasses off. Rubs his nose. Squints. An uneven line circumnavigates Hideo's skull, connecting the two hulls. Tadashi thinks of someone tapping at the side of an egg with a spoon. As fragile as that.

Another X-ray. This one of Hideo's neck. One vertebra shattered, dislocated. Marked C2 in blue. Hideo had hit the ground head-first.

❀

He calls her.

But I've been there, to Akiyama, Mrs Yamaguchi says. The long-distance line crackles. Her voice sounds metallic. To the footbridge. It's impossible. There *are* no rocks.

Can we meet at the inn? he says.

He takes the bus, as Katsuo would have done. The same bus. To imagine what it would have been like to be him, travelling up the mountain, this hideous thing already in his mind.

He sits at the front, talks to the driver.

Did he know Hideo Yamaguchi?

Yes, he did. Tragic, he says. Why would such a good man kill himself?

He wheels the bus up around another hairpin bend.

After a while: You know, I began to think it had something to do with me.

With you?

Yes, with me. Three deaths. In less than a year, the driver says. I know, people tell me it's just coincidence. But three of them, in one year? And all of them passengers on my bus at one time or another.

Three? Omura says.

The driver nods.

It wasn't just Hideo, you know. His daughter died as well. About eight months after he did. She died in childbirth, trapped in the snow.

He glances quickly over his shoulder to the road above.

And before that...Well, before that, I lost my only son.

The engine changes register. The bus slows. The driver's powerful arms pull at the wheel. The bus climbs up around another bend.

❀

The two of them, Mrs Yamaguchi and Omura, are talking on the bridge. They are only centimetres from where Katsuo had stood, although they do not know this. She has begun telling him about her family, her husband, her past. My sister was very stubborn, you see, she is saying. She hated village life. How small it was. How narrow. It's killing me, she used to say. From our verandah she would look down at our village and say to me: There's a world out there, Tomoko. Just waiting for me.

Then, just after she turned fifteen, my sister came home from school one afternoon and announced: I'm leaving. I'm going to Osaka. My mother forbade her to go. But my sister simply dropped her school bag where she was, turned, and walked out the door. Just like that. I remember waiting up with my mother long into the night. Waiting for her to return.

Don't worry, my mother said. She'll be back. She needs

her things. Then, when she didn't return, and it was after midnight, my mother went into her room. Opened her cupboards. And they were almost empty. She had already packed. She must have hidden her bag somewhere, or given it to someone for her to pick up on the way.

And she stayed away. For good. We rarely heard from her.

Then, one day, perhaps seven or eight years later, completely unannounced, this young woman arrived on our doorstep saying she was pregnant, that she needed a place to stay. And it was her, my sister.

A long time later my mother told me that she hadn't recognised her, not until she spoke.

Mariko, my mother said. Is it really you?

She did not tell us where she had been. What she had done. She kept to her room. Looking forward to the birth. Which came about a month later.

Not long after the child was born, however, Mariko began to change. She...

But Tadashi Omura has stopped listening. What was this sudden upheaval in his chest? Had Mrs Yamaguchi said Mariko?

There, she said it again. Mariko.

...withdrew into herself. She barely looked at the child. She kept saying what a mistake she'd made. That she should have waited.

She *had* said Mariko!

Could it be? Was this *Katsuo's* Mariko?

That she had given up everything. She realised now that she

was too young to have a child. A child whom she felt nothing for, whom she did not love.

Then Omura came back to her, Mrs Yamaguchi. Concentrated. Attended to what she was saying.

Early one morning, she was saying, I got up to go to the bathroom. I could hear Sachiko crying. She must have been about six or seven months old. I went into Mariko's room, but Mariko was not there. She had disappeared again. There was only Sachiko in her crib at the end of the bed. And a note.

She did not understand what was happening to her, she said. She no longer knew who she was. She felt crushed. She felt as though she was living in a fog. Life had once been so dazzling, she said. So full of promise.

And then her plea: Why, she said, do I not love this child whom I so longed for? For whom I surrendered everything. I can bear the pain no longer. Please, forgive me.

❀

I could hear Sachiko crying.

Omura told Jovert that, in that instant, the dam had burst. He had felt his thoughts cascading back through his life, bouncing from one memory to the next, had felt himself being swept along on this torrent, all the time desperately trying to grasp hold of something that would anchor him, hold him fast. Some memory, some incident, that would fix in his mind what he already knew was true. How old was Sachiko? What had

Katsuo said? Sixteen? Seventeen? When had Katsuo bought the house? When had he commenced his legal practice? When *exactly* had Mariko left?

He could see the three of them standing on the terrace that first day, looking down over the city to the harbour below as clearly as if it were yesterday. Mariko, holding a glass of wine. Radiant. Full of laughter. Katsuo, his hand on her shoulder, his fingers under the strap of her dress. Where her scar was.

But what year was that?

❀

I'm sorry, Mrs Yamaguchi, he said. Did you say Mariko? That your sister's name was Mariko?

Yes, she said.

And did she have a scar high up on her right shoulder? He reached up subconsciously to his own shoulder.

Yes, she said. She did. It was like a tiny map of Japan.

And then he thought the impossible thought: Sachiko was Katsuo's daughter.

Mariko had gone, Mrs Yamaguchi was saying. She had abandoned Sachiko. So we brought her up as our own.

He stood there, on the bridge, beside Mrs Yamaguchi, looking down into the darkening river. To the now corpse-less riverbank. Mrs Yamaguchi had been right, he saw now. There were no rocks below.

Chapter 43

IT was the saddest call he ever made.

Two days after his meeting with Mrs Yamaguchi at the inn, and, coincidentally, almost exactly two years after he had run into Katsuo that day in Osaka's garment district, Omura decided to pay him a visit unannounced. He had spoken to Ishiguro on the phone earlier that day.

I'm sorry, Tadashi. It's not my affair, Ishiguro had said. You need to speak to Katsuo.

He went in the evening. The taxi dropped him at the bottom of the hill. He had expected to have to buzz the house from the gates. But the gates were open. There were weeds growing up through its metal track, and around the base of the buttressed walls. Two rows of thistles—their ghostly, broken-headed spheres still glowing against the setting sun—lined each side of the driveway. Their heads were nodding in the evening breeze, as if to say: At last, you're here. Go on up, we've been waiting for you.

He walked up the hill through the untrimmed hedgerows. When he emerged onto the gravel forecourt, the house lay in darkness. Katsuo's once magnificent car sat abandoned some distance from the house, as if it had given up on finding a better place to die. All four tyres were flat. Its once gleaming bodywork was pockmarked with dust.

The house looked closed up, deserted. He cursed himself for not having asked the cab to wait. It was a long walk back to town.

He climbed the stairs to the first-floor landing. Pushed the button. There were dead leaves crowded into the corners of the portico. Others, still looking for a place to shelter, scurried from one unwelcoming group to another. Cobwebs hung from the light fittings. The house mat was leaning against the wall.

He pushed the button again.

They had been there, he and Mariko. On that first day. *They* had been the anointed ones. They had moved from one light-filled room to another, as if no one in the world existed but them.

Now the house felt abandoned.

But then he heard the sound of a key scraping in a lock. The door began to open. An old man appeared in the half-light. He was dressed in a dishevelled bathrobe. He had a soiled scarf tied around his head. The sound of a baby crying came from somewhere deep within the house.

My name is Tadashi Omura, he said. I am an old friend of Katsuo Ikeda, the owner of the house. I am wondering if he is in?

The old man did not answer him. Omura thought he might be deaf. He went to repeat his question.

It's me, Tadashi, the old man said.

He barely recognised his voice. The old man looked up at him so that Omura could see his face.

Katsuo?

Yes, he said.

Katsuo leaned inside the door and turned the light on. He reached up, removed his scarf.

See, he said. It's me.

The face Omura saw now was even more shocking than the old man's. The light from above cast deep shadows into Katsuo's eyes. His cheeks were hollow. His neck was as deeply ravined as the trunk of an ancient fig. He had not shaved in a long time.

Katsuo? he repeated.

Yes, Tadashi, he said again. Won't you come in.

❀

They sat opposite each other in the long room. As they had always done. Outside, it was beginning to get dark. Only the first metre or so of the balcony was visible. It could have stretched on forever for all he knew.

He told Katsuo about Mrs Yamaguchi coming to see him. About the diary. What it contained. He told him that she thought her husband's death wasn't suicide. That he had been killed.

Didn't Ishiguro call you? Omura asked.

Ah, old Ishiguro, Katsuo said. What would Ishiguro know?

Katsuo took a cigarette out of the packet on the table in front of him. He lit it. Inhaled. He blew the smoke out into the air above his head. Omura recognised the ploy. He could see it in the way Katsuo leaned forward, flicking the ash of his cigarette into the small bowl in front of him. Katsuo was waiting, wondering just how much he really knew. What had Katsuo once said to him, of his writing? It's simple, Tadashi, he had told him in the particularly condescending way he saved for such occasions. All you have to do is ask: What if? What if? What if? And then: How come? He decided not to waste time.

Etsuko, he said.

Katsuo nodded, exhaled.

Very good, Tadashi, he said. He leaned forward again. But what does that prove?

From a legal point of view, it proves that you were there. Don't you see that? And if you meant him no harm, why buy a bus ticket in Etsuko's name?

From a legal point of view? Katsuo said. My God, Tadashi, has *nothing* changed?

Omura ignored the slight. It was just another ploy.

Why Etsuko? he asked after some time. Weren't you worried someone might check?

Some lives are full of risk, Tadashi. What is it people say about tempting fate? Besides, who can remember back then? Etsuko Kaida? The name is meaningless. Just like the millions of anonymous people who have existed but who have never left a mark on the world. Meaningless. Except perhaps to you. And who else? Professor Todo? I heard he committed suicide. So clearly, not to him. And yes, you're right. I resurrected Etsuko! Maybe life is just a game, after all. Maybe I wanted to see who was the stronger, me or...

He hesitated, as if to say: Well, now I know.

...or fate? Katsuo said.

Some game, Omura said. You killed a man.

Yes, he said. I did. I killed a man.

Katsuo seemed to reflect for a moment on what he had said.

On the other hand, he went on, I've always known that, one way or another, I would never escape myself. That I would *always* have to pay. I think I just got tired of waiting.

And what about Hideo?

What do you mean? He drew on his cigarette. My God, Tadashi, don't you think Hideo got tired of waiting too? You know, he came to me, wanting to buy Sachiko back. He said to me he could not live with himself. He said he wanted to undo what he had done. But you can't do that, can you, Tadashi? You can't undo what you've done. Nobody can.

He flicked the ash from his cigarette into the bowl on the table again, waved the smoke away.

And how do you know, Tadashi, he went on, how do you know that Hideo was ever going to make it back across the bridge in any case? Back to the twinkling sanctuary of the inn? There *was* no sanctuary. Not anymore. The empty room was no longer empty. He could no longer keep his thoughts at bay. They were always there, waiting for him.

He got up and went to stand by the window.

No, he said. Hideo was finally cornered. Halfway across the bridge. And he knew it. And cornered not by me. But by himself. His thoughts. Thoughts that had tormented him for years, for what he had done. How could *any* father sell his own child?

Katsuo stood looking out into the growing darkness.

How many times had I imagined him, after every trip, walking up to the railing of the bridge. How many times do you think I actually followed him? I used to see him stop there on his evening walk. He'd stand at the railing, for five, ten minutes, peering over the side. Listening to the sound of the water swirling below, over which he could *still* hear the voices raging in his head. Knowing that, perhaps, this was the moment, the moment to atone for the ghastliness of what he had done. But he could never bring himself to do it. Even after he'd surrendered her. He always walked on.

Katsuo took the cigarette from his mouth, stubbed it out on the glass. He came over to the table. Picked up the pack, but finding it empty threw it back onto the table. He went to stand by the window again.

Don't you see what I did, Tadashi? I put myself in his skin. And *I* could not live with myself. I did not kill Hideo. I merely released him from his torment.

❀

They went out onto the terrace. The evening shadows had already spilled down the mountain, inundating the city, rubbing the edges off things. They talked on like this into the night.

It soon became clear to Omura that Katsuo had thought he was merely there because he had discovered the truth about Hideo's death. That, in a way, Katsuo was relieved now that this truth was out. He seemed strangely happy to chat. To fill him in on what had happened to him over the years since they had last seen each other.

He told him what it had been like after Mariko left. What a mistake he had made letting her go. How desolate he had felt. How empty. He told him of his self-imposed exile, and of his return. Of how cruel the chance discovery of Mariko's death so soon after his return had seemed.

And then he told him about Sachiko. How he had found her. How he had sent her books. Anonymously. Including his own. How having Sachiko around was like having Mariko back. As though he had been forgiven.

He told Tadashi how they used to talk to each other. How she had never tired of answering his questions.

And, after a long while, he told him of that fateful night, the night Sachiko died. They had gone to Ume's village in the mountains, he said. For a break. The week before, Sachiko had received a letter telling her that her friend Kimiko had been found floating in the pool at Takaragawa. She had drowned inexplicably during the night. Sachiko took the news to be an omen. She said she felt trapped. She needed to get away.

Get some air. So they decided to escape to the mountains. Just for a short time. Sachiko was not due to give birth for another six weeks. They would come back to Osaka when she was ready.

On the second afternoon we were there, he said, Ume took us up the mountain to see its famous temple. It was cold. Snow from the previous night blanketed the hills. I was worried, he said. But Sachiko insisted we go.

The sun is shining, she said.

She wore the snow kimono, the one her grandmother had made, the one she had worn that first night, under her coat. We followed one of the many paths up through the forest to the temple.

The shrine was beautiful, tranquil. The woods indescribably quiet. We were the only ones there. Each of us had felt the peacefulness that only newly fallen snow brings. Amid the stillness, the leafless trees, the snow, the mountains rising above them, we had felt blessed.

On the way down the mountain, however, the weather suddenly turned. It began to snow again, lightly at first, then more heavily. We were still within sight of the shrine when Sachiko said that she felt unwell. With me supporting her on one side, and Ume on the other, we tried to walk on, but Sachiko became more and more distressed with every step we took. All at once, she cried out: Oh, Katsuo. I need to stop. I think the baby's coming!

Ume and I lay Sachiko down on her coat. Ume felt her stomach. It was snowing heavily now. And the baby *was* coming.

We could not stay where we were. It was far too cold now. We tried getting Sachiko to her feet again, but she cried out again in pain.

It was then, Katsuo said, that I had a terrifying presentiment, a kind of falling into place. I felt suddenly, he said, as if we had been lured there.

Where are we? I asked Ume.

We're about a kilometre from the village, she said. It's not far.

Being so close only seemed to make it worse.

Sachiko had started whimpering. I could hear the fear in her voice.

Oh Katsuo, Katsuo. Help me, she said. Please, please help me.

It was late afternoon. The snow was falling. The trees, and the mountain, were already beginning to disappear. And there were so many paths.

I don't know the way, I said.

I will go, Katsuo-san, Ume said to me. I know which path to take. You stay here with Sachiko.

She stood up, prepared to go.

Don't worry, she said. It's not far. Just keep Sachiko warm. I will be back soon.

And Ume set off into the falling snow.

❀

Katsuo had taken Sachiko's gloved hand in his. Talk to me, he said. Just talk to me. It will take away the pain.

He no longer recalled, he said, the precise moment he realised—I remember the snow had stopped, and the moon had already appeared above the mountain behind us—that Ume was not coming back.

He recalled how still it was. How eerily beautiful.

And Ume did *not* return.

❀

Hours later he heard their voices, and saw their burning torches through the trees. In her haste, Ume had fallen from the path, into the steep ravine. And could not get out. She had lain there for hours, calling.

❀

On the outskirts of the village, in a small warm room, a man has stayed up late, working into the night. Eventually—they have been there for some time—he hears the faint cries of a woman echoing off the mountain. He puts down his pen. Listens. Walks out into the night.

It is this that saves Ume. And Katsuo. And a tiny, blood-spattered newborn child. But not Sachiko.

Chapter 44

WHO was it who said: There is another world—this is it.

❀

The time, they both knew, had come. It was the early hours of the morning. They had stopped talking. They had gone back to sit in the darkness of the long room.

I know you, Tadashi, Katsuo said eventually. You are still, I imagine, the man of principle I once knew. I know where this will end. Unlike you, I gambled. And lost. I am prepared to wait.

For what? I said.

For you, Tadashi. For the inevitable. You have my fate in your hands.

You make fate sound so puny, Katsuo. It's not just you who is waiting, I said. There's also Mrs Yamaguchi.

Ah yes, dear Mrs Yamaguchi. Sachiko's mother.

And her husband.

Again he waited.

The man you killed.

As I said to you, Tadashi, I merely released him from his torment.

I'm surprised, Katsuo, I said, how little you interrogate things that concern you. What was it you used to say to me? About writing? It's simple, I remember you saying. All you have to do is ask, What if? And then, How come?

Katsuo was sitting watching me closely now.

You know, I said. Mrs Yamaguchi? I saw her a second time. At the inn.

Still he waited.

What if I told you that Sachiko was not her child? That she had a sister?

I took out my own pack of cigarettes and threw it onto the table in front of him.

You know, Inspector, even as he was looking at me, I could see him trying to isolate what it was he had missed. He seemed somehow smaller now.

And still it had not dawned on him.

What if, what if, what if.

The atmosphere in the room began to change. You could feel it. It was as if every particle, every molecule, everything around us were now waiting, and Katsuo and I were somehow connected to the world, and to each other, in a way that we had never been connected before.

A sister. From a mountain village.

I saw the moment of truth arrive. Katsuo began rocking back and forth in his chair, a look of growing anguish on his face. He was clenching and unclenching his fists, his face was drained of blood.

And I knew he knew. He'd been looking in the wrong direction. The retrospective piece had fallen into place.

No, he said.

The sound of a baby crying came to us again.

He put his head in his hands. So that I could not see his eyes. So that *he* would not see the blow coming. He was leaning forward in his chair now, like a prisoner waiting to be executed.

Mariko, he said to himself. And then, under his breath, Sachiko.

Yes, I said. Sachiko was Mariko's child. The child you never wanted.

❀

You can't prove anything.

And what about the child I hear crying? I said.

Fumiko.

Yes, what about her?

Katsuo looked up at me.

If Fumiko were to find out one day that Sachiko was your daughter, what do you think that would do to her?

You know, Tadashi, he said, you've *always* judged me too

quickly, too uncharitably. If only I had done half the things I told you I had done, what a life I would have had.

Don't you think you've done enough? Mariko, Sachiko, Fumiko…

He reached for my pack of cigarettes. Took one from it. Struck a match.

Yes, he said. Mariko. Sachiko. Fumiko. What am I going to do about Fumiko?

The match was still burning. He shook it distractedly. Inhaled.

Fumiko, he said slowly. You're going to tell, aren't you, Tadashi?

Tell who?

The authorities. About Hideo.

No, I said. I knew he knew what was coming next. You are.

But then it will all come out, he said. Fumiko will know that I killed—

Who? Her grandfather? Her mother's uncle? A weak old man who had sold his own stepdaughter to you. And then wanted her back?

But what about Sachiko? *You* know I was Sachiko's father.

Yes, I do. But I can live with that. And so can you. Fumiko shouldn't have to.

PART IX

VALEDICTION

❀

Chapter 45

HE was fucking his own daughter, for Christ's sake, Martine said.

They were sitting at Le Bar l'Anise. They were both rugged up because of the cold. Soon it would be winter. Martine was smoking, tapping her cigarette lighter impatiently on the table, waving the smoke away with her hand, just as Jovert imagined Katsuo had done.

Yes, you're right, he said. But did he know? I don't think he did.

Of course he fucking knew, she said. Or if he didn't, he should have.

Perhaps.

Well, didn't you ask what's-his-name? Takashi? Tadeshi?

Tadashi. Omura. Professor Omura.

Whatever, she said.

You see, that's what's so strange, he said. That evening, the evening Omura told me all of this, when I looked up, he was sitting there looking at me. Just as he must have done with Katsuo.

Jovert reached for his coffee. Swirled the remnants around in the bottom of his cup. Some of the depleted grounds stuck to the sides. He drained what was left. The coffee was lukewarm. It tasted bitter now.

We were just two old men sitting in a room opposite each other, talking, he said. Something so simple. And yet, so strange. So...unfinished. As if we were two parts of an uncompleted whole. Do you know what I mean?

She didn't answer. She sat looking at him. As though she was still angry.

And what about the girl? she said after a little while.

What girl?

The girl on the ice. You remember, when Professor Omura took Fumiko to see her mother's grave. The girl whose baby was trapped under the ice. What about her?

I don't know, Jovert said.

Didn't you ask? I thought that's what you did!

No, I didn't. I remember Omura saying to me—it was when we were out walking, so it must have been that first night—I thought you might have asked.

About what? I'd said.

About the girl on the ice.

But we must have got sidetracked, because I never found out. And after that, we never came back to it.

He looked at his watch. It was already after four.

I must remember to ask him next time I see him.

He put his hand up, signalled to Daudet, raised an invisible glass to his lips. He looked at Martine.

You? he said.

She too glanced at her watch.

Why not? I'm still cold from walking here, she said.

He held two fingers up.

Deux, he mouthed.

It's strange, he said to Martine. When we were sitting in Omura's room, after he had told me about Mariko, about who Sachiko really was, what Katsuo had done, it was as though Katsuo were in the room with us. Waiting for us, waiting for *me* to answer some as yet unasked question. And suddenly I realised.

Oh, I said. I'm sorry, Professor Omura. Of course. You want to know—what would I have done?

Yes, Inspector, he said. What would you have done? Would you have told the police?

❀

Had he slipped that far? In such a short time? A matter of five months? Had he really relinquished the habits of a lifetime so quickly? He would never have accepted at face value some of what Omura had told him if, back then, it had been Omura who had been brought in for him to interrogate. Never.

He saw Omura leaning forward to peer into his room that first night, the night he had picked up the keys. He recalled how

Omura had seemed reluctant to leave. What had he said? 'Yes.' 'Yes.' That was all! And then he saw Omura standing there, waiting to be invited in.

He felt disgusted with himself. How *could* he have fallen so quickly?

He called the real-estate agent at nine the next morning. Yes, he could go through their records if Jovert wanted him to. Yes, twenty-five years, longer, they were all in the basement. He knew Jovert's apartment. The list would not be long. There had been few owners, fewer tenants.

Then it was evening. Night. The typing stopped. He looked at his watch. Twelve forty-five. The rest of the building already asleep. Five minutes later, he was standing outside Omura's door, knocking. He heard Omura's footsteps. The door opened. Omura stood there, a cigarette in his hand.

Insp—?

He was on the bus, Jovert almost shouted.

Who? Omura took a half-step back.

Katsuo. That day, when Sachiko came down the mountain with her stepfather for the first time. Katsuo was on the bus.

What do you mean, Inspector? On the bus?

Can I come in? Jovert said. Are you busy?

You know I'm not, Inspector. I was going to go out onto the balcony, but it's freezing out there.

It's mid-November, Jovert said. What did you expect?

I was just about to make some tea, Omura said. Would you like some? Or something to drink?

No, I'm fine, Jovert said. I've been going over some of what you've told me these past few months. And now I find myself saying, no, that can't be right. How would Katsuo know that? Sachiko can't have told him.

Cigarette? Omura asked. A small pyre of bent-elbowed butts already occupied the ashtray on the coffee table. Omura saw Jovert looking.

It's last night's as well, Omura said.

I'm sorry?

Nothing, he said. It doesn't matter. You were saying.

You remember you told me, Jovert said, when Hideo brought Sachiko down to Osaka, they stopped at an inn because of the rain. Then they went on. Down the mountainside. In the storm. And the bus broke down, it got stuck in this water-filled hole on the side of the road. And the bus driver's son…

Hiroshi?

Yes, Hiroshi. You told me how he had drowned when the bus fell back on him. Well, he was there. Katsuo. Katsuo was there.

How do you know?

Who told you the story? Jovert said.

Katsuo.

And where did he get it from?

From Sachiko. As I've told you, he would ask her the same things over and over again. Building up his account of things. Adding to what he'd missed. When I went to see him that fateful night, he told me how Sachiko had died in the snow. How he had tried to keep her awake by getting her to talk. How she had told him again of coming down the mountain with her father. Almost from the moment they left her village, things started to go wrong. It was as if these things were warnings, omens, which they did not heed.

And do you recall what he said about Hiroshi? What you told me?

Hiroshi?

When the bus lurched backwards. When Hiroshi was struck down. When he was stuck under it. They couldn't get him out. And you said something about his arm, how it rose up out of the water. You described his hand. You said it was like a...like a bloody mouth trying to suck air down into his body.

Yes, Omura said. I did say something like that.

But you said, Sachiko said, that she and the old people, the women, the old men, and the children were standing at the side of the road some distance away. With the rain still beating down on them. Didn't you? Even I can see them there, huddled under their umbrellas, looking on while this nightmare unfolds. Isn't that what you said? And when the bus begins to loom over them, the men jump out of the way to escape it. And down it comes, trapping Hiroshi. And the men are all there, in a semicircle, watching, except for the two who are trying to pull him out.

Omura did not reply. He was listening intently to what Jovert was saying.

He was one of them, Jovert said. Katsuo. One of the men standing in the semicircle at the rear of the bus. It was he who saw Hiroshi's clenched and bloodied hand rise up out of the muddy water, gasping for air. Sachiko couldn't possibly have seen that. She was with the women and children on the far side of the road.

Omura was nodding.

Don't you see? It would have been exactly what Katsuo would have done.

Pieces began to fall into place. Jovert could see Katsuo going to Sachiko's village dozens of times, disguised, just to catch a glimpse of her. He would already have been obsessed with her after that first night. Of course he would have ensured he was on the bus bringing her down to him.

It couldn't possibly have been Sachiko who told him, he said. It *had* to be him. And then, when they got to Osaka, at the bus terminal, the man who was standing in the stairwell of the bus, while Hideo went to get their luggage. The businessman who rescued her. That must have been Katsuo. He was watching over her.

Jovert did not stop there. There was one other thing he had figured out.

He was here, too, wasn't he? he said to Omura. Here in Paris. When Katsuo disappeared that time, after the publication of, what was it?

The Chameleon, Omura said.

The Chameleon. The chameleon, Jovert repeated. You said he was away for years, isn't that what you said? He was standing looking at Omura now. He was here, wasn't he, Professor Omura? In Paris?

There was a moment of silence while something other than Omura decided what his answer would be.

He was. Yes, Inspector, he was.

In my apartment?

Omura didn't answer immediately. He reached for the teapot, poured some more tea into his cup.

I looked up the tenancy records, Jovert said. This morning, at the real-estate office.

Omura still did not answer him. Instead, he waited, as though he were weighing up the consequences of what he was about to say.

Yes, he said.

So you weren't waiting there for me, were you?

What do you mean, Inspector?

The night you picked up my keys. That night you said you were waiting for me. It wasn't *me* you were waiting for, was it?

I'm not sure I follow, Inspector?

You weren't waiting specifically for *me*, he said testily. You were waiting for whoever lived in my apartment. So that, perhaps, if luck was on your side, you might get inside, look around. At the apartment your former friend had lived in.

I was waiting for you, Inspector.

But only because it was my apartment.

Oh, I see, Inspector. The coincidence thing again. As if it didn't matter who lived there now? As if anyone would do.

He drew on his cigarette.

Auguste Jovert, recently retired Inspector of Police, who

finds out he has a daughter he's never known two days before I knock on his door. That's just coincidence, is it? He leaned back against the kitchen wall. How very interesting, Inspector. How very western.

He took a sip of tea.

No, Inspector, it was you I was waiting for. As soon as I found out you were a former Inspector of Police, I knew. It was preordained. It was meant to be. The unfolding I had been waiting for, for so long, had at last begun.

But you knew he stayed here, in my apartment, all those years ago.

Of course. He told me. Paris. Rue St Antoine. He told me how he loved seeing the golden-winged boy soaring over the city. It was why he had taken the apartment. So bizarre, so surreal. He told me about the lift. He told me how much he enjoyed walking around the Paris streets at night, knowing that he could be walking in Victor Hugo's footsteps. Kawasimodo. How they still inhabited them. The Marais. The swamp. If only you knew what that meant to us—the swamp.

But I *could* have been anyone, Jovert said. And all this stuff about finding the right person, the person through whom we see our own lives—it's all nonsense, isn't it?

I don't know, Inspector. You tell me.

Chapter 46

WHAT happened in the days and weeks that followed this conversation, Jovert no longer remembered. He was sure there were still plenty of other questions he had forgotten to ask Omura. But he had to get his own house in order first. Decide whether he was going to Algiers to find Mathilde, or not.

❀

He awoke at some unknown dark hour. The room pulsed with a soft, amniotic glow. He had been dreaming, but about what he knew not. He lay for a moment, watching the pattern of the lace curtains magically appearing and disappearing on the ceiling. Shadowed tree limbs, clouds, flying birds, all suspended in an alien aqueous sky. His rectangled bedroom window now a beating membrane, delicate beyond belief, like some veiled, thin-veined living thing.

He rolled onto his side. The green-glow digits of his bedside clock were gone. He reached for his lamp, pushed the button. No light came on. He closed his eyes, put a thumb and forefinger to his eyelids. But his head still beat in time with his beating room.

He stood by the intermittent window. Pulled one corner of the curtain aside. It was snowing. Large feathered flakes floated down through the darkness into the cupped light of the streetlamps below. It was as if the light were conjuring them, as though stillness itself were falling. Once and for all.

❀

There are two police cars angled across the laneway below with their headlights on. On the pavement, an ambulance, its lights flashing. Wave after wave of reddish light surges up the walls of the building opposite. Jovert watches it fall back to the pavement and spill towards the roadway. This is how he comes to see it, the fallen figure lying in the gutter, snow settling on his coat, his legs, his hair. Softly, as if each individual flake is being placed there. And he knows.

❀

He will go down in a minute, he thinks. There is no hurry. Not now. It no longer matters. He watches one of the medics retrieve the gurney from the back of the ambulance. Another is on his two-way radio. Next to him, a policeman, smoking.

Fox-tailed plumes of breath escape his mouth and then slip away into the night.

❀

Just before the corner, he finds Omura's hat leaning against the wall, rocking back and forth on its rim. As if it could not bear being there. As if it is already in mourning.

Jovert speaks to the young policeman. He's wearing thick glasses. There's snow on his cap, his shoulders. It turns out he knows him, vaguely, from years ago. His father one of his former colleagues.

Inspector Jovert?

Gilles! he says. How are you?

Gilles shrugs, looks across to where Omura is lying.

Jovert remembers him as a boy. Unhappy. Withdrawn.

And your father?

You know, he says. He's my father.

Yes, he does. He remembers well.

The policeman, Gilles, looks uncomfortable. He glances at his cigarette.

It's okay, Jovert says. He touches him on his arm. I'm no longer working. That's all over now.

I heard, the young policeman says. He takes one last puff of his cigarette. Flicks the butt into the snow anyway.

Their breaths are fogged. It is much colder down here than he had anticipated. He pulls his coat around him.

Gilles rubs his gloved hands together.

I'd better go and help Jean-Paul, he says.

The ambulance officer is still retrieving things from the rear of the vehicle.

Jovert stands for a moment looking across to the snow covered form lying in the gutter.

I know him, he says.

Oh?

Yes, he's one of my neighbours, a friend. His name's Omura. Professor Tadashi Omura. He used to teach at the Imperial University in Tokyo.

He wonders if he could ask Gilles for a cigarette. He looks up into the darkened sky. They're both looking up now, staring into the darkness, their eyes blinking as the snow comes streaming down. It's falling more heavily now. The top of Jovert's building is barely visible. It could easily not exist.

I saw him, he says. From up there. From my window. I live up there. This is my building.

The two of them are still looking up into the dark swirling sky, as if they are both contemplating what Jovert has just said, what it could possibly mean.

❀

Omura is alone now. Lying in the snow. He could be sleeping. But when Jovert goes over to him, steps out onto the roadway, he sees that Omura's eyes are open. He could be looking down the snow-filled alleyway, as if, having seen the ambulance approaching, having seen its flashing lights, heard it pull up, its engine stop, he is still waiting for them, wondering what they're doing. He can't stay here.

His head is resting on one of his arms. The other is outstretched, as if pointing to something. Jovert follows the line he might be indicating. Then he sees it—the fallen notebook. It lies in the snow, in the gutter, almost completely covered. A few minutes more and it would have disappeared. Jovert looks around. The policeman, the medics, are still busy at the rear of the ambulance. He bends down, picks it up. Brushes the snow off it. Puts it in his coat pocket. He thinks of that night after the fireworks, of returning home on his crutches, seeing Omura outside his building, flipping through the notebook until he finds the page. He sees Omura holding it up to his face, tapping it with his fingertip. Then bending down myopically to punch his code into the panel beside the door.

Tonight, there is no light over the door. His building, the ones adjacent to it, the ones opposite, are all blacked out. It's the first day of December. The first big snowfall of the year.

Perhaps Omura had come around the corner to see what this month's new code was in the lamplight. But found, instead, his angel, the one sent to collect him, waiting to tell him it was over. This wondrous great adventure. No need to worry. You won't need that. Your notebook. Here, let me take it from you. Lie down upon the snow.

Jovert looked up to his window again, at the sky glowing dimly above him—the snow falling down towards him invisible until it hits the light, in which he is now standing, alone, with Omura lying at his feet.

❀

Can we contact you, Inspector. If we need to?

The two medics are circling the body. They could be animals in the snow.

He nods.

Gilles says something.

The medics lean down.

His body unbending.

On the stretcher, Omura looks like a child, curled up on his side. One hand outstretched, the other resting under his head. And the world is now weeping.

❀

Back in his room, his lamp has come on. His clock is blinking. He goes to stand by the window once again. Snow in his hair. On his shoulders. He has Omura's hat in his hand. He pulls the curtain aside. Places the hat on the cold windowsill. Drops the notebook into it.

They have gone—the ambulance, Omura. He looks for Omura's imprint in the snow. But there isn't one.

The snow is falling more purposefully now. The breeze has picked up. One of the police cars is still there, at the end of the street, half-blocking the laneway. The snow lies thick and soft on its roof, its bonnet. It is beginning to quilt. The car's emergency lights are still flashing. Soon they too will disappear.

The snow is dense in the lamplight. Great shoals of it are eddying fretfully back and forth in the narrow laneway, as if they are looking for Omura. There is something frantic about their movement, back and forth, back and forth, as if they can foresee a moment when they will have to account for why they had momentarily turned away. And when they turned back, he was gone! How were they to know?

Watching the snow swirling, the police car disappearing, Jovert felt as though his building were moving. As if it had become unmoored from the solid earth below. Was now adrift. The floor seemed to pitch forward beneath his feet. He put both hands out onto the cold windowsill to steady himself. The world.

❀

The snow has given up looking. It seems to collect itself, then, all at once, in one great mass, it minnows up through the lamplight into the darkness above.

The street is barely visible now. Like a fading photograph. The details are gone. Soon, Jovert knows, the world outside will be erased: there will be nothing left. Except for the barely perceptible glow of the streetlamps, the pulsing of the police car's lights, which themselves have begun to recede, as though they are a constellation that is growing dimmer and dimmer as he watches. The moment he turns away from the window, he knows, all of this will cease to exist. So he stands watching as this part of his life slowly disappears before his eyes. Then he turns, looks back into his room, to the still-unknown future which awaits him there.

Chapter 47

TWO days later, the police *had* contacted him. To ask if he would look after Omura's affairs. Act as go-between, given his, Jovert's, former status. His relationship with the deceased.

The following night, at around 10.30, just as he was about to go down to Omura's apartment—he had already collected the key—not to start packing up, but just to go down there, to sit perhaps, take a minute or two to say goodbye—there was a knock on his door. For one mad, irrational moment, he had thought it was Omura.

He went to the door, opened it, and an apparition of another kind was standing there.

Martine?

He must have stepped back. She too seemed to have been taken by surprise. Her right hand was still in the air. Her fingers clenched.

Oh, Inspector! I'm sorry, I was just about to knock again.

I wasn't sure if you were home.

How did you get in? he said. It sounded more harsh than he intended.

I followed someone in.

It was something he'd always worried about while he worked. That someone he'd arrested, put away, some crazed sociopath, would find out where he lived. And come looking for him. It had never happened. But it was always there, in the back of his mind, nevertheless.

I'm sorry, Martine said, to turn up on your doorstep unannounced. She looked at him standing in his coat. And this clearly isn't a good time, is it? I can see that you're on your way out. I knew I should have called.

She took two steps away from the door.

Martine. He raised his hand as if he was a traffic cop. Wait, he said. Slow down. He let his hand drop. Yes, I am going out. But it's only down to Omura's apartment. You remember Professor Omura. Yes, of course you do, how could you forget? Omura died a couple of nights ago. He was caught in the snowstorm. It's been left to me to sort out his affairs.

I'm so sorry to hear that, Inspector. You and he had become bound to each other in a way, hadn't you? Recently. From what you were saying.

Bound to each other. He would never have put it that way himself, but she was right, he now realised.

They were still standing awkwardly in the doorway.

Won't you come in?

No, look, I don't think so. I came to ask you for something. But it can wait.

Just a moment, Martine, he said. I know this will sound strange, but would you come down with me? You saw him. You know what he was like. How much time I've spent with him, these past five months. I'm not sure I want to go on my own. If I sit down there, I'm afraid I will turn to stone. Then there will be two of us they'll have to attend to.

Okay, she said. Yes. I will. I'll come down with you.

❀

Do you realise you're still limping, Inspector, if you don't mind me saying.

They were walking down the corridor to the lift.

Am I?

Yes. When did you get rid of the walking stick?

Sticks! I kept losing them. I don't know. A couple of months ago. When did we last see each other? September?

October, she said.

October. So it must have been just after that.

Maybe you ditched them too soon?

The lift arrived.

Then he was inserting the key into the lock in Omura's apartment door, opening it, reaching in for the light switch.

The apartment seemed darker now, now that Omura was no longer there.

God, it's dismal in here, she said.

It had only been three days, but the apartment already smelt musty, as though Omura had been dying in there for weeks.

Are you sure you're okay with me being here? Martine said. It doesn't feel right, if you know what I mean.

No, he said. It's okay. I'm glad you're here.

He walked over to the small table with the typewriter on it. The lamp had been left on, as if to lure him there.

Did I ever tell you that I used to hear Omura typing away at all hours of the night? And morning.

You did, she said.

God knows when he slept.

The typewriter was flanked by two piles of paper, one of them almost gone. There was an envelope on the thicker pile, a passport underneath. The envelope had Jovert's name on it.

I thought this might have been the case, he said. It's why I wanted to come down here. He picked the envelope up, opened it, began reading.

> *My dear Inspector,*
> *Could you do one last thing for me—could you send what I have written to Fumiko? Perhaps she will understand what I tried to explain to her that day, but could not. My shame. Please accept my apologies for lying to you.*

Strange, he thought, the note was dated 22 September. And yet here it was, December. At the bottom of the note was an address. He began to read it. Then he heard Martine.

Oh my God, she said. Inspector!

She had picked up the passport, flipped it open.

What is it? he said.

I think you should have a look at this.

She handed Jovert the passport. He too looked at the faintly blurred Hirohito-like photograph of Omura trapped under the plastic covering. At his face. His eyes.

So? he said.

It's-not-him, she said. It's not Omura.

Jovert looked back at the page—to the passport holder's details.

Nom: IKEDA, it said.

Prénoms: Katsuo.

The world began to reel. He felt dizzy, as though he were going to fall. He reached for a walking stick he no longer had.

Are you all right, Inspector? Martine said.

No, he said. I don't think I am.

❀

Later he read the note again. The address:

Miss Fumiko Omura

c/– Professor Tadashi Omura

Faculty of Law

University of Tokyo
7-3-1 Hongo Bunkyo-ku
TOKYO, JAPAN

Fumiko *Omura*. Not Fumiko Ikeda. How much had that cost him? To write that down, acknowledge that.

And then he thought of Mathilde. His own daughter, the daughter *he* had not had. And the photograph of her, her eyes looking back at him. Watching. Waiting.

Chapter 48

MARTINE was late. Jovert was sitting in Le Temps des Cerises, the café on the corner of rue de la Cerisaie and rue du Petit-Musc, a place he hadn't been to in years.

Except for a man in his forties—someone who looked as if he knew a thing or two about life—sitting alone at a table with a half-finished drink in his hands, there was no one else in the café.

On the way, he had walked past La Maison de Jerôme, the antique store where his *hippopotamane* had gone. It was no longer there. The space it had occupied was now full of junk. He felt guilty seeing it gone. At least he had known where it was, even though it was caged, even though it had nowhere to go. He wondered if he had walked past the store so often just to check on it. To see if it was still looking out at him. Waiting for him to change his mind, to take it home with him again.

He recalled the first time he had pointed Omura out to Martine. They were sitting at La Pointe.

There he is, he said.

Who?

Omura. Over there. At the bus stop.

I can't see him, she said.

See the man and the woman with the stroller. He's behind them. Wait. See, there he is. The little man in the coat and hat.

Why is he limping?

Is he?

Yes, look.

She was right. Omura was pacing slowly back and forth. And he was limping. It was slight, but it was definitely there, nevertheless.

I don't know, he said.

He reminds me of the Emperor Hirohito, she had said. With his hat, and those round wire-rimmed glasses. Even the way he stoops. It's just like him.

Jovert laughed.

Why are you laughing? she said.

Because that's what I thought when I first saw him, when he was standing in the corridor outside my apartment.

We did this project, at school, she said. On the bombing of Hiroshima. I remember seeing a photo of this little man, wearing spectacles, and a hat, hands behind his back, inspecting what was left of the city, the buildings that had been destroyed, the rubble...The caption below the picture said: *The Emperor Hirohito inspecting the devastation of Hiroshima*. I remember thinking not only how terrible it must have been to be there, but also how small he was, the Emperor. How could anybody that small be an Emperor?

Yes, he said. I know what you mean.

❀

Inspector!

He looked up to see Martine walking towards him. The door was still closing behind her. She was folding her wet umbrella.

I'm sorry I'm late, she said. This weather! She looked out the window, to where it was raining, to where the wind was gusting. Is it ever going to stop?

He got up, reached out, took her hand.

That's okay, he said. I just got here myself.

She looked down at his almost-empty glass.

Well, ten minutes ago, he said.

Fifteen, she said. You forget, I saw you at Le Bar l'Anise.

Yes, you're probably right, he said. Fifteen. Please, won't you take a seat?

The waiter came over and helped her off with her coat.

She sat down, rubbed her hands together.

What would you like to drink?

She took the wine menu, skimmed it expertly.

I think I'll have the Mont-Redon, she said.

A bottle, or a glass?

Oh, God no. Just a glass. She laughed. She looked away then, as though she were remembering something. Some other special time.

No, no. Just a glass, she repeated.

He signalled the waiter.

You know, she said. You have this habit. I was watching you when I came in. When you're thinking about something, or something someone's said to you, you turn away, as if the answer is written somewhere else. In the air outside, perhaps. On the roadway. I noticed it at Le Bar l'Anise that first night.

And she was right, he had been doing exactly that, looking at the people hurrying by in the rain, their coats folded tightly about them, their umbrellas held out, shielding them against the wind, looking for the answers that lay scattered there.

The waiter brought Martine her glass of wine.

I'm sad he's gone, he said. Omura.

Katsuo.

Katsuo.

You shouldn't be. Omura was right, she said. Katsuo was a selfish, insensitive, narcissistic…She searched for a word. But couldn't find one. Who used people. Who *always* put himself first. Who didn't care, or have any idea, about the impact of what he did on others. He was a jerk.

Katsuo? Insensitive? Or Omura? Which one was I talking to?

He reached for his pack of cigarettes. Loosened one from the rest. Offered it to her.

No, no thanks, she said. I think I'm going to give up. Once I've found Mehdi. I might as well start now.

Do you mind?

No, please. Go ahead.

He struck the match against the side of the box. It burst into flame with a hiss. He held it up to his cigarette, then placed the still-lit match in the ashtray, where it burned for a few seconds before extinguishing itself.

Well, whoever it was, Omura, Katsuo, I'm sorry he's gone, he said.

She looked at him again.

It's true. Tadashi. Katsuo. I miss him. His voice. It's as though a special sound in the world, something unique, has stopped. Forever.

That's how I felt when Mehdi disappeared, she said. I used to see him every day...and then there was nothing, he was gone.

I know, it's strange, isn't it? Even though it's only been a week, Omura always had something to tell me. Always. It was like I had access to another world. Even when I resisted, he'd still persist. I never really knew *where* we were going. Where we'd end up. But wherever it was, I knew we were going somewhere. When he was telling me about Fumiko, about

Katsuo—about himself—Sachiko, Mariko, I felt inhabited by him, by what he was telling me. And it all seemed somehow connected. Not just to him. But to me as well.

He picked up his glass.

The other night, he said, the night we went down to Omura's apartment, you said there was something you wanted to ask me. What was it?

I wanted to ask you…I wanted to ask you, if you decided to go to Algeria, to find Mathilde, would you take me with you? Help me find Mehdi.

I thought it might have been that.

He nodded to himself.

Yes, of course I will, he said.

When he looked up, her eyes were brimming with tears.

I'm sorry, she said. But I miss him too, my brother.

Then Jovert did something he had never done before. He reached out across the table and took her hands in his.

Yes, of course I'll take you, he said. I've already been there with you.

She did not look up.

Are you okay? he said.

She nodded. He went to pull his hands away, but he felt the small renewed pressure of her fingers, holding him there.

He recalled a colleague, someone from another jurisdiction, someone he hadn't seen or heard from in a while, who had told him about a young woman he'd once seen sitting in a café. She had been with this older man. The man had been holding the young woman's hands. His colleague had been close enough to see that, even though she had tears in her eyes, she was smiling. He remembered his colleague telling him how this image had stayed with him for some reason, how he had never been able to forget it.

He heard the man behind him put his glass down, heard the scrape of his chair as he got up. Jovert was still holding Martine's hands when the man walked by. They must have exchanged glances, the man and Martine, because she smiled up at him through her tears as he walked past, alone, unknown, to who knew what awaited him in the streets outside.

What was it called, the bar? The one his colleague had mentioned. He thought for a moment. It was something appropriate... Yes, now he remembered. The Winterset. The Winterset, he thought. How could he forget.

He thought again about Martine, this young woman, whose hands he held, and whose hands held his. He thought about her brother, who had killed their murderous stepfather. And the younger brother they had both lost. Four-year-old Luc. Who had stood there, looking silently into the eyes of his rage-blinded father, waiting for the fatal blow. Had he had any inkling of the final darkness that was about to befall him?

Perhaps, he thought to himself, another universe *did* exist. Some parallel, other life. If only we gave it a chance. That he should be sitting here with this young woman, holding *her* hands across the table; that there were tears in *her* eyes, through which she was smiling, wasn't a coincidence. It was something else, something greater.

He looked up at Martine. Her eyes. One dark tributary had survived her hand and now lay imprinted on her cheek. He felt her fingers moving in his. Perhaps it was not too late to atone, after all.

Chapter 49

WHENEVER Jovert stepped out the door onto rue St Antoine, he always had the feeling that he was stepping into history. Did he imagine it, or was there not, each evening, when he went to get his paper, some invisible flow against which he had to brace himself? He had often thought about the masses sweeping down rue St Antoine to storm the Bastille. He knew that this was not the case. There were no angry masses. It hadn't happened that way. But his boyhood imaginings had proved ineradicable, permanently resistant to the later truth. The crowds still swept by. So close to him he could almost hear their murmurings.

And from the time he was a boy, he had always been fascinated standing in the exact spot where something significant had happened: an assassination; the death on the Champs-Élysées of some poor poet whose name he could never remember, cruelly felled mid-thought by a falling tree. He had stood on the corner of rue Amyot, where Modigliani's eight-months-pregnant wife, Jeanne, had thrown herself from their fifth-floor window. He had mourned her loss, as if some vestige of what had happened that day lay indelibly inscribed on the pavement in front of him.

But hadn't this always been the case, for him? How many crime scenes had he been to in his life? Were there not hundreds of times when he had stood in the exact place where someone had died some brutal and unnecessary death? Had it not been his job to reimagine what prosaic horror had taken place there—in a bedroom, a kitchen, a sixth-floor balcony? How many times had he traced a trail of blood on a staircase from a now less frantically opened door down to the deserted landing below, where the bigger pool lay? And had there not been, each time, a smaller, more mundane voice of history still quietly sobbing there?

❀

Sometimes, when he thought about what Omura had said, he found himself going over it in his head, taking each individual word in his hands as though it were a pebble. Examining them. One by one. Then reassembling them in exactly the same order, trying to find the precise moment at which they ceased to be just a string of single words, and they were transformed into something else, something much bigger, that flowered in his brain. Or stopped him in his tracks.

He recalled doing the same thing when he was a boy, going over a phrase, a sentence, a paragraph in a book, reading the words over and over again, trying to prise them apart long enough to see into the secret cleft they had just described. But he never could. The words closed over as quickly as a woman turning on her bed.

He had seen Ichiro's father cradling his son in his arms. Had felt the crow's clawed feet tense on the young boy's brow before it launched itself into the air. But where, exactly, amongst these words, was *his* sorrowing? What strange metamorphosis was this? Why was *his* heart aching?

❀

Now, in his room, he thought that perhaps he *could* see the pattern of his life emerging. He had finally begun to piece things together, make sense of it. This is what you did, at sixty-three, or seventy, or seventy-three. You looked back, contemplated what *had* happened. Six months ago, he had felt that his life was over. Except for the final reckoning, there would be nothing new.

But he had been wrong. He could never have predicted Omura walking into his life. His present, his future, were so different from anything he could have imagined then.

He thought about how many deaths he'd come across these past six months. They were nothing compared to the number of deaths he had investigated in his career—sudden, ghastly, accidental deaths; homicides, acts of rage, mistaken identity; deaths that were premeditated; people burnt to death, shot or stabbed, run over, or killed mid-sentence on their way to pick up their child; people who had died on the operating table. Then there was the richly imagined field of suicides. Some people disappeared without a ripple, forever anonymous, never missed. Others were always there.

He was sixty-three. Probably half the world's population had died in his lifetime. Half! And how many billions before that? It made the microscopic teeming at the end of life's living tip seem so vulnerable. The difference was, he did not know most of them. But someone did. Everyone was at the centre of some more complex web that bound each of us to others. He thought of Omura. Katsuo. He thought of Mariko, Sachiko, Fumiko. And then he thought of Mathilde, his own daughter.

He could still hear Omura's voice in his head. He knew now what had happened. He had never wanted him to stop. He had been there with him from the beginning. He was there that afternoon, with Omura, on the snow-covered path, holding Fumiko's hand. He had stood on the ice. *He* had looked into the dead child's frozen eyes. He had held Hiroshi in his own arms. He had been on the bridge with Katsuo the night he waited for Hideo. Had seen the look of surprise on Hideo's face. Surprise, he imagined, that had turned instantly to understanding. I should have known. He had seen Sachiko dying in the snow.

And when Katsuo had walked out of the prison gates to see Fumiko standing waiting for him, he had been there watching on. He understood the impossibility of that day. Where *did* you start? How *did* you explain a life away?

Now the image of Omura lying curled in the street came back to him. He was standing by his window, looking down. Snow was falling. And Omura—Katsuo—was gone.

Acknowledgements

To my wife, Lee Kerr, to whom this book is dedicated, for keeping us afloat this past eighteen months. And not only that. To my daughter, Georgia, and my son, Harrison, for pressing the send button. To Michael Heyward and David Winter for their brilliant editing, and the rest of the team at Text Publishing. To Kensuke Todo and Jun Imaki—who read the manuscript, or parts of it—for their comments and invaluable insights into things Japanese. To Bill Fagan and David Foerster at Fuji Arts, Ann Arbor, for their unflagging generosity.

The following works were of use to me in the writing of this book:

Michel Déon, *L'armée d'Algérie et la pacification*, Paris: Plon, 1959.

David Galula, *Pacification in Algeria, 1956–1958*, RAND Corporation, 1963.

Edgar O'Ballance, *The Algerian Insurrection, 1954–62*, London: Faber and Faber, 1967.

Jules Roy, *La Guerre d'Algérie*, Paris: Juilliard, 1960.

An early version of Chapter 1 appeared in Helen Daniel and Robert Dessaix (eds), *Neo: Picador New Writing*, Sydney: Pan Macmillan, 1994.

The Snow Kimono is a work of fiction. Certain liberties have been taken with actual places and events. For example, the Bastille Day fireworks which occur each year at Le Trocadéro have been transposed, for fictional purposes, to Place de la Bastille. Similarly, certain Japanese festivals have been translocated. The Imperial University of Japan became Tokyo University long before the events described in this book occurred. Specific terms of address have been used more loosely here than they would otherwise be in Japan. Beyond that, as has been said elsewhere, all outright errors and omissions are my responsibility. It remains to say that all characters in this book are fictional. Any resemblance to actual people, living or dead, is entirely coincidental.